MAY 1 1 2011

10/12

His Other Wife

**Center Point
Large Print**

**This Large Print Book carries the
Seal of Approval of N.A.V.H.**

His Other Wife

Deborah Bedford

CENTER POINT PUBLISHING

THORNDIKE, MAINE

This Center Point Large Print edition
is published in the year 2011 by arrangement with
FaithWords, a division of Hachette Book Group, Inc.

This book is a work of fiction.
Names, characters, places, and incidents are the product
of the author's imagination or are used fictitiously.
Any resemblance to actual events, locales,
or persons, living or dead, is coincidental.

The text of this Large Print edition is unabridged.
In other aspects, this book may vary
from the original edition.
Printed in the United States of America
on permanent paper.
Set in 16-point Times New Roman type.

ISBN: 978-1-61173-034-0

Library of Congress Cataloging-in-Publication Data

Bedford, Deborah.
His other wife / Deborah Bedford. — Center Point large print ed.
p. cm.
Originally published: New York : FaithWords, c2011.
ISBN 978-1-61173-034-0 (library binding : alk. paper)
1. Divorced mothers—Fiction. 2. Life change events—Fiction. 3. Large type books.
   4. Domestic fiction. I. Title.
PS3602.E34H57 2011b
813'.6—dc22

                                                              2010052379

To those who need to look forward instead of looking back, to the ones looking for light at the end of the tunnel.
To the ones who want to run from the places that hurt them.

And they rose up in the morning early, and worshipped before the LORD, and returned, and came to their house to Ramah: and Elkanah knew Hannah his wife; and the LORD remembered her.

1 Samuel 1:19

I want to die before my wife, and the reason is this:
If it is true that when you die, your soul goes up to judgment,
I don't want my wife up there ahead of me to tell them things.

Bill Cosby

His Other Wife

Prologue

❧

Boo never moved until Hilary got up. Eric went about his same routine every morning; he rolled out when the clock radio turned itself on just after five, rummaged through the drawer in search of athletic socks, tugged on his sweatpants, stuck his arms through the sleeves of the T-shirt that was worn so thin you could have read a newspaper through it, and headed downstairs to work out on his home gym. For almost a half hour, Hilary could hear the *clank* of the barbell returning to the weight bench, the *whir* of the pulley as Eric worked the leg press, the final silence when she knew he'd be doing chin-ups on the bar that hung from the doorway. And still the dog waited for her, his head resting atop his two front paws, one eyebrow cocked in a question over his liquid eyes. When she adjusted the pillow, he lifted his head and cocked one ear.

"I don't know why he can't just go out for a *run*." Hilary covered her head with the pillow. "Then he could take you with him."

Boo, a Jack Russell terrier with a brown spot around one eye and a black ear, didn't move a muscle.

Hilary swung her legs to the floor. "Why does it always have to be *me?*"

The dog was gone in a shot. He barreled out of the bedroom before Hilary could even stand. He tore down the stairs, tumbling over himself with a thunderous clamor that could have come from a pack of dogs five times his size. He danced circles around his empty food bowl. Hilary came behind him much slower, cinching her terry robe around her waist.

"Calm down," she said, yawning herself awake. She opened the slider so he could go outside and sniff around the backyard. "How can *anything* have that much energy this early?" She scooped kibble from the bag in the pantry and ran fresh water into another and set both bowls on the floor. Then she opened the slider where Boo was already impatiently making nose prints against the glass. "Now," she said as he started eating. "See? You're going to live."

Hilary reached for the carafe on the coffeemaker and stopped short. It was empty. She'd forgotten to put in the grounds and set the timer the night before. As she reached for the French Roast overhead, she noticed the clock on the microwave and did a double take. "Oh *no.*" She gave up on the coffee and headed toward the stairs. She'd have to pick up a cup at the drive-through near the hospital. "I'm glad *somebody* gets breakfast this morning." She gave a rueful glance toward the dog.

She hadn't heard Eric finish his workout and go upstairs, but there was water spraying in the shower. Good thing they'd built the bathroom with room for two. Hilary rapped on the door, said "May I come in?" and walked in without waiting for his answer. She never waited for his answer. She always knew it would be okay.

Hilary unfogged a spot in the mirror with a towel. "Good morning," she said as she tucked strands of blond hair behind her ears and made a critical exam of her face. "Sleep well?" She set about polishing her teeth with the Sonicare.

Soap thudded on the shower floor. Eric must have dropped it.

"Can you make sure Seth makes it to the bus?" she asked. "I've got to get going."

She expected Eric's chatty voice from behind the glass, teasing her about being late again. She was always turning off her alarm. But he said nothing.

"Eric?"

"Yes. I'll take care of it."

She heard something in his voice. "Everything okay, Eric?"

"You getting in the shower?" he asked. "I'll leave the water running for you."

"I will in a minute. Let me make sure Seth's up."

"I'll take care of Seth," he said as he swung the door open. "Here. I'm out. You get in." Eric grabbed a towel to scrub his hair dry and stepped past her.

Their arms brushed as Hilary hung up her robe. Hilary shot him a smile. Here they were after a fifteen-year marriage and she still melted at the sight of him. Water ran in rivulets down his chest. Wet hair clung to his forearms in dark curls. She pressed her lips against his damp shoulder. He smelled like soap and aftershave. "Hmm-mm," she said, closing her eyes. "I love the smell of man in the morning. Minty fresh."

It was the perfect opening. He could have used it to tease her. *But what about the smell of a man in the afternoon?* Only he didn't.

Hilary stepped into the flow and let the water drum her shoulders. She raised her face to the stream. She felt so lucky. God had blessed her with so much. She had one great kid, a good job, a satisfying marriage. Never mind the days when things got stressful in PCU. As she soaped herself up and rinsed herself off, as she ran a razor up her legs and slathered on lotion, she thought how nice it felt to be secure with a man who loved her, to have a job where she helped people.

"I didn't make coffee—" she called to Eric as she stepped onto the bath mat. But he would already have gone to the kitchen. He would have already found the empty carafe and would be laughing at her for it. *Forgot to turn it on again, did you, Hil?* But when Hilary slipped her arms into the robe again and carried the used towels into the bedroom, she found him still there, sitting on the edge of the bed, waiting for her.

"Oh, sorry," she said. "I didn't mean to yell about the coffee. I thought you'd be downstairs."

He'd already dressed. He'd pulled on his pinstripe slacks and found the black shirt she'd given him for Christmas last year. He usually never got ready for the office until he made his energy shake in the mornings. He was on his vitamin B_{12} kick again. "Did you wake Seth up yet?"

"Hilary." He gestured to the bed beside him. His eyes, which never left hers, held something unfathomable. "Will you stop?"

She stared at him, uncertain. "Stop what?"

"Running around. Come sit down for a minute."

"Now?"

"Yes, now."

"But Seth needs to be up."

"Hilary, please."

"Something wrong?" In spite of all the changes this morning, the way Eric had acted different in the shower, she hadn't quite spent the time to decipher it. Here they were starting their day together, rushing on with their routines, getting Seth off to middle school, going on with their lives. Why would Eric act so somber?

"Yes. There's something wrong."

"What is it?"

"We have to talk."

A sense of foreboding began to creep up Hilary's limbs. Her skin had gone cold. What was this? "Can't it wait until tonight, Eric? I'll be late."

"No."

"What do you mean, no?"

"It can't wait."

"You can't be late, either." It took a quarter of an hour for him to get to his office at the investment firm in the Loop, a little less if he took the L.

"That doesn't matter right now."

"The traffic—"

"I've waited too long as it is."

She dropped the laundry on the floor and drew the robe tighter around her. Her hair was still wet. She was freezing. "Is it money?" she asked. "I know I put the tires on the credit card, but it's hard making things balance the month insurance is due."

"It isn't money," and, for a moment, Hilary felt relieved as she stood before him. "Well, what is it then?"

"Put something on." That was when her fear started, the moment he spoke and, at the same time, looked away. "Get dressed."

"But you said you wanted to talk. You want me to get dressed now?"

"I do, Hilary. Yes."

She'd asked all those casual questions in the

bathroom, the same script she followed every day. They never thought about the things they said to each other. *May I come in? Sleep well? Everything okay?* Only now did she realize. All those questions she'd asked, and he'd never answered.

Eric found her something to wear in the closet. Hilary had a dozen scrubs or more; she needed them for the long hours she spent on the PCU floor. Eric didn't thumb through them; he grabbed the first one he came to. She'd worn it yesterday, the blue shirt with smiling sunflowers. Her security badge still dangled from a Tweety Bird clip on the pocket. Bold letters read: **Hilary Wynn, R.N.** The yellow sun faces leered at her. "What is this, Eric? Just tell me."

Eric drew a deep breath. "It's not easy."

She reached for his hand. "Should it be? Is this something you want me to make easy for you?" Outside, the garbage truck turned onto their street. It picked up speed, its engine crescendoing as it roared toward the neighbor's driveway. Brakes hissed. A horrific clatter came as the hydraulic fork reached for a container, lifted it, and rained its contents into the hopper.

Eric squared his shoulders and said, "I'm seeing someone."

Hilary stared at him. "Seeing someone? What? Someone? Who, someone? A doctor? A financial advisor?" It took her that long to begin unraveling his meaning. "What are you telling me, Eric? I don't understand."

"I'm seeing *someone*," he said again.

Oh.

Oh.

"A woman," he clarified.

A hundred emotions ran through her at once. Shock. Disbelief. Confusion. She must have heard wrong. She reacted as if she'd been burned, jerking her hand from him before her nerves signaled pain. "A woman," she repeated, as if she had to say it herself to hear it. "You're having an *affair?*"

For the first time, he didn't speak.

"Eric, what are you saying?" *Deny it!* she wanted to scream. *Tell me it's a mistake. Tell me you aren't serious.*

"I never meant it to get this far."

The air had gone out of the atmosphere. Hilary couldn't breathe. She felt like she'd been punched in the stomach. "This is how you start my *day?* You're telling me *this?*" She could still be dreaming. She could wake up and find Eric sleeping beside her. The alarm would sound and she'd stagger out of bed and Boo would be dancing at her feet, waiting for his breakfast. The breath would rush from her lungs; she'd go limp with relief.

"There's no way else to say it," Eric said. "I'm sorry."

For long seconds she couldn't speak. If she tried, words might betray her. Words, spilling to the ground like blood spills from a wound. Her ears buzzed. Her hands started shaking.

"Hilary, I—"

"Don't say anything more, Eric," she said. "Please just *stop*."

It didn't make sense. Eric was the man who'd loved her, who'd actually gotten permission from her father before he'd asked her to marry him, who'd positioned an engagement ring precariously in whipped cream and hot chocolate after they'd gone skating in Grant Park. He was the man who had held her after her father died. He was the one who'd placed his hand over her belly to feel the baby move, who'd wiggled her stomach and talked to unborn Seth in "Mister Ed" horse voices, who'd brought her Jolly Rancher candies and let her squeeze his hand during labor and breathed cleansing breaths with her when the contractions got too fierce to bear. What was he thinking, that he could throw it away?

"That's all you have to say? That you're sorry?" Later Hilary would be furious. Anger would grow inside her like a geyser, ready to erupt. But for now she could only swim through a fog with everything upside down. She had no idea when they'd started living this lie.

The neighbors were coming awake. Hilary glanced out the window to see the Hartmans, the retired couple who had lived on this street for the past two decades, out for their morning stroll. They'd always been the sweetest couple around, making sure everyone knew when their grandchildren would be coming for a visit. As they walked, the elderly woman curled her fingers around the crook of her husband's elbow and gazed up at him. Mr. Hartman cocked his head and smiled at something she said. Hilary had thought she and Eric would grow old together like the Hartmans, celebrating milestones, amazing their friends with their exemplary marriage.

"Do you want to tell me more?" she asked, her voice a study in control. "Or do you want me to ask questions?"

She had *trusted* him. This couldn't be the man she'd pledged her life to, the one who'd promised to stand beside her through better or worse, through richer or poorer, in sickness and in health, until death parted them. Eric wasn't this man anymore. He was a stranger. Sure, they'd had their rough spots, everyone did, times when one or the other of them had been bored or unhappy, but they'd been honest with each other, hadn't they? Sure, there had been times when she'd worked the long night shifts at the hospital. That wasn't any reason to break a lifelong promise, to find someone else, was it? Her fists ached to pummel him. She wanted to hurt him the way he was hurting her.

"Mom!" Seth's voice came from the family room. "I'll get detention if I'm late again. How come nobody woke me up?"

Oh, Father, she prayed. *What do you want from me? How do I respond? How do I stay sane and guard my heart and do the right thing?*

Hilary adjusted her badge and locked eyes with Eric. There were so many things she would find out later, who the other woman was, how she and Eric had met, how they'd stolen time to be together. But now Hilary asked the only question that mattered.

"This other woman. Do you love her?" she asked.

When he nodded and whispered, "Yes," she felt like she'd been shoved to the ground.

Do I fight for this marriage? Do I try to work through this, Lord? Or do you want me to quietly let it go?

Downstairs she heard Seth rummaging through the pantry in search of the Honey Nut Cheerios. Seconds later she heard the refrigerator door slam shut and the chair scrape on the kitchen floor.

Because I don't think I can do either one.

He said, "Hilary. I want to marry her."

She stared at him, the shock beginning to ebb. Pain knifed her chest.

"Pam and I have wasted enough time. We'd like to do this fast."

"If you're asking for a divorce," Hilary said, her

voice even, "you'll have to file for it. I want everyone to know this isn't coming from me."

"I've already started the process with my lawyer." He turned toward the door as if he couldn't face her for this. "The papers will be served on Thursday."

Oh, Eric, she wanted to cry. *Isn't there some way to fix it? Isn't there something to make you forget her? Something to make you see what you're giving away?* But Hilary had too much pride to beg. "You're leaving the house," she said. "I'm not."

"We're dividing the house," he said, finding something fascinating on the ceiling. "It'll have to be sold."

She didn't flinch. She took a step toward him. "I'll have custody of Seth. I'm leaving you no choice in that."

"That's yet to be negotiated, Hilary."

All this time the little dog had been cowering at the foot of the bed, paws beside his ears, fearful eyes raised toward Eric. "Is it?" Hilary asked. "Is that what our life is now, Eric? Something to be negotiated?"

"It's the best I can do."

She sat on the bed and picked up Boo, holding the dog against her like a shield. "It *isn't*," she said. "It *isn't*, Eric. It isn't the *best* for anybody."

"It is for me," he said.

"So it's all about you, is it? The rest of us don't matter, I suppose. Especially your *son*."

"We have to leave Seth out of this," Eric said. "I refuse to make this a power struggle about my son. For Seth's sake, I expect that we can be civil."

"Oh, of course we'll be civil, Eric," Hilary whispered, and, to her horror, tears leaked from her eyes. She wiped the back of her hand across her nose. "And no matter how you'd like to twist this around on me, it isn't a power struggle. It's what you're *teaching* him. That he isn't important enough to you. That he's easy to leave."

Eric said, "He isn't the one I'm leaving."

Her tears came unbidden now. There was nothing she could do to stop the swirling storm, the emptiness. With jaw clenched and hands knotted into fists, Hilary stood her ground and watched her husband go, taking with him the marriage she'd always placed so much faith in, the man she'd never thought could betray her, the man she thought would never desert his family, leaving them stranded and alone.

Eric had met Pamela when she'd come to decorate his office. He and Hilary hadn't been talking much those days, that month, that year. She'd been coming to terms with her doctor's report that she couldn't have the second child they'd planned on, that Seth would be their only one.

When Eric had wanted to talk about it, Hilary wouldn't hear him. She'd be running out the door

25

with her nurse's bag in hand for another long shift at the hospital.

When he'd wanted to admit to her that he felt vague guilt because he'd been the one who'd wanted to wait, to get further in his career before they had another financial drain, Hilary had been off to another church activity or buying oranges to take to Seth's Little League game.

Their conversations had run the gamut from, *Did you feed the dog this morning?* to, *Weren't you going to make a tax payment? Did you do that?*

Simply put, Eric knew he had been wrong. But Pam had come into his office asking questions about his likes and dislikes, trying to define his tastes, at a time when Hilary had been distant. It had started when Pam had told him about a walnut desk she'd found. *It's quite the handsome piece,* she'd said. *It fits you, Eric.* There had been a lunch. A celebratory dinner out after her work on his office was finished. Phone calls and texts. There had been a second night, when Pam had come to town for a different client, dinner at an expensive steak house near the lakeshore, after which they'd sat on a bench beside the water, holding hands while a man played James Taylor songs on an acoustic guitar.

Sometime during the James Taylor street music, they had danced. He had pulled Pam up by the hand and she had moved into his arms, fit herself against him the way a water creature curls inside its shell. Somewhere during the song, he had told her she was the most desirable woman he'd ever known. After which he had tipped the guitar player a hundred-dollar bill because he'd been so grateful just to have a safe place to spend time with her.

He'd driven her back to her hotel and left his car with the valet so he could walk her to her room and kiss her good night at the door. Which was what he'd intended to do.

Only he hadn't. And he hadn't stopped to think what he could lose, not then. Later it surprised him that he'd so easily forgotten to think about Seth or his parents or his wife. He'd ignored all these sound reasons and drifted forward on the promise of intrigue, warmth, risk. He'd been excited. A little infatuated. Willing to add this forbidden thing to his life in the same calculating way that someone might add an extra room to a house.

He hadn't stopped to think of the people who would judge him, or the people he would hurt.

Those people weren't a part of this world. He didn't see how they could ever be.

Seth soon came to see his life divided into two parts. First, the part when his mom and dad had been together. They'd done things like going to Cubs games or riding the L all the way to the

Loop for pizza. They'd driven three days to camp in Yellowstone, where he'd drifted off to sleep watching the fire dancing beyond the wall of the tent and the shadow cast by his parents as they'd pulled their chairs closer to each other and to the flames. Second, the part after his father had decided he didn't want them anymore. When Seth's mom cranked the water in the shower because that might keep him from hearing her sobs. When the kitchen was as silent as church that one day even though his mom and dad were both sitting there. When the tension in their house felt as if it might shatter like glass and cut them.

"You're handling this well," his dad had told Seth over chocolate ice cream at Baskin-Robbins. "You haven't even cried. I'm proud of you, Son."

"When are you leaving, Dad?" he'd asked.

"Tomorrow."

"You don't have to leave if you don't want to," Seth had said, a twelve-year-old hating himself because he'd started to sob. Melted fudge ripple dripped down his cone. He let it drip, didn't try to lick it off. "You can stay, Dad."

"No," his dad had told him. "Things have gone too far for that."

That's the moment his mother started needing him. From that moment, he had felt like the statue of Atlas, with the whole world balanced on his shoulders. If he slipped or stopped trying or anything went wrong, the whole world would come crashing down.

That last day with his dad, Seth had told jokes, told them frantically, thinking if he could make his dad laugh, maybe he could make his dad change his mind, maybe he could make his dad realize what he was leaving behind.

Why did the kid eat his homework, Dad? Because the teacher said it was a piece of cake.

What do you get when you cross an elephant with a fish, Dad? Do you know? Swimming trunks.

"You're so good to take care of your mom, Seth," people he barely knew said after his dad had gone. "I don't know what she would do without you."

Or they'd say, "Look at you. You're so grown-up. You're the man of the house now."

Seth knew what his mother's friends thought about him. They thought he was the perfect kid. People thought they knew what they were getting with Seth, but they were wrong. He just wanted to be a kid everybody wasn't watching and depending on. He wanted to do stupid things; he wanted to make a mistake and not feel like the bottom of his mother's world was going to fall out because of it.

When he'd gotten in the fight with Chris Schorr on the playground, Seth had never intended to stop hitting. The principal had yanked him off by the collar and dragged him into the office. He wanted to keep pounding and pounding the kid who had told him his dad had a girlfriend.

"Liar," Seth had said every time his knuckles met Chris's face. "Liar. *Liar.*" When Mr. Baker asked why, Seth would have been vindicated if he had wailed out what had happened. But Seth sat in the principal's chair feeling like a mad animal lived inside him, something that took over his body and made him want to be mean. *It's none of your business!* Seth wanted to shout. Instead he sat silent, too proud to speak, his bloody hand throbbing in his lap. And when the school secretary, Mrs. Knight, had poked her head in and asked if he wanted her to make a call, Mr. Baker had shaken his head. "Don't phone Seth's mom, Nora," Mr. Baker had said as he'd offered Seth a conciliatory smile. "This isn't anything Seth and I can't work out together. His mom's got enough problems of her own. I'm sure Seth agrees this isn't something we should bother her with."

From then on Seth carried this anger beneath his skin. His frustration ran just below the surface, unseen and churning like an underground river, something he vowed he'd never let his mother see. That's when Seth had known the truth. Chris Schorr hadn't been the biggest liar on earth. His *dad* had been.

Chapter 1

❧

Six years later

*W*hen Hilary opened the door to the coffeehouse, a burst of conversation and the aroma of Arabica swirled out to meet her. She stepped into the front foyer and looked for her friends. *I don't* need *this,* she'd told Gina Minor, trying to beg off. *I don't even want to* think *about it.* Hilary had been doing her best to shelve Seth's graduation in the back of her mind alongside the other items she planned to think about later: the need to draw up a will, the need to add more insulation in the crawl space.

It had been Gina's idea that they meet on Tuesdays in that big corner booth at Spilling the Beans on North Central Avenue. They could brown-bag if they liked or buy a salad and order up a Brownlow or a coffee. Gina, who worked with Hilary on the nursing staff at the hospital, had always been the one to organize things. They were a group of friends who had known one another forever, several of them with kids graduating, another with a mother she'd just admitted to an assisted-living center, another going through a tough divorce. Gina was the one

31

who always reminded them how they needed to stick together and encourage one another, because they could give one another advice, a gentle hug, laughter, strength.

"Maybe you shouldn't count on me for coffee," Hilary had told Gina when the invitation had been issued. "I doubt I can get away from this new rotation schedule. You know me."

"Denial," Gina had said, laughing. "It's not just a river in Egypt." Which, although intended to be funny, hadn't made Hilary laugh at all.

"This won't go away just because you won't let yourself deal with it," Gina had pressed. "I have just as much time as you do. Trust me. I've been through this. I know how lost you're going to feel without Seth."

Well, Hilary reasoned as she stared at the menu overhead, trying to focus on the list of coffee drinks, *maybe Gina was right.* Only today she certainly didn't intend to be the one to soak up the sympathy at the table. She'd come to support Julie, the newest divorcée. *You'll make it to the other side of your divorce with flying colors, just like I did,* Hilary would tell her. Sure, she'd tell Julie, there were times when it had been rough. Sure, she could say, she still remembered that train wreck like it had been yesterday—the day Eric had stood in their bedroom and told her he loved someone else. But she hadn't let the pain derail her for very long. She hadn't let the

the anger stop her from moving
r life.

ta was making Hilary a decaf
the steamed milk hissing from the
, she took the cup in hand, she glanced
up to see Lynn waving at her from the designated
table. Hilary smiled back and wove her way
toward her friends. When she slid into the booth,
the conversation had already turned to the high-
school seniors, graduating this year from
Jefferson High on Chicago's North Side.

"They say these will be the best years of our
lives." Kim Draper was tucking a tomato inside
her sandwich. "I read an article by one woman
who got through her empty-nest syndrome by
putting tuition on credit cards. We could do that.
We could make a pact to earn frequent-flyer miles
together. Think of the places we could go with all
those miles."

Fay reached across the table and snagged one of
Donna's sweet-potato chips. "Next meeting on the
beach somewhere. Or maybe Times Square."

"Who can afford Times Square?" Doubt filled
Kim's eyes and Hilary could tell she wanted the
same reassurances Hilary did: *Mothering doesn't
go away when they leave home, does it? It just
changes? Right?*

She pictured her eighteen-year-old's face. If
she'd felt like she'd been drowning after Eric had
left, then Seth's presence in the house had felt like

someone bringing oxygen to her, allowing
breathe underwater. It had been so easy to
treating Seth like the man of the house. It had been
so easy to start depending on him.

I have to let him go, Lord. I know I do.

*And I don't know what I'm going to do without
him.*

Fay must have read her expression. "Just keep
the kitchen open, girl. He'll come home more than
you think."

"Just wait until Seth wants to move back in,
Hilary," Gina said. "We'll be here for each other
then, too. That's when you can cry."

But not one of them mentioned the major
difference, Hilary realized. They all talked about
Seth *coming* home. Rather than *being* home. Once
he crossed the gym stage and the school
superintendent handed Seth his diploma, she
wouldn't have anything left of him to hang on to.
No more nights curled up together reading *Go,
Dog, Go!* No more sweaty little head propped
beneath her chin. No more soggy bottom in a
bathing suit. No more epic drives to baseball
games with six players crammed into the seats,
babbling on about girls and their batting averages
while they shot spitballs at one another.

No more terror as she stomped an imaginary
brake on the passenger's side of the car, teaching
Seth to drive. No more mornings feeling responsible
when he couldn't drag himself out of bed.

Actually, Hilary admitted, it had been awhile since she'd worried about any of these mothering duties, even the teenager ones. She had this to consider: Was she really grieving her son's growing up and moving out for good? Or was she more afraid of being alone for the first time in her life?

Kim left the booth to pick up her order. Gina was talking to an acquaintance at the door. Donna and Fay were waiting in line to order lunch, deep in a conversation about whether or not to order the college-dorm package with extra-long twin sheets for their kids' beds. Which left Hilary and Julie fingering their mugs as they leaned toward each other, each waiting for the other to speak.

Julie's eyes filled with tears. "Oh, Hilary. I'm so sorry. I'm not great company these days."

"Been rough, has it?"

"Yes, more than I ever imagined. I shouldn't be here, I guess. So many of you are dealing with graduating seniors. And me, I'm dealing with this divorce and I'm a mess. I don't have anything worthwhile to add to the conversation."

Hilary reached for Julie's hand and squeezed it. "It's good you came, Jules. You know that. Anything any of us can do to help, we'll do it."

"His lawyer delivered the papers this morning, Hilary. It was awful."

There weren't many words of comfort for this,

Hilary knew. She held her friend's hand and let Julie cry. "I'm so sorry."

"How did you do it, Hilary?" Julie pulled her hand away and blew her nose on a napkin. "How did you get through it? Does it keep hurting like this forever?"

Hilary rummaged through her purse to find an extra tissue. When she found one, she handed it to Julie. "On the day Eric's lawyer showed up at the door, it was horrible." She remembered standing on the front step, the edges of the document in her hand rustling like dried leaves, hearing her own lifeless voice asking when the papers needed to be signed, where they needed to be delivered.

"Can you imagine having that job?" Julie touched the edges of her eyes with the tissue and offered a sad smile. "I'd hate it."

Hilary gave a wry laugh. "Yeah. Me, too."

"You never talked about your divorce much."

"You want me to talk about it?" Hilary propped her elbows on the table. "I was a blubbering, sobbing wreck of a human being for eight solid weeks. I don't think I missed an hour without crying." She locked eyes with Julie. "You really want to hear all this stuff?"

Julie nodded. "I wouldn't have asked if I didn't want to hear it."

"I just kept thinking, *How could he do this? How could Eric just throw away all those years* we'd spent together? *How could he give up on half our lives?*"

Julie watched a sparrow flit past the window. "No," she said. "Really, Hilary. It's *more* than half. At least it is for me."

"I used to wake myself up in the middle of the night crying. It was like there was some physiological thing happening to me," Hilary said. "Like my body required a certain number of tears every day just to sustain itself."

The diners beside them were clearing their table themselves, carrying their plates and baskets to the self-service tub. "It helps so much to hear it. Really." Julie lowered her voice as a restaurant employee followed them and wiped the table with a rag. "It helps so much to know that I'm not the only one to go through this."

"It gets easier, Julie. It takes time, but, eventually, it does pass. You stop trying to second-guess yourself. You stop asking yourself what you could have done differently."

As the other women returned to the table, it was Julie's turn to grip Hilary's hands. "Thank you."

"Call me any time you want to talk." Hilary scooted sideways to make room for Fay next to her. "And you'll see. You'll figure out who you are without him. You'll wake up and realize one day that you aren't thinking about your divorce all the time."

"You have no idea how much I need to hear this, Hilary."

"You'll see yourself through God's eyes. You'll see how much you're worth. How much you can *do*."

Yes, Hilary could speak with authority on this subject. This was exactly how it had happened for her. Somewhere along the way, after her pain had been replaced by anger, after her anger had ebbed into a dull sadness that had seemed to sap every ounce of strength from her body, she'd awakened one day and felt like someone had turned on the sun in the sky again.

Because of Seth, her sleep had started to come easier. Mothering Seth had become good therapy for her. Maybe, in Eric's eyes, she'd failed as a wife. But just let anyone try to accuse Hilary of not being a good mother! Now Seth stood six-foot-one and could bench-press 230 pounds. But he'd better know good and well that his mother still laid down the law around this place!

It was time to let him go. Although Seth wouldn't leave for Emhurst College until late August, Hilary had felt his presence fading from the house for months now, each milestone of his senior year at Jefferson—the SATs, the college acceptance letters, scholarship night, the senior prom—drawing him one more step away.

While Hilary had been in her own thoughts, the subject at the table had shifted to husbands. "I was looking at Don across the table the other night," Karen was saying, "and I kept thinking, *What did we do together before we had kids?* I honestly don't remember."

"There's that line in *Failure to Launch*," Fay said, "when Kathy Bates finally tells her son that she's terrified of being left alone in the same house with her husband. I thought that was the best scene in the whole movie."

Well, Hilary thought. *At least I don't have that problem.* Hilary caught herself eyeing her empty ring finger, the small indentation from her wedding band still visible despite the years she hadn't worn it.

When Fay glanced at her watch and announced she needed to get back to the office, Hilary knew she'd found her perfect exit. She needed to get back to her nursing duties; she had several new care plans to write up this afternoon. But as Hilary wadded up her napkin and gave Julie one more reassuring squeeze, her cell phone played its song inside her purse. The interruption sent her rummaging through the zippered pockets, trying to find her phone so she could silence it. She saw the flash of light to the left of her keys. Just as she reached to push the vibrate button, she saw the caller ID.

Eric. *Speaking of.*

Her breath caught in her throat.

What on earth does he want?

Hilary knew she ought to be able to ignore him, turn him off, pay no heed to his summons. But she was still programmed to answer to this man. Even after everything they'd been through over the years, after the way he'd hurt her, after all the promises she'd made to God and to herself, after all the promises Eric had broken, she read this man's name and her heart beat faster.

"I've got to take this."

Hilary slid sideways out of the booth. *I'm sorry,* she mouthed as Kim moved out of her way. She wove past the line at the cash register and shoved the door open with her shoulder. "Hello," she said, keeping her voice measured as the cell bobbled against her ear. But even though she tried, she couldn't totally erase the familiarity she'd once used with him. "Eric? What's wrong?"

Maybe it had been the way she'd opened her heart to her friend Julie that had made Hilary lower her defenses. She wasn't exactly sure why she felt more vulnerable than usual. But when she heard the woman's voice on the other end, Hilary felt like someone had wrung the air from her lungs.

"Hilary. Hilary? Are you there? It's me. Pam."

Pamela.

Eric's other wife.

"I'm stuck on these travel arrangements, Hilary. Do you have a minute to help me?"

Oh, Father, help me. Not for her I don't.

"I hope you don't mind me calling."

"Pam." After that, Hilary stayed silent, letting the silence answer for her. She wasn't going to lie.

"For Seth's graduation I'm interested in finding a hotel close to your place. It's hard to tell about these from the Internet. Could you tell me which is best?"

"You want my opinion about a hotel?" Hilary asked, incredulous.

"Eric told me about one. What's it called, the Omni? I'm worried that if I don't make a reservation now, everything will be full."

"The Omni," Hilary repeated. And then, pointedly, "I'm surprised you don't already have information on Chicago hotels. I know you've stayed here before."

If Pam recognized this as a jab, she ignored it. "You know how it is. Everything looks great in the pictures. I've read all the TripAdvisor reviews and the posted rates. But there may be better rates if someone phones directly."

"Eric isn't staying with his family this time?" The elder Wynns lived an hour-and-a-half commute to the north. Of course Eric would want to be close to graduation activities. "You're making the reservation for Eric?"

"For Eric. And for me, too. We're both coming."

"Oh. I see." Hilary hoped Pam didn't hear the catch in her voice, but there wasn't much chance of that. "I'll need to get back to you. Would that be okay? I'm having coffee with friends." How mundane a date at Spilling the Beans sounded compared to the impressive things Pam must be doing today, pursuing her career as an interior decorator. The last time they'd talked, Eric had told Hilary how Pam was designing an office for Liam Neeson.

"I'll send you a list via e-mail. You can look it over and phone with the information later," Pam said. "Or maybe you could find out if any of these places offer a local discount. I'll bet we could get a cheaper price if we used your local address. You could make the reservations yourself."

"Oh, I see."

"If it worked that way, you could call me with the confirmation number. Would you mind that?"

The words popped out of Hilary's mouth before she could stop them: "Why would *you* want to come? You aren't Seth's mother." This was always how she got into trouble. All this time she'd been picturing Eric coming alone for Seth's graduation, the three of them spending a few hours together, she and Eric sending their son off as best as they could, considering. The three of them pretending to be the family that they weren't anymore.

"We'll need two rooms for three nights." As easily as Hilary had ignored her question it seemed that Pam also ignored Hilary's. "We'll arrive the afternoon of the thirty-first."

"Two rooms?" When Eric and Hilary had spent

their anniversary there, they'd saved for months to be able to afford it.

"We're bringing the kids, too. They're looking forward to seeing their big brother in his cap and gown."

Hilary knew she ought to be praying, asking God to give her the right words. She ought to be asking for wisdom. *Father, why do I feel like she's trying to shake me up?* "You're asking me to make your hotel reservations? For all of you?"

"Well. After all, Hilary, you are the one who knows the area."

"Eric knows the area. You could have called him instead," Hilary pointed out.

A brief pause on the other end of the line. "You sound like you don't want us to come for Seth's graduation."

Maybe this was the time for Hilary to say something sarcastic or funny, something to make Pam realize that she couldn't step in and turn this family upside down anymore. Hilary had worked her way through so many emotions during these past years. She'd grieved. She'd grown stronger. She'd learned to be honest with herself. She wasn't about to say something that might open old wounds now.

After a lump of silence that felt like it was bleeding between them, Pam spoke in a lowered voice: "Hilary, what you're doing isn't fair. We're setting this up for Eric's sake."

"Are we? I thought graduation was a ceremony for Seth."

"Seth is Eric's son and I am Eric's wife. We have every right to be involved in this special occasion."

"*Eric* has every right to be involved." The rest of it hung between them without being spoken.

"Why don't you come right out and say it?" Pam asked. "Why don't you admit how much I threaten you, Hilary? Because Eric and I stand a better chance of making our marriage work than you two ever did."

A seagull drifted in easy circles overhead, his wings trained into the air, his unblinking eyes searching the ground. He was off-course, Hilary thought. What was he doing so far from the lakeshore? "What are you trying to do?" Hilary asked, her voice hard.

"Eric didn't think you'd have problems with me coming with him. I'm a part of Seth's life, too." Hilary realized that the two of them had discussed how she might react. Hilary was standing on the curb beside North Central Avenue, the ends of her hair and the hem of her skirt lifting and curling as cars whipped past. She screwed up her nose at the damp air tinged with sulfur; Chicago was known for its disagreeable smells. But that wasn't the reason Hilary felt like she was being smothered. Pam seemed to be waiting for her to agree to make those reservations. And she would never do it.

"I'm sorry, Pam, but I have to let you go."

"Oh, right," Pam said. "You were out with your friends. I forgot."

"Send me your plans when you make them. I'd like to know where you decide to stay." Hilary flipped her cell phone shut with guilt-ridden satisfaction.

When she hurried back to the booth inside, Gina, Kim, Julie, and the others were stacking plates, busing the table themselves. Everyone was in a hurry. Their time was up, and heaven only knew where their conversation had gone since Hilary had left them. It didn't matter. Hilary felt incapable of joining in again. She'd been blindsided by Pam's call. No more joking about frequent-flyer miles and trips to Times Square. When she caught her friends staring, she realized they must have been able to read it on her face.

"Who was *that?*" Gina said.

"I can't believe she called."

"Who?" Julie asked.

"I can't believe I let that woman pull me down to her level. I almost lost it. I can't believe anyone in the world could make me feel that *defensive.*"

"Who?" Donna said.

"Eric's wife," Hilary said, hating the way her composure finally crumbled, how her voice sounded as thin as a hurt child's instead of like someone who might actually be able to stand up for herself. "I guess Eric's bringing the whole

45

family for graduation. She called wanting me to make hotel reservations for them. Can you believe it?"

It encouraged her because her friends looked as shocked as she felt.

"As if you don't already have enough to deal with," Julie said, shaking her head. "The other wife."

"You can't be expected to entertain that *woman*," Donna said, throwing her purse strap over her shoulder like she was donning a military weapon.

It was Gina who stripped Hilary bare with her words, though. She was the friend who knew Hilary best of all. "What did you say? Did you tell her she's got more gall than a bladder surgeon?"

"Disgusting," Kim said. Hilary couldn't be sure whether Kim was referring to Pam's actions or Gina's bad joke.

"What's that Scripture?" Donna quoted something that sounded like it came from Proverbs: " 'The lips of an adulteress drip honey but in the end she is bitter as gall.' "

"You would memorize something like that?" Hilary said.

"Just sort of rolled off my tongue, huh?"

"Don't say it." Those words made Hilary's teeth clench. "I've gotten beyond that. Don't mention words like 'adulteress.' "

"Guess I just believe in calling a spade a spade."

Gina gripped Hilary's shoulders and made Hilary meet her gaze while, all around them the lunch rush began and people were jostling three deep at the counter. "Hilary, you're only barely making your way through as it is."

Hilary took a stab at humor: "Thanks for the vote of confidence, Gina. I'm glad you think I'm handling my life so *well*."

"We're your friends. Who's going to look after you if we don't?"

"We're not kidding, Hilary," Kim added. "What are you going to *do?*"

"Invite her to dinner and cook my best sage-chive steaks with arugula salad when she comes. Or maybe I'll run away. Set up a new identity in a new place. Which do you think would be easier?"

"Setting up a new identity," Kim said.

"That woman is perfectly capable of making her own hotel reservations," Gina said.

Life never gets easier, does it, Lord? Hilary thought. *Just when you think you've got everything under control, something else comes along.*

Why did she get the feeling that Pam was trying to initiate a competition between them? Hilary supposed that's where it started, two women having a go at marriage to the same man. Pam had ended up with Eric, after all, so why would she have anything else to prove? But Hilary was the one who had also gone through a divorce with him. Maybe that meant she had the edge. Maybe that meant she knew Eric better.

"You've got to come up with something more elaborate than steaks," Donna suggested. "You've got to make *girl* food. Maybe Thai. Something with peanut sauce. Show her who's got the edge in the cooking department."

"Having a Pillsbury Bake-Off is the last thing I want to do during graduation week."

Julie held the door open for Hilary. "I agree. You don't need to do that. Just eyeball Eric and see how much he weighs. That'll tell you who's the better cook."

Donna couldn't leave that one alone. "Or who's making sure he gets the most exercise," she commented.

"Get out of here." Hilary flung her purse in the general direction of Donna's arm. "Don't even say it." And finally everyone started laughing, even Hilary.

Donna wrapped her arm around Hilary's shoulder and hugged her sideways.

"See you at the hospital," Gina called.

"Thanks for everything," Julie said.

As Hilary waved good-bye to the others and steered the car toward Englewood General, where she worked, she prayed, *Okay, God. Help me get through this in spite of myself.*

She'd done fine up until now. Still, she had to admit that the hurt had lasted a very long time. Pam's phone call had reminded her of the struggles, the questions she'd asked, the long months when God didn't seem to be handing out any answers.

Chapter 2

⤜

*F*or as long as she could remember, this had been Hilary's mothering credo: *If you feed them, they will come.*

She walked in carrying the first of three loads of grocery sacks, filled with Doritos and enough mega-bags of potato chips to squelch the hunger of a small military brigade. She'd bought a case of brownie mix at Costco, along with massive jars of bean dip and peanut butter and a six-pack of squeeze cheese.

Hilary had learned that boys weren't like the tentative, polite girls who visited. Girls opened the refrigerator and made a careful study. *Oh, Lauren's mom keeps that same kind of juice; oh, I've never tried that salad dressing. Oh, you've got* croutons. Boys opened the refrigerator door and just started unloading. They moved through like flocks of starlings, devouring everything in their path. They would be happy for a while watching television or wrestling with each other or playing Xbox, and then they would move to the next location where they could find food. Yes, all this time, and Hilary knew she'd been buying love. But she happened to think it was well worth it.

After stowing the groceries, she headed to the living room. The boys had roosted around the television, howling with laughter as they alternately fast-forwarded and rewound the digital video on Charlie's camera, their dirt-encrusted socks propped on a coffee table that still needed polishing. Armed with an oily rag, Hilary moved three pairs of feet out of the way. *Of course I can handle Pamela,* she thought as she started to dust. With each swirl of the rag, *It's my choice if I let her ruin Seth's graduation.* With each stroke of polish, *Of course I won't let that happen!*

Hilary realized, as she glanced around the room at the boys, that she wasn't sure that Seth was even *here.* When she heard the car pull into the driveway, adrenaline shot through her. Okay. Maybe she wasn't as composed as she intended to be. She felt about as ready to have this flurry of Eric's family descend as she was to have a colonoscopy. She checked her watch.

Thank goodness. This must be Seth showing up in his ancient Plymouth Horizon. That car was ready to fall apart, and she didn't know where he'd been. She'd give anything to have another two hours, time to clean, time to run to the florist, too, to buy a bouquet for the guest room where her mother would be staying.

Hilary had just enough time to check her face in the hall mirror before Seth hit the screen door, all six-foot-one of him. He plowed past her into the

51

kitchen, throwing open the refrigerator door. He raked through the deli drawer for something to eat.

Every time he rounded a corner and Hilary looked up at him, she almost didn't recognize him. He was always bigger than she remembered.

She reached over his head for the mayo. "I'll make you a sandwich."

"No time for that. We're still working on the senior video." He spoke all this into the nethermost regions of the fridge.

Ever since this year started, it seemed like Seth had never stayed in place long enough for her to get a handle on him. In some societies he would already be considered a man. She couldn't understand some things going on inside him. She'd never been intended to understand them; they were *man* things, things she hoped he shared with Eric whenever father and son had a visit together. Hilary felt like her heart was always running to keep up with him, always disconnected.

Seth found the ham and ripped the package open, folding an incredible number of slices into his mouth all at once. "This video's going to be good. They're playing the pass I caught in the Kennedy game."

"Wow. You should be honored."

"Yep." A beat of silence before Seth asked, "When're Dad and Pam getting here? Have you talked to them today?"

Hilary nodded, hoping her expression divulged nothing. "They should be at the airport by now. Their flight was due about thirty minutes ago."

"Are Grandma and Grandpa picking them up?"

"I don't think so. I think they're renting a car this time."

Seth hesitated. "It's so weird that *she's* going to be here."

Hilary knew she had to pull this off; she owed it to him. "Pretty special, isn't it? All in celebration of you."

"Can't believe they're bringing the ankle biters, too."

"Pam will do some serious damage if she hears you call her children 'ankle biters.' Which reminds me." Hilary nodded toward the other room. "How about putting the couch cushions back on in there? Maybe throw away the paper plates and recycle the cans? Maybe tell your friends we're having company?"

Seth dashed his hands under the faucet and made a halfhearted attempt at drying them on the towel. He grabbed both of his mother's hands and pushed against them while she pushed back, this gentle wrestling a form of endearment that they shared.

Which also reminded Hilary, "How many thank-you notes have you written, young man?"

Silence. Hilary knew what that meant.

"Aunt Dorothy wants to hear from you. She

wants to make sure you got the check. She thinks Hank Bonner is stealing things from her mailbox."

"*Mom.* I'm *working* on it." Then a quick turn, a salute with his expensive smartphone. "I've got to go help with the video. I promised Emily I'd stop by and help her fix the gears on her bike, too." Emily was Seth's girlfriend. They'd been dating since the homecoming dance in the fall, and Hilary had to admit that she thought Seth had good taste. "I want to be done by the time Dad gets here."

As Seth's eyes lingered on Hilary's, it was strange, but this time it seemed like he was sensing it, too, the symbolism of his departure, the waning of a season, the progression of time. "You going to be okay, Mom, with her around?"

"Her? *Who?*" For a moment Hilary thought he was still talking about Emily.

"Pam."

Hilary almost flinched when Seth said her name. *Just like that,* Hilary thought. *Was it that easy to give myself away?* Maybe she spoke too quickly, but she couldn't help it. "Oh, I think I'll manage."

"It doesn't seem weird to you or anything? She'll be in our *house.*"

"Nope," Hilary lied. "Not weird."

She saw both pleasure and relief fill his eyes. "Mom, you're the best."

"Yeah. You just keep telling me that."

He bear-hugged her. His letter jacket smelled of all the places he'd gone these past months, faint leather and wood smoke and school locker. It occurred to Hilary how remarkable it was, how he towered over her now, how she kept remembering holding him when he was small, his head tucked beneath her chin.

While the boys downloaded digital video into the computer, Hilary overheard them discussing the *other* senior party. Not the chaperoned function, sanctioned by the school, which the PTA had been planning, but the one the parents all pretended not to know about even though it happened every year.

Hilary straightened a picture frame on the bookshelf while, bit by bit, the boys slipped casual details to her. They intended to camp together; they'd been gathering sleeping bags and gear for weeks. There was a huge spot reserved for the whole class in a campground, not too far away. That's when Hilary realized what they were doing. They were trusting her and testing her at the same time. They wanted to know what she thought about their plans. Finally, Ian asked, "Seth's Mom, if you knew about a party like this, would you let Seth go?"

The frame in her hand contained a photo of Eric and Seth together. Eric was teaching Seth to cast a fishing rod, their arms in perfect sync, their hands on the reel, their eyes on the red and white bobber. "You want an honest answer?"

But of course they did. This was where Hilary had stood so many times before, her heart straddling a fence. If she was too strict, she faced the possibility of pushing them away. The more she showed Seth that she trusted him, the more worthy of trust he became. Yet she was also aware of this: Seth's age group didn't always think things through to the end. She'd read somewhere that a young adult's brain wasn't totally developed until twenty-five or so. And they were still decades away from understanding their own mortality.

"I don't know. You'd be far away from anyone who could help you—"

"We'd be okay," Will said.

"—and it seems like a lot of effort after the parents have already put something together."

Even Hilary could see past what she was telling them. They wanted to be on their own.

She set down the frame and did away with a cobweb on the lampshade. "What I'm going to tell you is what I've told you before, you guys. You can be responsible for yourselves, but you can't be responsible for someone else. When you get a group together that big, something usually gets out of hand."

Chase said, "We'll be careful."

"Everybody feels the way we do, Mom. It's tradition. The seniors do it every year."

"No matter how careful you are, guys, you know someone's going to be drinking." They stared at Hilary with innocent, round eyes, like they'd never heard that word before. *Drinking.* "That sort of thing comes with a big responsibility. You've got to make good choices. And you've got to think how you're influencing other people." There, she had said her piece. Seth knew how she felt about it.

"We know that." A couple of them inclined their heads in assent. She could almost believe they would heed her warning. Ian asked, "You had a senior party when you graduated, didn't you?"

Only then did Hilary exercise her right to remain silent.

"See?" Seth said. "It's the last chance our whole class has to be together. *Ever.*"

And he was right about that, too.

Maybe she was going against her own better judgment, saying yes. But she knew how it worked. If she didn't give permission, Seth would sneak around behind her back and do it anyway.

Hilary suddenly felt flippant about her son's freedom, flippant about her own qualms. Why was she taking everything so seriously, anyway? Seth was graduating tomorrow. In spite of Pamela and Eric, they were supposed to be having fun. She was tired of grieving. She was tired of not being able to get past her own feelings so she could be happy for her son.

"I wouldn't have you miss it, Seth," she said.

Will jumped on it: "You'd let him go, then?"

"Wouldn't your parents let you go?" Hilary asked Will. Then she turned to Seth, but she was perfectly aware she was answering them all. "You're eighteen. You've gotten good grades and you did great on your AP tests. You're accepted into college with a scholarship." Not three months from now, he wouldn't even be *living* with her anymore. He could be staying out all night and never going to class, and, for a while at least, he wouldn't have to answer to anyone. *There has to come a time to let go, doesn't there, Lord?* "You know how to make the right choices. Right now, I don't give a . . . a flying flip what you do."

"A flying flip?" Seth repeated, grinning. "A *flying flip,* Mom? Really?" He loved to critique her when she said something that was outdated or embarrassing, heaven forbid. He especially teased her when she said "I'm jazzed" about something. She couldn't blame him, really. That phrase had stuck with her a long time. She happened to like being jazzed about things.

She brought in the vacuum cleaner and began to un-snake the hose while the kids turned their attention back to the senior video. "Should we run this picture of Laura welding metal in the art studio or should we run this picture of her without teeth when she was seven?" Chase asked Hilary.

"Do you have to choose?" she asked. "I think

they're both cute together. As a set. Laura then and Laura now."

"Okay," Chase agreed. "We'll use both."

That's how their time together ended that afternoon, with Hilary standing in front of the TV screen, the vacuum upholstery nozzle forgotten in her hand. She watched the video shots as they came up, enjoying them as much as the boys did. She gave motherly suggestions of what they should include in the senior-class video, and what they should avoid. The same way Hilary had given them her opinion about the party. And for a moment, she felt smug, mistaken into thinking they might have been *listening*. Mistaken into thinking that a mom might actually be able to influence a group of teenagers to be careful.

Chapter 3

❧

*H*ilary did find the time to rush out to buy fresh flowers for her mother in the guest room. She picked out fistfuls of red gerbera, yellow tulips, and blue royal iris from the tall buckets inside the shop cooler. While the florist arranged Hilary's selections in a vase, Hilary roamed the small aisles lined with mysterious ornamental plants. The water fountain. The rich smell of soil. The scarlet etchings of an orchid bloom.

The door opened, and even though Hilary recognized the woman who stepped inside, it took her one beat, two, to remember the woman's name. She was Seth's AP English teacher. Mrs. Winkler. Patty. Yes, that's what it was.

"Here you are." The florist set the arrangement beside the register as Hilary pulled her check card from her purse. Mrs. Winkler, as Seth had always called her, recognized Hilary, too. She smiled.

Hilary started off on a chatty, polite conversation. "I'll bet you were ready to have those AP essays over and done with." The florist handed back her card and the receipt. "I know Seth was sure happy to get his finished."

"Absolutely," the teacher said, laughing,

nodding toward the vase. "You getting ready for graduation?"

"We are."

"Is it bad for a teacher to admit she's almost as glad to be finished with a term as the students are?"

Hilary laughed. "I wouldn't think so. Not at all."

They continued chatting for a few minutes, talking about this and that, until Hilary said, "Thank you for what you did for my son." Maybe it was sappy, she thought as she shouldered her purse and picked up the vase, but a little encouragement was always nice. "You've been a great teacher for Seth. He likes expressing himself on paper. He's talked to me about your class; he's enjoyed it."

"I've sure enjoyed reading what he's written. Are you going to be okay after Seth leaves? You'll be an empty nester. He's your only one, isn't he?"

Hilary hated that term, "empty nester." It had been coming up way too often lately. "I *will* be." A bell tinkled above the door as another customer arrived. Hilary took one step toward the door. "I'll be fine, though. I'll get through it."

"You sound like you've been saying that a lot lately."

"I have." At the compassion in Patty Winkler's eyes Hilary decided to confide the rest. "Mostly to myself."

The woman hesitated as if she wanted to say

61

something more. "I have to tell you—" she started, but then stopped.

"What?"

"Seth's final essay. Did you get a chance to read it?"

Hilary thought back. "No. Actually, I didn't."

"Well, I have to tell you how much I admire you. With everything you've dealt with, the divorce, keeping Seth's world so *even*. And now, agreeing to spend quality time with Eric for Seth's graduation."

Hilary was confused. Why would a teacher think it unusual for a father, albeit an absent one, to attend commencement exercises? She narrowed her eyes, trying to figure out what Mrs. Winkler could be talking about.

"It's the first time I've ever heard of something like this, divorced parents willing to take a trip together with their son. It's such a great gift for Seth. Such a confirmation for him that you both do love him. He wrote an excellent paper about it."

Hilary's stomach took a dive. "But we're not—"

"It says so much about your family, that you as a couple would put aside your differences for him."

There had been times since the divorce when Hilary had known Seth to lie. Occasionally she had challenged him on it. Other times, she had let it go, deciding it wasn't worth a confrontation.

Seth had been through so much stress, after all. And when he'd fudged the truth a bit, it had always been a tactic to get more freedom, which was normal for a kid, wasn't it? Saying he'd spent the night one place when she'd found he'd really been at another.

But was this what Seth had been telling everyone he was getting as a graduation gift? Her and Eric together on a trip? Hilary wasn't usually at a loss for words, but she felt like her tongue had been skewered.

When Hilary closed her eyes, she could still see the tears pooling in Seth's eyes as he'd asked her why she and his dad couldn't stay together anymore. She could still see the dark confusion in Seth's face those first months as he'd condemned himself for his parents' mistakes.

And wasn't that what Hilary had done, too, as she'd moved through the stages of pain and guilt? Had she noticed Eric spending more hours at the office but chosen not to speak? Had she ignored her intuition? Hoped things would fix themselves?

In the reeling aftermath of the divorce, how easily she'd condemned herself for her husband's mistakes! But six years had passed and she'd gained perspective. Her friends, especially Gina, had bolstered her by pointing out that the blame for the divorce lay almost entirely on Eric. *Hilary* wasn't the one who'd an affair! *She* didn't decide to marry someone else. *She* didn't decide she didn't love her husband anymore.

She launched herself into full lecture mode. *Don't go there, Hilary,* she reminded herself. *Don't walk down a road already traveled.* But the flowers in her arms suddenly smelled so sweet, so wrong, that she wanted to give them away. Every direction she turned today, she second-guessed herself again. "Has Seth told anyone else about this?" she asked her son's teacher.

"As far as I know, he only mentioned it in the essay. A trip down the Grand Canyon in a raft. It sounds like such fun." Patty Winkler smiled her admiration. "I hope you don't mind that I shared it with a few others at the school. I told him I'd wring his neck if he didn't keep a journal. What an experience!"

Hilary stood speechless. Had Seth thought this was a fiction project or something? If she told the teacher it wasn't true, then she'd be telling her that Seth was a liar. And the three of them had already gone through so many levels of sadness and anger and guilt, they'd made so many apologies to one another, nothing was black and white anymore; they balanced on an edge, living in the shades of gray of survival that the teacher might not understand.

"I'm going to miss having him as a student," Mrs. Winkler said. "Seth's a great kid."

Hilary handed the teacher the vase of flowers

she'd just purchased. Really, she sort of shoved them against the woman's blouse buttons so she had no choice but to grab them before they fell.

"Oh no," Patty said. "I couldn't, Hilary. Weren't these for you? They're so pretty."

"Thank you for saying that. That my son is a great kid," Hilary said. "I think so, too. Please. Enjoy the flowers."

Hilary left Patty Winkler standing in the middle of the shop, hugging the vase. When she stepped outside she could smell rain. The clouds moved across the sky as the wind whipped up, seeming to chase her.

Of course, she would always be able to trust Seth.

Yet Hilary knew firsthand how quickly a relationship between two people could unravel. She couldn't shake this uneasiness that followed her. She wondered, like all parents do, if her son could ever become someone she didn't know.

Driving the rental car in from O'Hare, Eric couldn't help but compare his Chicago birthplace to the gleaming, sunlit freeways he'd just left in L.A. Where the California breezes seemed to always be sweeping the clouds out to sea, the Illinois horizon seemed to always be tainted by them, greenish gray and ominous even this time of year, roiling overhead like the seaweed that littered the lakeshore.

In L.A., everything glittered. The bright light could leave a person dazed. Churches made of glass throbbing in the sun. Gleaming ribbons of road leading from the latest open-air shopping promenade to the megaplex theater. And the surprise of palm trees arrowing into the sky.

Everything in Chicago was gritty, built from bricks or huge blocks of quarried limestone, two centuries of determination woven throughout the deep roots of hackberry, maples, ironwood trees.

Today Eric couldn't help but feel like he might be returning to a place inside himself that he didn't want to see.

"Don't miss your exit," Pam was saying, navigating from the road map even though they'd paid extra for a GPS unit at the rental counter. "You'll take the next one to get to the house." Then, "Lily, stop bothering your brother. Leave his basketball alone."

"Mom, it's taking up my whole seat."

"In fifty feet, exit to the right," said the GPS navigator. By the way Pamela had insisted on renting the navigation system, you'd think she had forgotten how well he knew this city. And maybe he didn't blame her so much, considering. Except for a couple of stilted visits to his family's place at Christmastime, Eric had been perfectly willing to pay for Seth's commute to LAX so they could have their regular schedule of visitation suggested by the court. Eric told himself that he'd been totally satisfied to see his son bounding out of the Jetway with a stewardess in tow and the plastic tags around his neck to show he was a minor traveling alone.

Eric felt like he'd been gone from this place a long time.

He felt like he'd left only yesterday.

"At the next intersection, turn left," the navigator said.

Had he subconsciously let the novelty of Disneyland and the beach and the Santa Clarita skate park fill up his and Seth's time so Eric, too, wouldn't have to think of what he'd left behind him? Had he relied on an amusement park to make up for their stilted conversations? The dashing waves to fill silences that might have contained questions from his son: *Don't you love Mom anymore, Dad? Why did you decide to leave us?* Questions that Eric didn't want to answer.

You're handling this so well, Eric always said instead of answering him. *You're growing up so fast. You're so strong about what's happened between your mom and me. It makes me proud of you.*

Now, in the car, Pam laid a hand on Eric's knee as if she knew what he was thinking. "We'll get through it, Eric. Everything's going to be okay."

He turned and smiled at her. "Yes. It will."

"It's his graduation. We'll be glad we did this."

He breathed deep and tried to relax his shoulders. It didn't work.

She reached across and massaged his neck. "It's understandable, you being so tense. Don't apologize."

"Are you tense? How come?" Ben bounced his basketball against the seat in front of him.

"No."

"Are we there yet?" Lily asked.

"You two stop asking questions," Pam said. "Ben. Hold the ball still or you won't get to bring it next time. Lily, your dad is trying to drive."

A bell rang. The navigation system told him to take a "slight right." He was passing landmarks he recognized, a day-care center Seth had once attended, a pizza place he and Seth had once frequented after Cubs games.

That moment, Eric wished he hadn't taken this exit into his old life. He wanted to keep driving in any direction—Indiana, New York, Canada, whichever direction the rental car would take him. He wanted the navigation system turned off.

Pam's fingers kneaded his neck. "You okay?"

He didn't answer that question. "I think we need to stop first. We don't know how long the visit at the house is going to take us. I think we need to take care of the . . . gift."

"No," Pam said. "It won't work if we do it now. Let's get the visit at the house over with. We'll take care of the other on the way to the hotel."

And when she explained the logistics, he saw her point.

"Okay," he agreed. "House first."

"House first!" Lily sang.

"Seth told me he'd shoot hoops with me when we got here," Ben said.

"Daddy?" Lily asked in little-girl innocence. "When I graduate from high school do I get a present like Seth's?"

"Why would you care about that?" Pam asked their daughter. "You're only five."

Eric told her in all honesty, "You'll get something else. Something especially for *you.*" He didn't say the rest of it: *You'll get a graduation gift that's reasonable.* But this was for Seth. Because, with Seth, he had so much to make up for.

Chapter 4

❧

*T*he doorbell rang three times in quick succession. All of Hilary's good intentions flew out of her head; she was a bundle of nerves. She peered out the peephole as she scrubbed her palms on her slacks legs.

The glass in the peephole made everything on the porch look compressed, as if she were peering down on them from a bigger world. How it pleased her that her ex-husband appeared somewhat small.

Through the hole, Hilary watched Eric as he prepared to face her. He straightened his collar with short, sharp jerks. When he didn't get it right, Pam reached over and fixed it for him. Eric beckoned eleven-year-old Ben away from the doorway, offered him a chummy high five followed by a shared bop of the knuckles. Pam crossed her arms over Lily's collarbone and rocked this child, this one she and Eric shared, back and forth in front of her.

Pam shot Eric a look of reassurance that any other woman could read: *You're going to be fine, honey. Just enjoy this as much as you can.*

Hilary opened the door so fast that she almost caught them. But no. Instead, she got them standing in the door frame as if they were posing for a portrait, Pam with her dark hair and symmetrical features, Eric with his fixed, dazzling smile, the children's faces eager.

"Hello, Hilary," Eric said.

The warmth in his voice actually surprised Hilary. She found herself doing the unthinkable, examining the physical changes in her ex-husband, the lines that ran from his nose to his mouth, the skin thickening around his eyes. He looked older. Good. Handsome, in fact.

"Hello, Eric."

There were all sorts of things they could say to each other, but nothing came. They spoke in scripted sentences. He asked, "How have you been?"

"Fine. And you?"

"Fine."

As she searched for words and analyzed the changes in him, she could kick herself for the moment she found herself awash in the loneliness again. Not from missing Eric exactly, she'd gotten beyond that, but just from missing *someone*. Someone stepping through the door at the end of the day. Someone in the bed next to her, a warm body that left an indentation in the mattress, a fading warmth on the pillow, a body spooning against hers, someone who would tug the covers and she could tug back.

All those feelings, which Hilary had managed to

71

tame into submission, rose again while this man and his wife and their children stood on her front porch.

The important thing is to watch out for Seth's best interests.

This has nothing to do with protecting myself.

Pam's two children—not ankle biters, thank you very much—peered past Hilary's legs as if they expected the Magic Kingdom to materialize behind her. "Hello," she said to the boy. "Ben, isn't it?" For the first time, she realized he was carrying a basketball against his hip.

"Yeah," he answered. "That's me."

"That's not the way you act when you meet someone, Ben." Pam stopped her son mid-exchange and directed him what to say; heaven forbid he wouldn't introduce himself properly.

This time, Ben extended his hand toward Hilary as prompted. "It's nice to meet you," she said.

"Nice to meet you, too." When Ben spoke again, his voice was oozing with hope. "Do you think Seth will shoot hoops with me?"

"Oh, I'll bet he will."

"You really think so?"

"I'm pretty sure. You'll have to talk to him about it, though."

The little girl, Lily, gazed past Hilary into the house. "Where is he?"

Hilary honestly hadn't known the kids would be this excited. "He isn't here right now, sweetheart. He's gone for a little while."

"Oh."

Hilary had never seen such dejected faces in all her life. She hadn't expected hero worship. "He'll be back soon, honey. I promise."

Their moment of greeting stretched into something awkward. Hilary took an abrupt step back so the Wynn family could enter. "Come in. Come in." She gestured. "Oh, Pam. What are you doing still standing out there on the porch? The airports are the worst, aren't they? You've been traveling all day." And after Eric entered, she watched him stand in the middle of the living room with his arms crossed as if he wasn't certain how to move inside her space anymore.

"I'm glad you finally bought this," he said at last. "There are such bargains in this market. And Pam likes the waterfall beside the front gate."

Hilary's pride took over. Hadn't he lost the right to tell her if he thought something was wise or not? *This is what you get with a household divided, Eric. A modest house with a water feature.*

Luckily, she had her nurse's salary to rely on. Hilary had only agreed to let Eric help with a small amount of child support, which would end when Seth turned twenty-one. She'd refused the alimony payments Eric had offered. She'd turned down Eric's offers to send money when she and Seth had gone through the rough spots. And, even without that, she'd managed to scrape together enough to get them into a neighborhood where Seth could stay in the same school district where he'd started. She'd managed to put together a comfortable home for the two of them, although there hadn't been room in the budget for many extras. The nurse with the purse, Gina had called her. Thank heavens for that. "It's been good for me and Seth. Good for him to feel settled."

The little girl began to twirl in the middle of the living room, her skirt billowing around her like a morning-glory blossom. Hilary remembered loving to twirl at her parents' house. She recalled falling down, seasick, as the floor pitched and she couldn't stand up anymore. If this had been any other child, Hilary might have found her charming.

"Lily," Pam said. The one word, "Lily," and the child stopped. "You don't behave that way when we're guests."

"Oh, please," Hilary said. "Let her. I don't mind."

Pam turned to Hilary. "The last time I let her do that until she stopped, she wore the wax off my mother's floor."

"Well, I don't wax my floors," Hilary said, and was instantly sorry for the disclosure.

Lily took a seat on the sofa. Ben sat beside his sister. He held the basketball between two hands and stared at it the way he would stare into the face of a friend who had forsaken him.

"You told Seth what time we'd be here, didn't you?" Eric crossed the room and rumpled the boy's hair. "I can't believe he isn't here waiting for us."

"Of course he's not here waiting for you, Eric." She couldn't keep the sarcasm from her voice. "He's *eighteen*."

The rain had cleared, but the air was damp. A breeze ruffled the limbs outside the window. The sun, which had broken through the clouds, slanted across the carpet. A reflection of leaves danced on the coffee table. Hilary hadn't meant to sound so sharp. She tried to soften the words a bit. "They had to finish the senior video. Then he went to work on his girlfriend's bike."

"He has a girlfriend?" Ben asked, shifting in his seat.

"Yes, he does."

"Daddy didn't tell us he had a girlfriend," Lily said.

"I don't think"—Hilary met Eric's eyes—"that your dad knew."

Eric interrupted her. "Why did you let him go out with friends when we've come all this way to see him?"

"They make a senior video every year. They'll show it at commencement tomorrow." Hilary kept her voice as even as iron. "It's a big deal. It's *important,* Eric."

"This is a disappointment to the kids," Pam said.

Only later, when Hilary called up memories of this day, would she realize that this was the moment she should have started to worry: these few sentences, this slight misunderstanding, how she had to explain to this family that they weren't the center of Seth's world. At the time, she'd taken it only as a slight offense (this was her domain and Eric and Pam were walking into it . . . the life she and Seth had managed to build together . . . *their* territory) when she ought to have recognized it as a red flag of danger. "I promised I'd call him the minute you got in. My mother's going to be here in a few minutes, too."

Which made Eric flinch. Hilary enjoyed that. The last person he probably wanted to see was her mother.

"Well, we've gotten in," Pam reminded her. "Why haven't you already called him?"

"He'll come home, Pam," she said. "He wants to see everyone, too." At that exact moment, Hilary's Nokia rang with a download from The Fray, Seth's distinctive ring. Hilary couldn't resist a smile of satisfaction. That's the way things happened with them; they usually stayed so in tune, it seemed like one of them always knew when the other was about to dial. Hilary touched the screen, feeling vindicated.

"Hey, sweetie. What's up?"

In the background she could hear about four different conversations, the grinding of an ice-maker, the steady beat of hip-hop. "Is he there yet?"

Only for a moment did Hilary's mood darken, as she remembered the story Patty Winkler had told her. But now wasn't the time to ask Seth about the essay, not with everyone standing there. "I have something to ask you about later."

"What is it? Mom, is something wrong?" He must have heard it in her voice.

"We'll talk about it when you get home, okay? And yes." She glanced toward Eric. "Your dad's here. They just got in."

The hesitation on the other end of the line made Hilary both surprised and alarmed. She'd given Seth pep talks when he'd been twelve and anxious about flying alone to California. But he'd always returned from L.A. with stories about the beach, carrying a new guilt gift from Eric, usually a skateboard or a new computer game, and talking about his baby sister. Maybe she'd been crazy, but Hilary thought Seth had accepted the situation over time.

After a while, he'd stopped talking about it. To his friends and to his mother, he had remained warm and steadfast. He had become a great support to her; month by month her son's presence had helped her grow stronger.

Hilary wasn't about to pursue the question right now. You lived through what you couldn't change. And Eric had paused beside her momentarily, his shoulders squared, as if he might be suspecting some secret language passing between them in their conversation.

So she fudged. "Are you at Emily's?" she asked lightly.

"Yep. Fixed her bike. Now there's a bunch of us hanging out."

"Does Emily have family coming in today, too?"

"Yeah. She's got to go to the airport to pick up her gran."

"Well, you'd better get over here pronto. You know how it is. Everyone's getting antsy."

"Will you tell him something for me?" Eric asked. "Tell him we want to take him to dinner before baccalaureate. Baccalaureate is tonight, isn't it?"

Seth must have heard his dad. He groaned. "Mom. *Baccalaureate?* Tell me I don't have to go to that thing."

Hilary let her silence speak for her.

"Who wants to sit in a room and listen to more people talking behind a microphone? It's time to *celebrate*. Besides, I need to write my *own* speech." Hilary tried to remember if she'd even mentioned the speech to Eric yet. A few days ago, Seth's friends had elected him to speak during the ceremony.

"So *you* can stand behind a microphone. Make people listen to *you*."

"Right. It's sure better than the other way around."

Hilary finally laughed. "Just get your sweet self over here," she told him in that tone of voice that implied she was almost exasperated. "I'm going to let you deal with this."

"The video went great. We got this great close-up shot of Remy dissecting a frog in Biology. It's going to gross everybody out. Then we got my touchdown reception and the parade when the swim team won regionals and Jess Forney's mom turned in about a dozen pictures of girls having a mud fight at Jess's birthday when they were four."

Ah, Hilary loved the parts of his life that Seth was willing to share with her. She also knew that he was trying to divert her attention away from baccalaureate. "Sounds like it'll play well to an audience."

"Oh, it will, all right."

"Ben said you promised to shoot hoops with him."

"I did. Oh, and Mom? When we get a minute, I need to talk to you about the senior party."

Once more, Hilary's mind went to the party the parents had been planning, the rental of the rec center with the pool, the DJ they'd hired, the ice-cream sundae bar and the inflatable outfits for sumo wrestling.

"I'd be willing to pay big money to see you in a sumo suit," Hilary said.

"No, Mom. I'm talking about that *other* party."

"Oh. The campout."

"Yeah."

"I just—"

"What?"

"Well, I'm so lucky. I know I can talk to you about anything."

"Yeah. So?"

"Well, a lot of the other parents don't know about it. A lot of the other kids didn't tell. So you shouldn't say anything."

Hilary had to be honest. Her son's request made her feel half-proud and half-uncomfortable. "Seth. If there's this much secrecy attached, maybe you guys shouldn't go."

"Mom, you know how things are. It's got to stay quiet. Somebody might call the police or something."

Silence.

"It's just one night. You know nothing's going to happen."

"No, I don't know that."

"Dad's standing there, isn't he? You're not going to let him have anything to say about this, are you? He isn't even a part of our lives anymore."

"Oh," Hilary said, smiling at Eric, who had stopped beside her. "I'd say he's very much a part of our lives right now."

Hilary had a disappointed little boy sitting on

her couch spinning a basketball with small, dusty hands, and a campout seemed like such a fleeting, small detail. She had a woman waiting in her living room with her two perfectly behaved children, a woman who probably waxed her floors weekly. "Seth. Are you coming home now, or not?"

"I'm on my way."

"That's better."

"Okay."

"Yeah."

"Love you, Mom."

Lily had started spinning again, her tiny feet crossing one over the other, toes barely touching the floor. And when Hilary hung up the phone, all she could see was the child her husband had given his new wife. The little girl turned dizzily, laughing, her arms splayed, spinning, spinning. Hilary couldn't take her eyes off Eric's daughter. And she couldn't help feeling that she was just like the little girl, slowly spinning out of control.

Chapter 5

❧

Emily waited at the end of the driveway, gripping her bike handlebars. Seth shoved his cell into his pocket and turned to her. "Guess I'd better get home. My dad's here."

"Is he?" Emily watched her boyfriend, trying to read his eyes.

"Dad wants to take me to dinner tonight. You want me to ask if you can come with us?"

"I can't," she said. "Mom wants me here to do stuff with Gran."

Seth shrugged. "So I won't see you until graduation tomorrow?"

"Guess not." She tucked a strand of hair behind her ear. "Got to keep the relatives happy, huh?"

She'd thought he would go to his car then, only he didn't. He didn't move for a minute. She wondered if it had something to do with his dad. Whenever Seth's dad came, Seth got quiet. He never liked to talk about their time together. "Seth? Are you freaking out or something? About your dad being here?"

"That's stupid. Why would I do that? He's my dad."

"You know," she said. Sometimes when she and Seth had been out together and alone, when the stars had cloaked them and the rest of the world had seemed far away, she had sensed that he was still mad at his dad for leaving them.

"Give me your bike."

"Seth. You said you had to get home."

"Come on. Just let me ride it."

"Why?"

"I'm not going to take it or anything, silly. I just want to try out the brakes before I take off."

"But you tried them in the garage."

"We need a road test."

She walked it to him and he swung his leg over the seat. "Get on," he said, motioning for her to hop on the handlebars in front of him.

At first Emily was able to balance in front of him. She fell against Seth's chest when he took the corner. As he steered up Walnut Street, she could feel the slow, steady drum of his heart behind her shoulder. She closed her eyes and lifted her face to the dappled sunlight as they passed beneath the trees. She held on for dear life as they turned onto a four lane and Seth shot to the middle, cars whizzing past on both sides. They veered into the 7-Eleven parking lot, hung a U, and headed toward her house again.

"You haven't tried the brakes yet!" she shouted.

"I will when it's time. Not yet."

So this was how it felt to be alive and young. She couldn't believe high school was over! Tomorrow they would graduate! And, after that, so many other things would happen. During the next years of their lives, so many things would change. They would leave home, pick careers, fall in love, get married, maybe have their own children. They'd make big plans. Maybe they'd make big mistakes like some of their parents had done.

Who knew where any of them would end up a few years from now?

Today was the start of everything they had waited for.

Behind her, Seth pedaled hard. His heart felt like it might hammer out of his chest behind her. He didn't throw on the brakes until they'd hopped the curb, careened up the sidewalk, and bumped halfway across her front lawn. That's when they finally jerked to a stop.

"Brakes work fine," Seth growled as he helped her off and then dropped the bike on its side in the grass. Right in front of the house where everyone could see, he hugged her against him longer than he had before, kissed her hair, and whispered, "I'll miss you until I see you tomorrow, Em."

"I'll miss you, too."

So happy. So full of promise. It was a moment as fragile as glass. Emily stood on her front porch after he'd left, remembering the feel of his lips where they'd touched her, not wanting to go inside.

• • •

The Jefferson High School football field stretched before Hilary like an oval emerald. Hilary caught her mother's arm and led her toward the folding chairs. Above them, in the stands, the benches were filling. Thank heavens they'd reserved seats on the grass for family, Hilary thought. Every time her mother came to visit, it was harder for her to get around.

Pam walked ahead of them, wearing a dress Hilary envied, a brilliant navy Dior with a white belt that made her waist look about as big around as a twig. Ben and Lily skipped ahead of their mother, sidling into one chair after another, glancing back at Pam for her approval.

"No," she kept calling to them. "A little farther. We want to be close to the podium."

Eric strode along in front of them, too, although he was lagging behind Pam. The folds in his suit changed color in the light, from brown to gray then brown again. He walked with his hand shoved inside one pocket, which wrinkled his sleeve, revealed his gold watch on his wrist, hefted the hem of his jacket. The whole effect made him appear altogether too relaxed and amiable. But Hilary knew better. He was as uncomfortable as the rest of them.

She saw him wanting to hurry, wanting to catch up with Pam, but he was slowing down to keep tabs on Hilary's mother and his own parents,

George and Ruth. "That's okay, Eric," Ruth called to him. "Save us seats. We'll get there. We're right behind you."

Hilary watched Eric's steps shorten. The next thing she knew, he was offering his elbow to her mother. Hilary knew her mother had missed Eric. Alva had always loved and relied on him, ever since the day Hilary brought him around so Alva could meet him. She had told Hilary she thought he looked like Harrison Ford. Since he ate the entire bowl of Alva's banana pudding, the one with the recipe on the vanilla wafers box, in one sitting that day, Hilary's mother had nothing but praise. Eric and Alva walked along in front of Hilary with their heads together, and her mother stood a little straighter and moved a little faster now that Eric was at her side. His lips were lowered to her ear. He told her something that made her pat his arm.

So much for me, Hilary was thinking. *So much for loyalty.*

Pam and the kids were waving at George and Ruth from way up the aisle. At last they'd found a row of seats that were acceptable. When the rest of them finally got there, Eric allowed Alva to enter the row first, which seated her beside Pam and the children, himself beside Hilary, and George and Ruth Wynn on Hilary's other side. Pam didn't like the arrangement, Hilary could tell. She kept glancing in their direction. Hilary thought about suggesting that Eric trade places with her mother, but she didn't. She wasn't sure whether she let it go because it would take so much effort for her mother to rearrange herself or because she was feeling spiteful. Hilary didn't have time to analyze her motivations, though, because in that instant she was surrounded by friends and other families from the high school. Gina adjusted the zoom on her camera. Kim hung her purse on the back of a chair and sat beside her husband.

Each hug that came Hilary's way was accompanied by knowing smiles, melancholy glances. Seth's third-grade teacher asked about his plans for the future and Hilary listed them with pride: the substantial scholarship to Emhurst, the liberal-arts college in Springfield, and a writing class he'd enrolled in.

"Where has the time gone?" the teacher asked as she shook her head.

Some in this group had known Hilary long enough to recognize Eric. Others hadn't. Hilary was caught in an endless round of introductions: "These are Seth's grandparents. This is Seth's father, Eric . . . his wife, Pam . . . their children," Hilary said, and pointed toward the kids, and they replied, "Nice to meet you. Nice to meet you," under the scrutinizing eye of their mother. "Eric. Pam. Kids. This is Julie." Or "Donna" or "Fay" or "Kim." Others crossed the aisle, too, the

MacCleods and Remy's father and Emily's parents and grandmother. The small talk continued until the women's choir filed onto the bleachers and sang "Graduation (Friends Forever)," a song from the band Vitamin C.

"Pomp and Circumstance" began and then came the graduates, two by two, the boys in black and the girls in white, their caps angled in every direction, their tassels dangling. A small uproar began each time a new face appeared in the aisle. Cheers and flashbulbs erupted simultaneously. Everything moved in slow motion until Hilary found her son. Suddenly here came Seth, moving toward them with Emily at his side, tilting his head to make sure Hilary knew he'd found his family in the crowd. How proud she was of him; he'd been waiting so long for this moment! Hilary found herself shouting his name with all the others, standing on tiptoe to see as much of him as she could, as the music played and he mounted the steps to the stage.

The student-body president spoke and an orchestra ensemble played something that made Hilary and Eric glance at each other because it was a little out of tune. The jokes from T. J. Williams, the class clown, seemed ridiculously funny. He talked a lot about picturing all of them in their underwear—which was an overused topic—but he spoke with such a great throbbing Roman-speech voice and talked about envisioning everyone's grandma in diapers so that he almost toppled everyone off their seats. Hilary glanced at her mother, halfway worried that she'd be offended by the irreverence. But Alva chuckled right along with the rest of them.

Next came Seth's speech, which Hilary hadn't warned Eric about. Better to let him find things out as they came along. Hilary sat forward on the bench, so close to the edge that the seat bit into the back of her legs. Seth told a couple of stories about his friends; he reminded his audience how it felt to own a new box of crayons on the first day of kindergarten. He reminded them of the smell of the glue. He challenged them to look and see how far they had come, how far they had yet to go. He thanked Eric and Hilary for being his parents. He thanked his grandparents for coming to graduation. He thanked Hilary for always being there for him, Hilary only. He didn't thank Eric for this.

Hilary swallowed and her throat felt full of needles. She hadn't realized she'd be so nervous for her son. He'd done an amazing job up there behind the microphone. Still, she felt Eric sitting stiffly at her side. She spoke quickly to cover the obvious omission in Seth's speech: "Good job, huh? He did great, didn't he?"

If she hadn't felt self-conscious about Seth's speech, she might have reached for Eric's hand. How good it might have felt to hold on to something of their past while they celebrated their son's future. She couldn't erase those years between them when they had a son standing there, no matter how hard she tried, no matter if it was awkward because they weren't together anymore.

Not until the Teacher of the Year began speaking did Hilary realize that she'd forgotten Pam. Mr. Schuster addressed the kids first, told them how much they'd meant to him, what a challenge and a source of pleasure it had been to instruct them. He encouraged them to do their best in the future, to work hard and play hard, to seek happiness, to be kind to others and to themselves. Then the honored gentleman finally turned his attention to the audience.

"I don't care what else might be going on in your life," Mr. Schuster said. "I don't care what else you're proud of, or what else you're fighting for, or what else you might be thinking about at the moment." He gestured toward the young adults onstage. "I want you to know that, when you look up here, you are looking at your greatest accomplishment."

The speaker had Hilary from the beginning. Everything he said gave credibility to the grief and pride she'd been juggling. She glanced across at her mother, feeling a surprising kinship with Alva. *I wonder if she grieved when I left home. If she did, I never knew it.* Hilary made a note to ask about it later in the day.

Mother did it with such grace, her letting go of me.

Mr. Schuster was telling the parents how proud they ought to be. Then he said, "Anyone who has participated in raising these young people onstage, please stand so we can give you what you deserve. A round of applause."

Eric and Hilary stood together as an ovation filled the gym. Hilary realized this was why she hadn't wanted Eric to trade chairs with her mother. *I wanted to sit by Eric. I wanted this to happen.* Pam was watching them together, and, for one horrible moment Hilary thought Pam might stand and try to take some credit for raising Seth, too. Hilary knew it was her pride speaking, but she felt a lovely sense of justice that Pam could not join them. *She may have Eric now,* Hilary thought as she looked down at her husband's new wife, *but she will never have this position in his life. She will never be the mother of his firstborn son.*

The rest of the ceremony went by quickly. The students stood row-by-row. They stepped forward when their names were called. Seth swung his tassel from one side of his cap to the other after he received his diploma from the superintendent of schools. Seth gave a high five to Remy and Ian and T.J., he hugged Emily, and the beach balls started to fly.

The senior video played on a gigantic screen.

Hilary cheered for almost every frame, baby pictures and sports videos, the mud-wrestling birthday party that Seth had warned her about, the funny pictures of Laura. When the football segment began, Hilary leaped from her seat. She knew where the ball was going, who was going to catch it, who was going to score. "It's Seth's touchdown catch. This is it." She grabbed Eric's sleeve (he'd draped his jacket over the chair because of the heat) and tugged like a child trying to get an adult's attention. "I'm so glad you're getting to see this!"

The next thing they all knew, Mr. Schuster was announcing, "Ladies and gentlemen, I present to you the graduating class of 2011."

Mortarboards flew. The band played a raucous, off-key song. The crowd went wild.

As the graduates tried to march down the steps the way they'd practiced, families converged on them from every direction. Hilary realized she should have made plans to meet Seth in the crowd.

"I see Seth!" Ben shouted. "He's over there."

Eric's parents appeared at her side. "Can you find Seth? Oh, that speech was wonderful!" Ruth gushed. "Oh, honey, it's so good to see you again. We've missed you so much."

"I've missed you, too," Hilary told Eric's mother. Which was an understatement. Ruth had raised the man with whom Hilary had fallen in love. She had taught Hilary how to reupholster her dining-room chairs and how to grow aloe in her garden and how to phone the insurance company repeatedly to get a reimbursement.

"I've wanted to talk to you," Ruth said, "but I didn't know what to say. We're sorry things turned out this way."

Yes, Hilary wanted to say. *I'm sorry, too.*

Thankfully, Hilary was saved from having to answer. The crowd swept them up and propelled them forward. "Seth's over there!" Ben shouted. "Let's go."

During the graduation ceremony, Hilary had discovered something she'd somehow known deep down for a long time: Her joy, her esteem, her self-image were all tied together, bound up with her child. She had no thought for anything else. "You lead the way," Hilary told Ben, forgetting everything else except finding her son in the chaos. "We're right behind you."

Suddenly the whole group of them, half sister and stepmom, grandparents and parents, formed an excited tangle around their newest high-school graduate. The Wynns and Myerses took photos of every imaginable combo of family: Seth and Hilary. Seth and Hilary and Eric. Eric and Pam and Seth with the kids. Eric surrounded by grandparents.

They filtered from the stadium into the parking lot to find that the traditional picnic had already been laid, with leaning towers of paper plates, orange coolers of lemonade, mountains of chicken. As Hilary helped her mother fill a plate, Seth's classmates weren't standing too far from them. Cameras flashed from every direction. Friends hugged. About half of the boys had kept on their gowns for pictures. Seth had lost his gown but was still marching around in his cap, the black dress pants Hilary had practically had to pay him to wear, his tie, which was loosened clear past the third button of his shirt, and his flip-flop sandals.

Even as Hilary shook her head at her son's attire, she admired how he interacted with his peers. The way he drew Emily close, a possessive gesture that made Emily stand taller and smile. The way he cuffed Remy on the shoulder. The way Seth greeted his principal and shook his proffered hand.

Emily whirled away once more, caught in a new round of hugs and laughter, each of the girls so fresh-faced and beautiful that she made Hilary's heart ache. Suddenly Hilary saw Lily, a flash of white skirt and hot pink Crocs darting among a forest of lanky teenager legs. Lily yanked Seth's tie to get his attention. Once Seth spotted his sister, he didn't hesitate. He swept her into his arms.

By the rapt expression on her face, she had been swept into the arms of a prince. As the two talked eye-to-eye, Lily's nose almost touching Seth's,

Lily draped her small hand, no larger than a maple leaf, over Seth's shoulder.

Seth swept off his cap and set it sideways on Lily's head.

What happened next was instantaneous, so unexpected and sweet that Hilary felt like she was privy to something she almost wasn't supposed to see. She watched as Seth carried Lily to a parked car and showed Lily her reflection in the window. Seth righted the hat on the little girl's head. Lily's bottom lip protruded as she pondered her reflection.

"How cute is *that?*" Hilary heard Eric ask.

Hilary admitted that she was one of those Christians who forgot about God sometimes. She'd roll along with her morning, steeping her hot tea, watching the clock, hollering at Seth to get moving or he wouldn't have time to take his shower. She'd check phone messages, pitch a load of clothes into the washer, follow her own plans. Then something would come along that reminded her of the bigness of things, God's nearness, her own helplessness, a sharp, stunning revelation. This became one of those moments, something she couldn't miss. A fist tightened in Hilary's chest, as she saw how happy Seth was with his sister, when the girl's existence brought Hilary so much pain.

Chapter 6

❧

$\mathcal{H}$ilary was standing a few yards past the teeter-totters when a woman approached, extended her hand, and introduced herself as Abigail Moore, Laura's mother.

"Oh, hello." Hilary gripped Abigail's hand and nodded. "I know Laura." *Probably more than you do.* Once again, Hilary prided herself on being the parent whom all the boys could talk to. "She's on the track team, isn't she?"

"She runs mid-distance. And the sixteen-hundred relay."

"I loved the shots of her in the senior video. The boys had such fun putting those in."

"Is Seth responsible for acquiring that toothless-wonder picture? She's ready to kill him for that. Those second-grade photos. They bring back such memories."

"They do for all of us," Hilary said.

"My daughter thinks your son and his friends are the best. I'm glad she's met them through Emily."

"Seth speaks highly of Laura, too." *Laura's hot,* he'd said yesterday. *Remy missed out.* Hilary had no experience, but she decided that girls' moms must have different sorts of conversations with their offspring than mothers of sons.

But Laura's mother was already on to a different subject. "Can you tell me something about that camping party that's going on tonight?"

Oh. I see. Now Hilary realized why the woman had approached her in the first place.

"Laura says your boys are going."

"Your boys" meaning all of Seth's friends. Hilary loved them, but she didn't want to be held responsible for *all* of them. "As far as I know."

"You've given Seth your permission?"

Hilary knew where the woman was going with this; moms all did the same thing. She was checking up, comparing stories. "Yes, I have. They're responsible kids. They know how to take care of each other. I asked plenty of questions, believe me."

"Laura's been begging me to let her go. I've given her a tentative 'yes,' but I still have my doubts."

Hilary reminded her, "These kids will be at college in no time, without any parents around to set rules."

"Yes, but a big group like that? I'm worried it could get out of hand."

"Maybe I'm wrong, Abigail, but I trust them. I think it's better to let them have a little freedom now so they don't run off and go wild later." Abigail was still dubious, Hilary could tell. But this was Hilary's "raising-Seth" philosophy, and so far it had worked. "I mean, every kid is different," Hilary clarified. "It's important to know what each one of them can handle. But Seth's told me about your daughter. Laura sounds like she's got her head screwed on straight."

"Yes. Yes, of course she does." Abigail still sounded like she was trying to convince herself. Hilary couldn't help but be proud, handing out advice. Advice was something she would always give freely.

Groups of graduates still posed for pictures, their arms braided across one another's shoulders. People had gathered beside their cars after the ceremony, but no one was in a hurry to drive home. Some were still finishing up after the picnic. Others sat and visited in folding chairs or gathered beneath the shade trees.

On the blacktop beside the football field, Seth and Ben played a pickup game of basketball. The two boys—one big, one small—were taking it to the rim as Hilary watched. Seth stopped dribbling at one point and coached, "Like this. Here's what you do. Shoot your passes chest high."

Ben caught the ball right in the breadbasket. "Will you teach me how to do a behind-the-back?"

"Only after you tell me you've been working on your jump shot," Seth said.

They hadn't been playing very long before Eric stopped them. He said something to Seth that Hilary couldn't hear.

Hilary saw Seth looking around to wave her over. He looked a little sheepish as he called, "They want to give me my graduation present or something. Dad says they want everyone to see."

Two days ago, Hilary had given Seth a wristwatch that she'd ordered engraved with this quote adapted from Thoreau: *Live the life you have imagined.* The gift satisfied Hilary in ways that she couldn't explain. It would last a long time. It was practical; he wouldn't be late to class with this on his wrist. (At least, Hilary hoped not. If he *was,* it would be through no fault of his mother's!)

Pam and Eric hadn't asked for ideas and Hilary had no clue what they might be giving her son. She couldn't help but be a little skeptical of their motives, as they called everyone over and made a big production.

Then Eric dangled a set of keys and placed them in Seth's hand. That was when Hilary's heart felt like it was being squeezed inside a trash compactor.

"Here are the keys to your graduation present."

"Dad?" Seth's voice was weak. His confused gaze traveled from the keys in his palm to his father's face.

"Go ahead." Eric cuffed his son solidly on the shoulder. "Go get it. It's in the parking lot."

Seth didn't move. "But what *is* it?"

"That black Ford F-one-fifty over there." Eric

cuffed Seth's shoulder again to fill in the awkwardness. "Not brand-new, of course, but it's in great shape. Congratulations, Son. Pam and I are proud of you. We want you to enjoy this truck."

Hilary hadn't even been breathing. How could they have done this without even asking her opinion? She felt like she'd been sucker punched.

"It's *mine?*" Seth glanced in Hilary's direction. She rearranged her face but not fast enough. She'd turned away, but she'd seen Seth catch her displeasure. Which irritated her even more. It wasn't fair for Seth to get trapped in the middle of this. And that, she suddenly suspected, was the reason Pam must have encouraged Eric to do it this way, so Hilary couldn't fight back.

Seth's friends had erupted. "Totally *chron!*"

"Amazing!"

"Emily, get over here and see this."

"I call shotgun."

"Word!"

"Emhurst is a long way off," Eric said. "And Springfield's a big place. You'll be needing something to get around."

"But it's too much, Dad."

"It isn't too much," Eric argued. "After all, I'm your father."

Looking dumbfounded, Seth headed toward the parking lot. "It's locked," Pam called after him, the pride evident in her voice. "Punch the button

100

on the key chain and the taillights flash." Pam touched Eric's sleeve. "Honey, go with him. Show him what he needs to do to get it started."

Hilary felt like she'd been trapped. "Your dad has a little money to go along with it," Pam added. "We thought you could use a little help getting settled into your new place."

The school grounds were still packed with high-school graduates and their families. Pam and Hilary stood a distance apart from each other, their arms crossed, their eyes locked on the hoopla in the parking lot. "He'll have to apply for a parking permit on campus, of course," Pam said.

Exhaustion swept over Hilary. She didn't want to be bitter anymore. She longed to close off her heart and just feel nothing. But Seth was the only thing she had left of her family. She had only a few precious weeks left with him. A new truck? Offers of money? What were they doing, trying to buy her son from her? "Why didn't you and Eric talk to me about this? How could you do this without discussing it with me?"

"It didn't seem like anything we needed to discuss."

"It isn't? It's a new *truck,* for heaven's sake."

"It isn't *new,*" Pam reminded Hilary. Pam's voice sounded as if Hilary were committing some major offense by questioning her.

"You know what I mean," Hilary said as the fever rose in her voice. "That isn't the point."

"It's just a graduation gift."

"No, Pam. It's a little more than that. You should have warned me."

"Can't you just relax and enjoy the moment?" Pam asked.

Hilary had no practice at this. She was stepping into uncharted territory. Pam might as well be saying, *Can't you see that I'm better at this than you?* "I'm sorry if we've put you on the spot," Pam murmured in an undertone, as if she were confiding something Hilary couldn't have known, something Hilary would rather other people didn't hear. "We knew you couldn't afford to do anything like this. Seth needed something dependable."

Dependable. The thought pounced on her like a cougar. She didn't see it coming in time to push it away. *Like the father he would have had if you hadn't stolen him.*

Seth had climbed into the front seat of his new truck, his fingers gripping the steering wheel. Hilary saw Remy cupping his hands against the glass, trying to look in through the tinted window on the other side. Seth's friends were drooling all over themselves!

The dashboard sloped around Seth like the instrument panel on some sci-fi starship. As Hilary and Pam talked, Hilary saw him marveling over his gift, fingering the gearshift knob, feeling it smooth and commanding beneath his hand. One press of the clutch, one flick of the key, and her son would be rolling forward. As they talked, the engine roared to life and then shut off again. The lights switched on and off; the windshield wipers arced across the glass. As Hilary watched her son's profile through the glare on the windshield, she expected him to be memorizing the intricacies of his new dashboard. Only he wasn't.

Hilary watched her son get out of the truck, slam the door, and check to make sure it was locked before he left it. Emily followed him, creases of worry between her brows. Hilary realized what Seth was going to do, and she was heartsick. *Seth. Don't. Not for my sake.* But it was too late. Seth shoved the keys toward his dad.

"Dad," he said. "This means a lot. But I don't want it." There were so many things he could have said; Hilary knew it. He could have given so many excuses. He could have said he didn't want to worry about parking on campus. He could have said that he didn't feel right taking it or, *It looks like a gas guzzler and I can't afford to pay for the insurance and neither can Mom.* Or he could have said he couldn't afford the registration. But Seth didn't bother. "Maybe this isn't the best idea."

"What's this?" Eric asked. "You don't want the truck?"

"You should have talked to Mom," Seth said. "You shouldn't have done this without her."

A muscle bulged in Eric's jaw. His mouth tightened in quiet anger.

Ben, who was too young to understand the friction among everyone, appeared at Seth's side, the basketball tucked against his hip. "Do we have to leave yet? Can't we shoot some more?"

"Come on, kid." Seth held out both hands, splayed as if he already held the ball in the tips of his fingers. "Let's do it."

"Yeah!" Ben grabbed Seth's hand.

After the boys headed toward the blacktop, Eric turned to Hilary, furious. "This is your fault. Seth knows you disapprove. He turned me down to satisfy you."

"He made his own choice," Hilary said in her own defense, her voice weak. But deep down she knew that wasn't true. She'd gone for years thinking she'd healed, that she'd moved forward, that she'd mastered her grief. Then here came Eric surprising everyone with a truck and Hilary felt like he'd found a deep wound in her, something that made her wince with pain. "You and Pam can't just spend money on him and expect everything to be all right between you."

Later, when Hilary was alone, she would examine this moment, draw the hurt out of her pocket the way she would draw out an apple, and she would examine it. She would pray, *What is this, Lord? Why did this one episode make me react this way? Why do I feel like Eric and Pam poked a sore spot?* She would wait then, listening for some answer. Maybe she'd robbed them of a lovely moment between father and son. For now, she could only salvage what little respect she and Eric had between them. "He turned a *truck* down, Eric, not you."

Pam stood with her feet apart and her arms crossed over her chest like a general ready to reprimand an army. "We're trying our best to be a healthy blended family for him." Pam's mouth had thinned to a grim line; her spine stood straight as the trunk of a box elder. "Everything we try to do for him, you undermine us."

"We'll talk this through," Hilary said, finding her composure. "It's fair for you to give him a good vehicle, something practical he can use while he's away. It was also fair for us to discuss this first."

Pam joined her husband. She kneaded the muscles in his shoulders as if preparing him for a knockout in the twenty-first round. "I'll tell you what isn't fair, Hilary. It isn't fair for you to turn your son against his own father."

"If you had talked to me first it would have been different," Hilary stated, her voice steady in spite of Pam's charge. What an absurd accusation! "Seth wouldn't have seen my shock. I wouldn't have stolen his joy at your gift." Then, "I'm doing the best that I can, Pam. You have to realize that."

But Eric's wife wouldn't be convinced. Pam shook her head with her chin raised in censure, disapproval oozing from every pore.

Chapter 7

❧

$\mathcal{A}$s she prepared for the family meal, Hilary aligned plates along the table with military precision, *plink, plink, plink*. She set silverware alongside each napkin with the same attention as she would have laid out sterile surgical instruments. The growl of the ice maker spitting ice into glasses suited her mood. She balanced a head of lettuce on the board beside the sink and severed it in one slice. Anything to keep her mind off Pam's finger-pointing. Anything to keep from taking offense at the woman who had come into Hilary's life and seemed intent on disgracing her.

The sun, still bright in the kitchen, was giving Hilary a headache. George and Ruth came through the door, George carrying a Tupperware carrier with a three-layer chocolate cake. "Oh, that cake looks *wonderful*," Alva said. "Ruth. You've outdone yourself. That'll go great with my homemade ice cream."

Alva had been working on the ice cream ever since they'd left the school grounds after graduation. To Ruth, she listed the entire roster of ingredients she'd used, starting with the eggs and not stopping until she reached the vanilla. Hilary knew that was how her mother dealt with stress. When Alva felt people were tense around her, she talked a mile a minute to fill in the spaces. And as Hilary loaded food on the table, there were plenty of spaces. The air in the room felt as explosive as lightning.

"Mom. Come sit down." Hilary set a pitcher of ice water beside Alva's chair. She stood on tiptoe as if that would make her voice louder. "Seth? Where's Seth? Are the boys outside? We're ready to eat."

Looking grim, Eric escorted Pam to the table, his hand touching the small of Pam's back. Lily came out of the bathroom with wet hands. "Honey. Use the towel," Pam said.

George spoke a brief prayer and they unfolded their napkins, smoothed them in their laps. Serving dishes passed, chicken and wait-a-day salad and bean casserole, as the silence swelled. Alva babbled on about a neighbor who had thought she'd let her dog inside only to turn around and find that she'd opened her door and let in a stray goat. At the end, realizing that no one was going to pick up the conversational slack, Alva let the story fizzle.

After that there was nothing but the sound of silverware against the plates. Hilary glanced around the table and just happened to catch the look passing between Pam and Eric. Eric began by clearing his throat. "Son," he said. "We'd hoped you could clear your schedule for us. We'd like to spend a little more time with you tonight."

Hilary's breath caught in her throat. She almost blurted it out: *Oh, he's not doing that. He's got big plans.* But she bit back the words. That was the worst thing she could do right now, make it sound like she was trying to interfere.

Seth looked her way for help. Hilary shook her head. *You're on your own with this one.* There wasn't anything she could do.

"Dad. I've got—"

"We were thinking we might ride the L downtown. Show the kids where you and I used to fly kites by the lakeshore. Have a walk and see the sights." Then, after a slight hesitation, "Hilary, Alva, we want you to come with us, too." Although it was obvious they didn't really.

"We're eating," Hilary said, trying to warn Eric off. "Can we discuss this after?"

"Well," he said. "Pam and I thought we might talk about it now. While we're all together."

Pam said, "He's a part of our family, too, Hilary."

If the atmosphere had been unsettled at the table before, now it became downright stony. Seth said, "I've got plans tonight, Dad. I can't come with you."

"Can't we just all eat?" Alva pleaded. "We have this lovely meal. We ought to enjoy it. And for the dessert there's the ice cream, the chocolate cake.

You should see the chocolate cake your mother baked, Eric, three layers. I'll bet she made those cakes for your birthday parties."

Ruth jumped in: "He asked for one every year."

"Eric," Hilary said. "You mustn't take this personally. Pam, it's not that he doesn't want to spend *time* with you."

Eric went straight for his son: "You're leaving tonight, Seth?"

Pam narrowed her eyes as if this were unthinkable. "I've never seen anyone so possessive of a child." She skewered Hilary with her gaze.

The words drove like a fist into Hilary's throat. "I haven't done—" But she made herself stop. Oh, how she ached to argue! But what good would it do? *I'd only make it worse, Lord.* Hilary refused to add fuel to the fire. She refused to let Pam bring her down to this level!

"I'd planned to be home for this family meal," Seth said. "But after that I'll head out."

Eric frowned. "You'll *head out?*"

"You know what they say," Seth joked, something Hilary knew he'd always done when he was trying to lighten the mood between everybody. "You know. Make like a baby."

"What?"

"Make like a baby and *head out*. You know. Make like a tree and *leave*." Eric was still glaring at Seth, so he clarified. "I'm not spending the

109

night at home, Dad. It's graduation night. A bunch of us are going camping."

On the road trip they'd taken to Yellowstone once, they'd piled out of the car at McDonald's and not until they'd consumed their share of Big Macs and given themselves brain freeze passing around one enormous chocolate shake did they realize they'd locked the keys in the car. Eric had gotten a clothes hanger from the restaurant and had whittled away at the door's rubber stripping while Hilary had blamed him for their delay and Seth had danced around the car bumper telling every knock-knock joke he could muster. *Knock knock. Who's there? Dwayne. Dwayne who? Dwayne the bathtub; I'm dwowning.*

Hilary had gotten so frustrated at all those jokes that she'd almost given Seth a time-out because he wouldn't be quiet. Only later did she figure out that he'd been working as hard as any stage comedian to make them laugh. He'd been trying to make them feel better.

Eric set his water glass on the table. "Your mother gave you permission to go on an overnight camping trip the night after graduation? You have no idea what could happen at a teen party like that."

"Things won't get out of hand, Dad. I already promised Mom."

Ben had been stirring his beans in figure eights. It amazed Hilary that Pamela hadn't corrected

110

him. The little boy stopped now, gazed at Seth like he had just been told Christmas had been canceled. Ben said, "You won't come with us?"

Seth spoke slowly, trying to make everyone understand. Maybe he could say no to his father, but Hilary knew that Seth's heart must feel knotted, refusing that little boy. "This is my class. The friends I've had since I was Ben's age. We may never see each other again after tonight. This is our graduation day."

Ben stared at his plate. Lily, such a girl, climbed down from her chair and went to pat her brother on the shoulder.

Hilary's heart suddenly felt as protective of her child as it had when he'd been six and dancing around saying things like: *Why does the teddy bear cracker wear long trousers? Because he's got crummy legs.* She rose to his defense by outlining plans for the night the same way those boys had casually divulged plans to her. She used only the words with a positive connotation. Words like "a tradition," "the seniors do it every year," "they're old enough to be responsible."

"But it's camping?" Eric asked Seth. "Without any chaperones? Your mother really gave you permission to do this?" And Hilary was thinking, after the truck incident, that she shouldn't be surprised that suddenly Eric and Pam were blaming her.

"I don't mean to be disrespectful, Dad," Seth

said, squaring his shoulders. And Hilary knew he could have said more, too: *If you'd wanted to spend time with me, you could have done it when I was thirteen.*

"Well, what do you call it?" Pam asked. "We've come all this way to see you." Pam swept Lily into her arms and sat the little girl in her chair. "Stay in your seat, you doodlebug."

"Couldn't we do something tomorrow?" Seth asked, glancing in his mother's direction for help.

"A whole group of seventeen- and eighteen-year-olds unsupervised?" Pam made it sound awful, like Hilary was an absolute idiot, like Pam was ticking off items on a list to prove Hilary an unfit mother. "I would never agree to a thing like that."

But your oldest is in grade school, Hilary wanted to say. *Give yourself time. You'll see how things change.*

Hilary reached for George's plate, stacked it on top of her own. She reached for Ruth's plate, her mother's, and Eric's. Others began to stack forks and knives on top. As Hilary headed toward the sink with the wobbling stack of dishes and utensils, Alva rose to help her. Ruth went to dig around to find a cake knife.

Thank goodness this was almost over! Hilary couldn't survive much more. She felt suddenly afraid, as Pam made her second-guess herself. Pam's objections were all the same that Hilary had listed to the boys just days ago. *We've talked about it,* she told herself. *They've promised they'll make good choices. They know they need to take care of everybody.* But at this point Pam made her feel like such an utter fool, she felt so *attacked. Was I wrong? Should I have agreed to it?*

If ever Hilary had reasons for giving Seth permission to go to this party, she certainly didn't remember them now. "Don't you know what happens at parties like this?" Pam asked as Hilary came back from the kitchen with dessert plates. "I've read about them on the Internet."

"They're a great group of kids," Hilary said flatly. "Seth has my permission and that's all he needs." But should he go? Had she gone against her better judgment? Or did she feel this adamant about the party now because it was a reason Seth couldn't go with *them?* She reached toward her ex-husband. "Help me. It's supposed to be a special day. Please don't let this escalate. *Please.* For my sake." Then, "I trust him, Eric. He isn't going to get into trouble."

Seth stuffed belongings into the duffel bag on the table. In went his headlamp and a pillow. In went his bug spray and a warm jacket while, outside, the solo sound of Ben's dribbling basketball sounded a reproach. In went a T-shirt and a swimsuit while Lily laid her chin on the table and stared at Seth's bag. From outside came the faint whir of someone mowing a lawn down the street.

Ice cubes dropped in the refrigerator with a dull clatter.

"You go on and have a good time, Seth." Hilary handed him a pair of boxer briefs. "It isn't your fault that it worked out this way." *They should have talked to you before they got the kids' expectations up.* She hoped her eyes spoke volumes to her son. *Don't let them lay this guilt trip on you.*

Seth slung the duffel bag over his shoulder and stuffed the clean underwear where it wouldn't be seen in a side pocket. "Thanks, Mom, but I'm a boy." He kissed her cheek. "I'm not going to need those."

"And I'm a mom." Her heart flooded with happiness. Maybe things hadn't changed all that much. "So I have to make sure you have them."

"I meant what I said about doing something with them tomorrow."

"Which means you better get some sleep tonight."

"Not much chance of that."

She caught Seth staring at the truck keys where Eric had dropped them on the counter. "You could drive it, you know. It would be okay with me."

"I meant what I said to Dad." Seth shouldered the bag higher. "I don't want the truck."

"Are you sure? Really? Seth, I know what you're doing. And there isn't any need to punish yourself—"

He interrupted her, brushed off the subject. "Emily asked Laura to pick us up. We thought it would be better to go together. We don't want too many cars up there. It would make the police suspicious, you know?"

"Look," she said, the small fear needling her again. "You're a legal adult, responsible for yourself and, unfortunately, responsible for others. When you mention that word 'police,' it makes me worry about underage drinking, drug use, disturbing the peace."

"Mom, you know there will be a little of that. There's always some of that at high-school parties. But you also know you can trust me. There's a whole group of us that just want to be together."

She made him stop and face her one last time. "You ought to drive the truck. It isn't going to kill me."

"I know that."

"Don't let me stand in the way. I didn't mean to react the way I did. We all need to be fair."

"I'm making my own choices, remember?"

"But you could take it up to the campsite. It might be safer. It's bigger than other cars on the road."

"I'm riding with the girls. It's okay." A honk sounded from the driveway. She didn't kiss him good-bye. He'd already taken that into his own hands and she didn't want to overdo it.

"There they are." She couldn't imagine why tears sprang to her eyes. "You go have a good time, you hear me?"

In spite of everything, Eric knew Hilary. He'd been married to her for over a dozen years, and during those years they had shared a life that had knit them together.

Once, when Hilary had been driving to his parents' for Thanksgiving dinner, he remembered they'd hit a patch of black ice and, the whole time they'd been spinning out, sliding forever to a stop, her voice had remained deadly calm: "Pump the brakes, right, Eric? That's what I'm supposed to do." They'd crossed into the oncoming lane, with the headlights of another car bearing down on them, but she hadn't panicked. Instead she had steered them up over the curb. When the world had stopped spinning, she'd looked at him and burst out laughing. "I've always wanted to do that."

"Well," he'd said, his own heart pounding. "Maybe next time you get the urge for some trick driving, let me know and we'll go to a track somewhere. It'll be a lot safer that way."

"You think?"

There had been childbirth classes and the pillow from their bed she'd insisted he carry to class and the way she'd needed him when Seth had been born. She'd been in transition (Eric kept teasing her and calling it transmission), the stage of labor that the nurses had all told him she would blame him for, and he'd been astounded by the way she kept asking, "How are we doing, Eric? Are we doing this right?"

"*You're* doing fine," he'd told her as he'd washed her face with a cloth the nurse had brought him. He doubted Hilary even knew she was crying. "*I* don't have anything to do with it."

"You have *everything* to do with it." She'd clenched his arm bruise-tight. "You're not getting out of this."

If she'd given Seth permission to go to this party, she really thought she was doing the right thing.

It saddened Eric, seeing how he'd missed the chance to know all he could about his son, to understand how to be the daily parent of a teenager. There was always that awkward coming-up-to-speed when he and Seth got together, the careful questions (so hard not to be an interrogator when you wanted to find out so much so fast!), Seth's first vague answers, and then finally, finally his getting around to details.

Now, Eric stood beside the truck he'd found on CarMax, the one Seth had rejected. Through the window Eric could see Seth and his mother with their heads together, discussing something serious, and Eric couldn't help feeling jealous. He heard the pounding bass a good thirty seconds before Seth's friend's car rounded the corner. It bumped over a dip and bounced into the driveway, an old Pontiac, with a rust ring around the exhaust pipe and so many decals on the rear window, it was a miracle anyone could see to drive. THE GIRL ON MY FAKE ID IS AN HONOR STUDENT, said the bumper sticker. It made Eric think twice, seeing this part of Seth's life, knowing he wasn't a part of it.

That was always the question with life, wasn't it? You had to let go of one thing to pursue another. Which discontent did a person want to live with? Maybe he'd only traded one set of problems for another when he'd fallen for Pam. When he'd been disillusioned by the pale exhaustion on Hilary's face whenever she came home from her PCU shift and he could see she had nothing left to give him. You got to pick your own poison, didn't you?

The door opened and music spilled out. "Come on, Seth," called a boy from the passenger side. "Let's roll."

Here came his son, bounding down the stairs with his bag hoisted over his shoulder. "Hey, Seth." He wanted to say something to make it better between them, like telling one of those knock-knock jokes or just saying, *I'm proud of you*. But Eric had waited too long. The kids were listening. "Son, wait up."

When Seth turned to him over the roof of the

car, the boy's face was unreadable. "Dad, don't. Please. I knew this was going to happen."

"What?"

"Not in front of my friends, okay?"

Eric didn't like his son telling him what to do. "How do you know what I was going to say? Maybe I was—"

"Everything I do ticks you off."

"What are you talking about? I just wanted to tell you that I'm not upset, all right, Seth?" Eric's anger rumbled up, ignited by the way Emily reached across and grabbed Seth's hand, a sense of conspiracy. Oh, Seth thought he knew everything so well, did he? All the kids did. *He* had when he'd been that age. "I don't care about you driving the truck. I don't care if you don't come with us."

"I'll see you tomorrow, Dad." He was being pushed away again. It irked Eric how Seth's voice stayed so calm. "Tomorrow I'm all yours. Make any plans you want."

Emily said, "Don't be mad at him, Mr. Wynn. It's just that it's been tough for him, fitting into your life when you want him to but not having you around when he needs you. It's been really hard. For Seth."

The air in front of Eric's eyes turned red. So Seth and this girl had talked it to death, had they? Probably for hours, days. His mistakes had been a main conversation topic while his son and this girl had been hanging out.

"Mr. Wynn," Emily said.

"Emily, don't," Seth said.

"You go," Eric told him. "You just go."

"I will." Calm. Seth's words, so calm in front of his friends, with that steel edge to them. "Thanks for your permission, Dad."

Chapter 8

⟡

"*H*ey." Remy nudged Seth. "Get over it, why don't you? We're supposed to be having a good time." The girls were crammed so tightly into Laura's front seat that she almost didn't have elbow room to drive. There weren't nearly enough seat belts. Megan, Laura's friend, sat wedged between Laura and Emily.

"Yeah," Seth agreed. "A good time. I know that."

As the car entered the Eisenhower Freeway, it felt like light-years to Seth before he would be leaving for college. But his mother seemed obsessed with him moving out of the house, living in a different town. He loved his mom, no doubt about that. His dad had left him to take care of her. That responsibility made him feel like he was moving underwater with a barbell on his back sometimes. Add to that the conversation he'd had with his dad in the driveway. His dad, who couldn't figure out why money, stuff, vacations, and promises wouldn't be enough! Couldn't his dad *see* it? Couldn't his dad ever be loyal to *anybody?*

Remy rolled down the window and stood halfway in his seat, shouting to the world and anyone else who happened to be driving along I-290, "Freeeedom!" They weren't the senior class of Jefferson High anymore, were they? They were graduates. They had tonight left, and then the whole summer if they played it right—two long months of late nights and freedom-packed, sun-seared days. It had the potential to be *great*.

From the backseat, Remy teased Laura's hair with the corner of his smartphone.

"Cut it out." Laura tried to swat his hand. "I hear they've got meds for ADHD."

"Sit still, Remy." Ian was already pressed against the door. "You're killing me."

"We'd have *plenty* of room," Will noted, "if Seth had driven his new truck."

Megan changed the song on the CD. A motorcycle thundered past. Seth scowled out the window as if he hadn't heard.

"Stop torturing me," Laura demanded. "Remy, stop it." But her flirty smile in the rearview mirror spoke otherwise.

"Seriously, dude. That truck is amazing. If my dad gave me that truck, I'd have it clear to Madison by now."

"Shut up, Remy," Emily said. "Don't talk about it anymore. We're supposed to be having fun. You're the one who said it."

"Oh, what's this?" Ian said. "You standing up for your boyfriend again? Just like you did with his dad?"

"Shut up, Ian."

"Too bad *your* parents didn't get a nasty divorce," Ian told Remy. "I hear the guilt gifts are amazing."

Seth felt squeezed tight, smashed together inside himself the same way his elbows were smashed against him on the crowded seat. He felt a beast coming alive in him. Maybe it had been hiding there for months; he didn't know. But after the conversation with his father, this thing had risen inside his chest until, like the osmosis they'd studied this semester in biology class, it had pushed its way out and filled every cell in his body. "Take the next exit," he said.

"What?" Ian asked.

"Stop the car. I want to get out."

"You're weirding out, Seth," Remy said. "Why do you want to do that?"

"Laura, stop the car *right now*."

She took the ramp as he'd said, darting across an extra lane of traffic to get there.

"Seth, *don't*." Emily grappled with him for the door handle. The car skidded onto the shoulder. "Don't. Nobody's going to talk about it anymore." But Emily was no match for him. He lurched outside the minute the car stopped, into a funnel of road dust and wind.

"You're kidding me," Remy said. "He wants to fight?"

Laura craned her neck to see Seth. "How should

I know what he wants? What's wrong with him?"

"Remy," Emily said. "Don't get out. Just let him get over it. I don't care what he tells you."

Seth's face leered outside Remy's window. "You want to fight or something?" Remy said through the closed window. "Find somebody else. I'm not up for it."

"Get in the car, man," Ian urged. "Come on."

The thing inside Seth was speaking lies. It made him want to act like a demanding jerk. But then if his dad was going to treat him that way, why not? "Who died and left you king of the world, Ian? Remy, stop freaking out. Just let me stand out here a minute. Just let me *breathe*."

"Fine," Remy said, slumping against the seat. "So breathe."

Seth rubbed his neck, tilted his face toward the sky, and stared at the airplanes strung into the night like a kite's tail as they made their final approach into O'Hare. He clenched his fists. A wind draft from a passing car plastered his shirt against him.

Emily climbed out of the car to stand beside him. She didn't reach for his hand and Seth didn't offer. He didn't get why everything triggered his anger lately. Even Emily made him mad, her standing there and she didn't deserve *anything*.

He thought if he acted like a self-centered idiot, maybe he'd turn into one; maybe someone would have to take care of him instead of the other way around for a change. Anything that would drown the angry ache in his chest. But Remy had stopped trying to talk him into the car. Laura hadn't honked to make him hurry. They'd given him time to get over himself. Which made him feel better.

Seth reached for Emily's hand. "You ready to go?"

"Yeah. Are you?"

"Yes."

He held the door open, watched his girlfriend duck inside. "Gosh, man," Remy said, rolling down the window in relief. "You were acting so weird. You were freaking me out."

"Remy—"

"But all is not lost."

"No?"

"Look where you stopped us, Seth." Remy pointed toward the strip mall, its lights pooling on a sparse mix of cars just off the frontage road. "Just where we needed to be. You found the mother lode, baby. The liquor store." Neon beer signs beckoned through the window. "Finally, the chance to try out my new fake ID."

Ian growled, "You're kidding, right? You haven't used it yet? What were you waiting for, Remy? College?"

"Laura, go and park beside the building." Remy yanked his wallet from his rear pocket. "I'm buying the booze. Who's chipping in?"

The girls dug in their purses and the boys

thumbed through their wallets. Crumpled bills and odd change passed to Remy from every direction. Seth slapped two tens in his friend's hand.

"We're getting beer?" Megan asked.

"Beer? Are you kidding me? How about the hard stuff? Bottles of Jim Beam."

"Beer," Laura said. "I just want beer."

"It's your money."

Emily called out the window, "Get us a twelve-pack!" as Remy hopped the curb.

"Beam, baby." Remy's eyes challenged them before he squared his shoulders and headed in like a man. "We've got celebrating to do. I dare any of you lightweights to try to keep up with me."

Even now, even as many years as it had been, sometimes Hilary still dreamed she was breast-feeding her baby. She dreamed she was sitting in a rocking chair with tiny Seth bundled against her, his little cap tugged down around his ears to keep him warm, a night so still it could evoke carols. She dreamed of that delicious moment when her milk let down, that stunning tingle of her body responding. And then in her dream, the shooting milk, the relief of the baby's mouth suckling. After which she always woke chasing something. As if it might be a moment she could catch. As if her shirt might still be wet. As if her breasts might still be laden.

But Seth was eighteen years old. Seth, the proof

that she and Eric had done some good things together.

After their son had left in the car crammed full of teenagers, Hilary had stepped outside. She'd leaned against the doorjamb, watching in the direction where the car had disappeared. As she'd shoved her sweater sleeves up over her elbows, she'd felt Eric's eyes on her. She touched her hand to her neck where the cardigan fastened. His gaze followed.

"It was a horrible dinner," she said.

"You could say that again."

"I tried."

"We're all trying," he said.

"I'm sorry." Even as she spoke them, she knew those words could mean many things: *I'm sorry Seth left the way he did. I'm sorry he didn't accept your gift. I'm sorry our marriage didn't work.*

"What were you and Seth talking about before he left?" she asked. "It looked like you were still arguing."

"Hurt pride, I guess." Then, "Mine. Not his."

"Probably both."

"You look exhausted," he said.

"Don't I always?" She tugged a piece of hair at her neck while a fly droned around their heads and the fountain in Hilary's front yard bubbled. For a moment they stood looking at each other, each of them realizing that they had done this together, this hurting of each other, both of them; it hadn't been just one.

"It's been a tough day," he said. "You should come to dinner with us."

There was a dog park several blocks away named Wiggly Field, and Lily had been begging Pam all afternoon to take her. Eventually Pam had given in and they'd walked over. Just as Eric had issued the invitation, here came Lily and Pam returning from their walk. They appeared around the same corner where Seth had departed, two girls, one big and one small, their elbows swinging, their heads bent at the same angle. Even from here, Hilary could hear them laughing.

"Thanks, but no. I've got to go in and work a shift," Hilary told him. "The hospital's understaffed as usual. And I wanted to spend time with Mother."

"You're sure? Alva could come, too. You'd both be welcome." But Hilary knew they wouldn't really be welcome, at least not as far as Pam was concerned.

"I'm sure." Still, it felt nice to be invited. "Thanks, Eric. Really."

Hilary and Alva had gone to one of those neighborhood places instead, one with poster-board signs and plastic checkered tablecloths that felt greasy even after they'd been wiped. They had Chicago-style pizza, with a layer of seasoned crushed tomatoes double-decked with Italian sausage. They sat across from each other, their elbows on the table and their cupped hands propped beneath their chins. As they talked, Hilary realized how much she'd been missing her mother. The mother Alva had been when Hilary had been, say, eleven. When whatever had been wrong, Alva had known how to fix it.

The two of them leaned toward each other over the table, sopping up olive oil with hunks of focaccia and discussing what young girls saw in Rob Pattinson. That had been one of the most terrifying things about becoming a mother herself, Hilary admitted—finally understanding that the wise, perfect mother, the person on whom everyone relied, hadn't really existed. Alva, too, must have sorted it out as she went, muddling through the process with the help of gut instinct and prayer, self-help books and teacher conferences.

"I'm exhausted," Hilary admitted. "What a day. It's impossible, trying to make everybody happy."

"You think that's what you're supposed to do?" Alva pushed the bread in swirls, mixing together the oil and vinegar. "Make everyone happy?"

Hilary thought about it. "Yes." Then, "No, I guess not."

"Hilary? Can I ask you a question?"

"Of course, Mom. What?"

Alva had plopped the bread in her mouth. "How long has it been since you've listened?"

"What?"

"Sometimes you get so busy trying to do what you think is right, you don't give yourself a chance to *hear*. Christians stay so busy trying to think what they should *say,* what they should *do*. But they don't always think how they should *listen*."

"Are you talking about this weekend? With Pam?"

Alva put a hand on her daughter's knee. "God's plan is often different from what you *think*. I don't know what it is, Hil. But that girl is hurting about something."

"Who?"

"Eric's wife."

"Pamela?"

"Yes."

"You called her *that girl?*"

The television overhead was playing a Chicago Cubs baseball game. Hilary stared at the screen as a ball sailed toward the scoreboard at Wrigley Field and the crowd went nuts. "Do you remember the morning of the wedding?" Hilary asked, and suddenly all she needed was to laugh uproariously at something. "When the choir director called and Eric's best friend had brought a *horse* to the church? So I'd see it tied up outside the door and think he was going to ride in and rescue Eric from me?"

"Where did they get that horse, anyway?" Alva started chuckling, too. "It was such a swaybacked nag, it wouldn't have made it more than a half block before it gave out."

As fast as that, they began one-upping each other about the wedding that didn't even matter anymore. The little lady who stood up and talked about riding the train to her own wedding and no one could figure out who she was. The flower girl who kept hiking up her dress to keep her tights from falling down. Alva's father ad-libbing the tango.

"And Eric's hair!" Alva said. "He looked like a bowling ball, remember? He had it cut way too short. Do you remember Eric's hair?"

"Of *course* I remember Eric's hair. He sunburned his whole head on our trip to Mexico." Maybe it was the mention of Mexico that made Hilary stop laughing and turn somber. It brought to mind Seth's English essay.

Alva's humor subsided, too. She took a deep breath.

"It was all supposed to be perfect, wasn't it?"

Alva didn't reply.

"Eric and I were young together," Hilary said. "There can never be a substitute for that, can there?"

Alva said, "I don't think so, sweetie."

"I can't help it," Hilary admitted. "Pam brings out the worst in me. I don't even think I *want* the things she has now. But I don't want to give any more ground, either."

"What does that mean?"

"She took my husband once. She took the children I wanted to have. And now it's like she's trying to take Seth, too. She walks in the room and she's just so *competitive*. Why is my son so important to her? Seth is all that I have."

"Ah. Are you angry at her still? I thought you'd been doing so well."

"I don't know *what* she makes me want, Mom. Maybe it's the life Seth *could* have had if I had done things differently. If Eric had been a better father. If I hadn't shut myself off from my husband. If I'd been thinking of him instead of myself. If I had known he needed me."

By this time Alva had paid the bill and they were headed outside. "Or maybe it's the life *you* could have had when you were Seth's age, Hilary. If your dad and I had stayed together. Is that what you're still wanting?"

"Oh, Mother." Hilary touched Alva's arm. "I have no idea."

Chapter 9

❧

Seth hadn't meant to be drinking at the campsite, not really. He'd slapped the money in Remy's hand for one reason alone, to compensate for his friends' having to wait for him so long. He'd promised his mom he wouldn't screw up, especially now with his dad around.

But someone had set up a plywood bar beneath the trees and his friends were the bartenders. They kept mixing different concoctions and everyone wanted him to taste them. There was cranberry juice and something green and something mixed with Red Bull.

Finally Seth decided he was being stupid. He couldn't make either of his parents happy anyway. These days, it seemed like he was always wondering what he would do wrong next. But then, what *didn't* he do wrong?

What did it matter, after all? No one was driving until morning.

He'd started out with a paper cup full of soda with some shot of something dropped inside. He'd followed up with a swig of something that tasted like cough syrup. Next he'd downed a few beers and left the cans stacked on the hood of someone's car for some drinking game they were playing.

Even the stars were spinning now. Seth lay with his head on a rock, squinting at the sky, trying to bring the night into focus. He'd thought if he drank enough booze, he'd get to the point where he didn't *feel* anymore. Seth didn't remember much, just something vague about punching T.J.'s lights out. Something T.J. had said, taking Remy's side about something. He remembered Emily standing behind him, that small jolt of electricity that hit his body every time she came near, trying to convince him to give it up. He remembered her ducking beneath his arm, bearing his full weight on her shoulders. Had she made him walk away?

The flames of the bonfire looked like dancing arms reaching for the darkness. That's the way Seth felt, too. Like he was trying to grab something he never could reach.

Seth had lost his sleeping bag. Which didn't matter, not really, because who planned on sleeping tonight anyway? Once the drinks had started coming, he'd lost all sense of time. He had smoked a few cigarettes. The night's refreshments had accomplished exactly what he'd intended. They'd taken the edge off.

He remembered Michael and Chase shouting and racing through the trees. Someone had brought a football and had been passing it back and forth as it got dark. Somebody else had brought out some sick speakers and had plugged in an iPod. The girls had danced.

The social groups, which had formed and morphed like amoebas from Mr. Fraser's Biology class, had been less predictable tonight. Tonight everyone had belonged, a moment in time without hangout boundaries. For a long time, Seth had chilled out by the fire, alternately growling sharp answers to those who asked about his new wheels, talking about nothing, or nodding off into a stupor. Someone had pressed another whiskey into his hand. He'd lost count of the times Emily's face loomed at him like a moon in the firelight. "You okay?" "You going to make it?" Several times she'd settled down beside him to rub his shoulders. "You still mad at T.J.?" "I'm worried about you, all right?"

That's when he'd pulled her down. She sort of fell against him, and he'd kissed her. She'd smelled so good, like wood smoke, shampoo, and peppermint. He loved that she tasted like peppermint.

"You got any gum? I've got booze breath, don't I?"

"Yeah." She'd laughed. "That and nicotine. But so does everybody else, so it doesn't matter."

"Oh, so you've been going around kissing everybody?"

"You'll never know, I guess. Too bad you're too drunk to try and keep up with me."

"Oh, I'd find out, all right. You know how they all talk in high school. Word gets around faster than fire."

"Yeah," she'd egged him on. "But we're not in high school anymore, remember?"

Seth was vaguely aware he kept slurring his words. But his guard was down and this was something he kept thinking they should talk about. "Are you breaking up with me? When we go off to college?"

If she'd answered him, he couldn't remember what she'd said.

Emily had disappeared for a while after that. When the Jim Beam ran out, they'd moved on to tequila, and after that gave out they tapped the keg. By now the party had mellowed, which was nice. Pockets of conversation surged and waned beside Michael's car. Earlier someone had been stomping Dixie cups. The ground was littered with smashed knots of paper. In the trees beside Seth, a random couple had started making out. Seth wondered if they were steadies everyone knew or if this was something that had started up tonight.

"Hey," he said when he saw Emily coming toward him again. Maybe he was starting to sober up. "Where did you go? I was looking for you." He sat up and picked dead leaves off his sweater.

She was rubbing her hands against her arms to keep warm. She looked a little worried. "Hey. Laura sent me to find you. Do you think you could get a ride home with someone else? I think we're going to take off."

"What?"

"Laura wants to go."

"Why?"

"It's a long story."

"You guys can't go. It's . . ." He tried to see his watch in the dark, but he couldn't. "I'll bet it's three in the morning. And you guys have been drinking, too."

"Not as much as you have."

"So let Laura go by herself. She'll be okay."

"I can't do that. She's my best friend."

"Can't girls ever do anything by themselves? You can't even go to the *girls' room* without each other."

She smiled, but it was a worried one. "You're right. Got to have a buddy."

He finally got around to trying to unfold his legs and stand up. He felt a little wobbly. "I don't get it. Why the quick decision to *vamos*?"

She offered him a hand. "Don't want to talk about it. Because it's one of your friends and he was a jerk and she doesn't want to be anywhere near him right now." When Seth finally got upright, he sort of stumbled into her again. "And I'm not telling you who it is because I don't want you swinging at anybody else tonight. The sound of fists hitting flesh makes me cringe."

"Tell her to get tough, Emily. She can't let guys get to her like that."

She steadied him with a hand on his chest.

"Look, she's got her period. She's got cramps and she's cold. And she just doesn't want to stick around and deal with it right now, Seth. Okay?"

Which was enough to sober Seth up and make him give his full consent immediately. Too much information. Don't start talking about the girl stuff. That stuff was just too intense. "I'll walk you to the car."

"If you think you can make it."

"I'm fine."

It wasn't the sort of night where you bid people good-bye. Seth helped Emily find her purse. When he spotted Laura coming toward them, she was lugging her sleeping bag like it weighed a ton. "Here. Let me get that." He took it from her.

Laura handed the sleeping bag over just as Emily stubbed her toe on a tree root. Of all the camping supplies they'd thrown together, how come no one had thought to bring a flashlight?

"Here." Seth powered up his phone and directed the pale green light in the vicinity of their feet. "This works." But now that Seth had stood up, his head was spinning. He wasn't feeling so hot. They staggered across the dark parking area with the girls' phones open, too, casting a ghostly glow in front of them.

Halfway to the car Emily glanced at her phone to see the time. "That's weird. We're not that far from home and I don't have any signal."

Laura checked hers. "Me, neither."

"That's what we can do, Laura." Seth's mind was an X-wing fighter, darting between stars, unable to land anywhere. "You need to call your mom. You've both been drinking. You've got to get a sober parent to come pick you up. You can't drive drunk."

"But there isn't any signal."

The idea had cemented in Seth's head. He'd promised his mom he'd be responsible tonight. What if he let the two of them go off alone and something happened? He took care of women who needed him; that's just what he *did*. Thanks to his dad, he'd been training to be a hero for six years running. "Either you call her or I don't let you drive."

"We've both sobered up enough to drive by now, Seth." Laura poked her hands in her sweater.

"Are you sure?"

"Yeah."

"Okay, then I'll go with you."

Laura shook her head. "No. You're the one that's messed up. You don't want to show up at your house like this. Your mom would go ballistic."

"My mom's cool about stuff. She trusts me."

"Stay here and have fun," Emily told Seth. "You'll want to hang out with your boys in the morning."

"Will I?"

"Yeah."

"Besides," Laura agreed, "Emily sleeps over all the time. She's just going to crash at my house. I'd have to take you home and that would take an extra half hour."

But Seth was pointing to the rock promontory that rose above the parking lot. "There's cell signal. All you have to do is just get to the top of that rock."

"Right." Laura followed his gaze up the limestone cliff.

He took Laura's hand and started pulling her. High overhead, the broad crown of a tree gleamed in the moonlight. Earlier during the night, Chase had scrambled to the top of the butte and had pounded his chest, bellowing like Tarzan. Several of their other classmates had scaled the wall, too, even a group of girls, because they needed to go up and make a call.

"I don't think I can do that," Laura said, shaking her head. "I really don't."

"You can," Seth reminded her. "You're a track star."

"Yeah, but track stars do their thing on flat ground. This is perpendicular."

"It's not that high. Everything always seems higher when you look up at it from below."

"Not true," Emily said, trailing them. "That's backward. Everything seems higher when you're at the top looking down. Seth, are you up to this?"

"Of course." He offered his hand to Laura. "Come on. Humor me. Let me once more be the knight in shining armor, make sure you get home safe."

The three of them stood at the base of the outcropping, eyeing the hollows and ridges, picking places where a hand could grasp, a foot could rest, a body could lean against a plane and stay balanced. Through the leaves that rustled in the night breeze above them, the moon cast a glow that fell over them like a lace doily.

"I don't want to climb all the way, Seth. I just want to go until I get one bar. Or maybe two."

"That'll work," Emily said.

"You start," Seth said. "I'll stay right behind you."

"Aren't you going up?" Laura asked Emily.

"He's okay," Emily said. "He's okay. He won't let anything happen to you."

They ascended with little effort at first, even though he stumbled a couple of times. He balanced on Laura's shoulder. They'd gotten two-thirds to the top before things got scary. He held her arm stable each time she hoisted herself to the next ledge.

"You're almost there," he said. "You can't stop now."

"Yeah," she said, "but then I have to climb back down."

The limestone felt cold and sharp beneath his

grip. Even Seth had started to shiver. "Why don't you check your phone from here? See if it works. Maybe there's signal now."

A light burst from her screen. "I've got signal. A couple bars."

"Oh, great."

"I think it's enough. I think it'll do."

With both hands gripping a root above him, he swung and listened to the faint song as she dialed. The party voices had faded to nothing. The only sounds besides her cell were the trill of frogs and the scurrying of a raccoon maybe, or a fox, something above them. The animal must have gotten close to the edge, because a storm of small, sharp stones rained around them. Suddenly Laura squeaked an expletive, her voice thin as wire. Her phone spiraled into space after it bounced off the outcropping at Seth's feet.

She clamped Seth's arm with fingers as cold as stone. "I'm freaking out. I'm really messed up. I'm so scared." He felt her shaking. "I looked down, Seth. I . . . I shouldn't have."

"Laura, look at me," he said, keeping his words even, knowing they were both in trouble. "Don't panic."

"I . . . I can't help it."

"Laura. You can't look down again. You have to look at me."

"It's cracking, Seth. The rock I'm standing on. I don't have any place to—"

"Grab this branch, Laura. You're almost to the top. Think where to plant your foot. Now. *Move.*"

"Seth. Please. Don't let me fall."

"I—" But she was right. Her footing was shifting, breaking away. Her half of the ledge had vanished. He watched in horror while the last of it shattered. He wasn't a hundred percent, oh no, not by a long shot. He tripped over his feet, sort of stumbled against the rock when he tried to reach her.

Overhead the stars shot from their circles and spread like a maze across the sky.

Later Seth would wonder if there'd been a second when she hung in the air like the characters did on the Saturday cartoons—Wile E. Coyote frozen in time, his eyes round and horrified—before he plummeted. Seth grabbed for her wrists and came up with air.

Seconds passed as he tried to make sense of what had happened. The sound of something sliding below him along the face of the cliff. Stones scattering along the rock face like pearls escaping from a string. Somewhere in the bottomless distance Emily started to scream.

Chapter 10

∽

$\mathcal{H}$ilary hadn't wanted a shift at the hospital during the graduation festivities, but she'd agreed to take this one. It seemed like every time she wanted off, they had unstable patients and nurses out sick. Guess it made sense, didn't it? A hospital. Always in some state of emergency.

In the wee hours of the morning, halfway through her nursing shift in the PCU, they'd paged her to help out in OB. Even if OB/GYN hadn't been short-staffed tonight, they would have been shorthanded. Three women had delivered babies in a forty-five-minute span, and one had been a nineteen-year-old without any family support.

"They'd better start taking advance reservations on those birthing rooms," Gina Minor said wryly as Hilary finished up her paperwork at the PCU station. "I hear they've got two more couples practicing Lamaze in the lobby."

"What was going on nine months ago today?" the charge nurse asked.

"Don't want to know," Hilary said, adjusting the stethoscope at her neck and waving them good-bye.

Every time a baby appeared at Englewood General, the intercom played a lullaby, and during the past hour it had sounded three times. No matter where a person happened to be in the hospital, you could hear the birth song. Whenever the melody repeated itself someone would laugh and say, "Boy, they're really pushing them out now, aren't they?" You could be stanching blood or administering electric shock or setting a broken bone. You could be administering a catheter or holding clamps for a surgeon or sitting with a family as someone died. The strains of Brahms's Lullaby would play and you'd breathe a sigh of relief. You'd think, *New life.* Whoever else might be dying; whatever else might be falling apart. *New life.*

Hilary had already read the young woman's Kardex. The girl had asked for help feeding her baby. Hilary knocked on the door to announce her presence and the girl lifted her face. "Hi."

"You ready to try?" Hilary asked after she'd introduced herself and admired the baby.

"I—I don't know." And as Hilary scanned the girl's features, she recognized the same expression she always found on a new mother's face: astonished, a little starstruck.

"You're going to do just fine. You're going to love it."

"Will it hurt?"

"A little," Hilary said. "Not right at first, but later." And Hilary thought how she might be talking about so much more than the subject at hand. "You'll be a little tender. But there are tricks to make it better. I promise you, once you get started, it's one of the easiest things you'll ever do. And it will be so good for this little munchkin here." She grinned at the newborn.

Ten minutes later the young woman sat against the pillows, beaming. The baby nursed with a tiny hand fisted in his mother's hair. Hilary's pager sounded. She made sure the girl could reach her call button before she gave the AOK sign with her fingers and backed away. *You're doing a good job,* she mouthed as she passed through the door.

After Laura had fallen, after Emily had screamed, Seth had scrambled down to see what he'd done. He hadn't searched for footholds or where to place his hands. He'd grabbed the next root and propelled himself down, daring gravity to make him fall, too. When he'd reached the bottom, he'd pushed his way through the group, trying to get to Laura. Nobody stopped him, which surprised him. No one grabbed his arm and shouted, *You did this! You stay away!*

He shouldered his way through the kids who were closest to the center of the circle. There he saw Emily swaying beside Laura, folded across the girl's torso, protecting her friend. The eerie sound coming from Emily's throat could have been the cry of the wind, the keening of an Illinois snowstorm along the lakeshore.

Emily rocked back on her heels, holding Laura's head in her lap. When Seth saw Laura, his stomach revolted. One leg folded sideways at an impossible angle. Her head fell backward against Laura's knee. Leaves, brush, and blood tangled her hair.

"Should you be touching her?" someone asked Emily.

"I don't care," Emily said.

Laura's face had gone gray as the moon. Her breath came in horrible rasping gasps, one deep, then two, three that could scarcely be heard.

After Seth saw Laura, he elbowed his way through the other kids and started to run. He thrashed through the black underbrush, tripping over fallen logs and shoving branches out of his way. He ran and could hear nothing except the sound of his labored breathing, the crack of the world breaking beneath his feet. He saw nothing but the net of tree limbs descending on him below the pale arc of moon. He didn't slow until he thought his heart would explode. He didn't stop until his lungs caught fire.

Even then, even before he pulled up, Seth knew he had to go back. The police would be there and they would be searching for him. But he waited with his chest heaving, letting the pain engulf him. He dragged his hand roughly across his chin, didn't know whether it was tears or blood, didn't care.

Night sounds sprang to life around him, the owl's hollow call, something with glowing eyes scurrying beneath a stone. The specter wail of sirens coming closer.

"Hilary Myers?" Her small pager sprang to life. Hilary lifted the small electronic device where it clipped to her scrubs and pressed the button. "What's up?"

"Hilary?"

It was Gina. Hearing her voice again was a jolt. Instead, Hilary had been expecting the charge nurse asking her to return to PCU. She didn't know why, but Gina's voice sounded knot tight. "Gina? Are you okay?"

"We've got something coming in."

"They need me back up there? Are you going to ER? Do you need to gown up? I'm on my way."

"We've got something coming in that you need to know about, Hilary."

"Oh." A beat. Then, "What have we got?"

"Couple of minutes out."

"Injury?"

Until this moment, it hadn't registered that anything might be personal. "A girl. Multiple crush injuries, open fractures, puncture wound in torso."

Hilary stood rooted to the spot. "A teenage girl?"

"It's a fall injury." Then, "Some accident that happened at some big outdoor party."

148

"Some party?" Hilary repeated, trying to get her mind around it. But there could be hundreds of big outdoor parties in Cook County tonight, couldn't there? *Couldn't* there?

From somewhere in another world, a cart rattled past, its test tubes tinkling like chimes. An alarm sounded on a distant heart monitor. A light blinked over a patient's door. "It's a girl?" *Thank you, God. It's nothing to do with Seth. It's not.*

"They haven't officially ID'd her yet."

"But do you know who it is?"

"Julie got me on my cell. Chase called her before the EMTs had even gotten there. Dirk left right away to pick up some of the other kids and drive them home."

From the way Gina rushed past Hilary's question, there was something she wasn't telling; she was testing to see what Hilary knew. "Gina? Is my son okay?"

Silence.

"Gina? What is it? What's wrong? What does Seth have to do with any of this?"

At her friend's hesitation, the sound started in Hilary's head like a keening wind. All she could hear was the roar. She was drowning; her head kept going under.

"Why don't you come up to the ER before the ambulance gets here," Gina said. "It's best if you hear this from me."

Case Number: IL 05/29/3462

Incident: Consumption of Alcohol by a Minor (MUI), Willful Trespass

Reporting Officer: Lt. J. Meehan

Date of Report: May 29

At about 0230 hours on 29th May, I was dispatched to a recreation site where a group of teens had been camping without adult supervision. Many of the girls were crying. Upon arrival, I came upon the unconscious victim, white female, age 17. I immediately requested medical rescue and an ID unit to respond for photos of the victim's injuries. One teen was performing CPR on victim. I aided volunteer. Victim began breathing on her own.

Paramedics not able to get girl to regain consciousness. Still working to stabilize victim en route. ID Unit C-190 on scene to take photos of injury and scene. After ambulance transported victim, I asked what had happened, if there were any witnesses, and how long ago had it occurred. They said that it had just happened, fifteen minutes before I arrived. I immediately requested a description of "Seth" and placed a BOLO to all units in area.

Described as white male 6' tall, weighing about 165, with short brown hair. He had on a long-sleeve hooded sweatshirt and blue jeans. Witness advised that they didn't think male had left the scene. Backup Rescue Unit 25 arrived; Lt. McCullough searched for "Seth."

Cordoned area obviously a campsite. Trash was full of bottles and cans. Witnesses appeared to have been drinking heavily. Parents arrived but were advised no custody of their children until Breathalyzer tests complete.

Note: All involved in incident are under-aged. Most at scene ID'd, written up, and released on own recognizance. Eighteen-year-olds transported to jail via police van.

Detective John Taylor, Unit 109 from felony crime section, notified of the incident. Before legal adults transported, "Seth" questioned by detective. A copy of the report is being forwarded to him for further investigative follow-up and disposition of the case.

• • •

Hilary wondered. Were there parents who imagined this feeling before it happened? Did they prepare themselves in some way for this news in the night?

Did they pray as they listened to the officer's voice on the other end of the telephone, describing the incident, listing the details without emotion? Did they imagine how their ears would buzz, how the adrenaline would settle into their fingers as they tried to make sense of what was being said? Did they know they wouldn't be able to find their car keys in the nurse's bag, that they would struggle with the arms of a sweater, trying to put it on?

When she'd been a girl at the state fair, she used to beg her parents for carnival tickets. Her father had to pay money for her stomach to be pitching this way. Like nothing was beneath her for a thousand miles. Like the bottom had dropped out and everything inside her was going with it. At the same time Hilary's insides were riding the Kamikaze, she heard herself at the graduation picnic, reassuring Abigail Moore: *They're responsible kids. They know how to take care of each other. I asked plenty of questions, believe me.*

She shouldn't be driving. Gina had offered to take her, but Hilary had gotten away too fast. She'd been wrong not to take her friend up on the offer. In spite of the arcing headlights, the painted lines along the shoulder, Hilary couldn't see the road.

Hilary replayed what had happened at the hospital as she'd been running to her car, frantic to get to Seth, to help him. The ambulance pulling up, the Moore family tumbling out at the same time. Abigail crying over and over, *It isn't Laura; it's* not. Abigail shrieking as the paramedics unloaded the stretcher and she barely recognized Laura. Abigail retching and sick in the parking lot. Abigail blocking Hilary's way, staring at her with pure hatred. *Look what your son did to* my daughter. *Look what he's* done. *If she dies, it's going to be on his head.*

Hilary had already been flying toward the jail before she thought she ought to phone Eric. Any other weekend, he would have been across the country instead of at a hotel near the Loop. This was the type of emergency that, had it happened the past few years, she would have dealt with solo. This was the type of thing Eric had left her to take care of alone.

Of course it was being discussed now, all over town. The kids were texting. Jefferson High parents were clustered blearily around kitchen counters everywhere, squinting into the unwelcome overhead light, hanging on to mugs of fresh-brewed coffee as if they could hang on to the innocence their children had lost since yesterday.

Beyond the pools of streetlights, beyond the

early-morning trash truck that was beeping and lifting a trash receptacle on its rusty arms, the sky was still onyx dark. She pulled to the side of the road and sorted through the business cards she'd never bothered to clean out of her purse. She found the card, its edges frayed because she'd been carrying it so long. And she could still read the name: Roundtree, Gates, and Mulligan, Attorneys-at-Law. She dialed this number first.

She made her second call, this one to Eric. After several rings, Eric's phone switched to voice mail.

"You've reached the voice mail of Eric Wynn, financial advisor with Stearns, Madison, and Levy. I'll return your call as soon as possible. If the call is time sensitive or you'd like to buy or sell holdings, contact my assistant Mary Woods at . . ."

Up until now, Hilary hadn't given any thought to how she would tell Eric what had happened, let alone what to say in twenty seconds or less. She blurted out the first thing that came to mind. No list of events in sequential order. No details of Laura Moore.

"Hello? Call me when you get this. Please." She hated herself for being this honest. She hated herself for the many times she'd longed to say the same words before. She hated herself because it was a one-sided conversation and somehow that made it easier to be intimate. "Eric. Seth and I need you."

Chapter 11

❧

*W*hen Seth had returned to the campsite, gasping for breath and exhausted, he found Laura gone and the clearing cordoned off. Every police car, and there had to be at least seven of them, had a spotlight trained on a different area of the campground. A detective approached him the moment Seth stepped into the light. "Do you mind answering a few questions for us, son? Would you consent to that?"

Here I am, Seth had almost said. *No need talking to anyone else. I can tell you anything you need to know.*

The guy's badge read: **Detective John Taylor, Unit 109. Felony Crime Division**. "What kind of questions?" Seth asked.

"General information. You know. Name. Age. You tell us what you witnessed here tonight."

"I don't know if I should," he said, doubtful. "I'm Seth."

"Have you been drinking at this party?" the officer asked. "Can you tell me where you were earlier? Why didn't you stay with your friends? Where were you going just now? Did you see her fall?"

It didn't matter, really. Seth knew he deserved

everything that would happen to him after he told the truth. He would deserve the condemning glares of his friends. He would deserve the cold bite of the handcuffs and the shove into the police car. "I don't think I'm supposed to talk to anyone about this," he said.

"So you're Seth, huh?" John Taylor held up two fingers and asked Seth to follow the fingers with his eyes. He jotted a note on his report. "I'm required to give you a BAC test. Do you know what that is? A Breathalyzer?"

Seth shrugged. "I know what it is." And it surprised him, but after he blew into a straw and Taylor recorded the results there wasn't a special armed unit waiting to take Seth in. They loaded him into the police van with the others.

He lost track of his classmates during the endless wait in the holding cell before they called his name, the assembly-line search to make sure he wasn't bringing in weapons, the threadbare uniform pressed within an inch of its life that they thrust into his hands. He went through all that before a precinct officer about as big around as the John Hancock Building told him his lawyer was on the phone.

"I don't have a lawyer. I don't want one," Seth said.

"You expect me to feel sorry for you, kid?" the massive man said. "You've got somebody looking out after you. Deal with it."

Seth jammed the ancient phone receiver against his head like it was a wall he could knock his head against. "Hello," he said, his voice a low growl. He had no idea who he'd be talking to.

John Mulligan introduced himself and the conversation went downhill from there.

"I don't have to talk to you, do I? You're just a crook out to get my parents' money."

"You'll talk to me if you have an ounce of sense in your head," the voice growled back. "I'm a friend of your mom's, did you know that? Do you know she hired me?"

But if the guy thought that would make it better, he was wrong. "I don't have anything to say."

It didn't matter to Seth. The damage had been done. And the most bizarre part of all, Seth felt a strange sense of relief. He didn't have to *be* anything for his mom anymore. He didn't have to feel guilty about not being what she expected. But this lawyer was throwing a barrage of questions out there; he still didn't get it.

Address? Birthday? You're already eighteen, aren't you? That poses a problem.

What happened last night when you and Laura Moore were together? Approximate time you started on the climb? How much alcohol had you consumed? How much have you told the police?

Did the officer force you to submit to the Breathalyzer test or did you consent? To your knowledge, had Laura been drinking, too? Has she ever mentioned being unhappy?

Did she seem depressed? Is it possible she was suicidal? Could she have done it on purpose?

Seth choked back a sound of grief halfway between a sob and a shout of rage. "You don't get it." He slammed his hand against the cinder-block wall. His knuckles were bleeding again. "How can you make it sound like it was her fault? It was *me*."

"Look, Seth. You may have already condemned yourself to a life behind bars. But like it or not, unless you go out and do something else stupid, that isn't going to happen. Other than an MUI, which is a pretty hefty problem, they can't charge you with anything else. It was an *accident*."

"But it was my fault. I was the one who convinced her to climb with me."

"You said so yourself, Seth: You were the one who convinced her. But she let herself be convinced, didn't she? I know how you feel, but she didn't have to agree."

Seth leaned his head against the cinder blocks. "I *did* it, don't you see? If not for me, it wouldn't have happened. Don't tell me you know how I feel."

"Oh, believe me. I do. My wife died four years ago. I know how it feels to deal with pain. I know how it feels to blame yourself for something."

When the lawyer added nothing to that, Seth

asked, "How do you know what blame feels like?"

"Because my wife died in a car accident. I was driving."

The news hit Seth like a fist in the stomach. He didn't know what to say. The silence hung between them, as firm and solid as the cinder-block jail wall. It took Seth awhile before he could even speak at all. "So are you doing this as some big favor to my mom or something?" he asked at last. "No lawyer would want to take this case."

"What I'm doing is this: We all have to deal with what we have to deal with. I don't care that you feel sorry for yourself because you aren't perfect. So you made a big mistake that hurt someone. You don't get to check out; I'm not going to let you. Life doesn't work that way."

Seth didn't have to take this. He hung up. The guy was lying. Seth slumped against the wall and tried to make the disembodied lawyer voice fade into background noise.

Once Seth was finished at the phone, they dragged him back for the health check, when they went over every inch of him looking for diseases and took his weight, his height, as if he were going to belong to the state forever. When they slammed the stethoscope against his chest during the health exam, he felt so empty that it surprised him they even found a heartbeat. Seth's biggest fear wasn't that Laura Moore would die. It was walking out of this place and knowing he didn't fit into his world anymore. It was walking out of this place and knowing the person he'd been didn't exist anymore. A black hole had been ripped in Seth's universe and he'd been the one who'd fallen through.

Pam awoke to Lily's voice from the adjoining doorway. "Mommy?"

She sat up in the bed and held out her arms to her daughter. "Lily? What is it? Little goose, come here. Did you have a bad dream? Why are you awake?"

"Daddy's phone was ringing."

"Was it?" Pam patted the hotel mattress beside her. "Here. Climb up. I don't think it rang. You must have dreamed it. We didn't hear anything."

"That's because it's in Ben's and my room. Daddy left it there when he tucked us in."

Eric had rolled over and was surveying them through sleepy, squinted eyes. "Why are you two awake?"

"Honey. I think your phone rang."

"I didn't hear it."

"Lily said it woke her up. You left it in the kids' room."

"My phone? Really?" He rolled out, taking half the covers with him, and went in search of it. He came back, still bleary-eyed, trying to read the screen. "Yeah. It says I got a call." He punched a button and held it against his ear.

From her place beside him, Pam could hear the request for a password, the first words of a message. She sat up straighter and hugged Lily against her chest. "Honey, who is it?"

His brow had furrowed. He held up his hand. After he'd listened, he punched it off. "That was Hilary."

"Oh my word."

"What's she doing? It's crazy."

"Something could be wrong, Eric."

He was already dialing Hilary back. "I know."

Ben appeared in the doorway, too, scrubbing his eyes. "Mom? What is it?"

Pam certainly hoped Hilary had a good reason, disturbing them all. Yes, Hilary worked crazy hours on her nursing shifts. And yes, she was the mother of a teenager. But surely the woman had enough sense of reality to understand that other people tried to sleep during the night.

Pam's next thought: *Seth.* Fear clawed the back of her throat.

"Your dad's phone rang; that's all." Then, to Eric, touching his arm: "Honey. The party."

When the central air turned on in the hotel room, the curtains opened a crack to reveal the high-rises of downtown Chicago. Even so early in the morning, the buildings shone in a collage of silver and glass and light. Pam propped her head on the top of Lily's and absently scratched Ben's shoulder.

"Hilary?" Eric asked when the call rang through. "I saw you called."

Pam watched her husband as, in the light that fell in through the curtain, his face went the color of stone. With her children wedged on either side of her, she waited for him to reveal clues about what had happened. The knot bulged in his jaw again, the one she'd grown accustomed to whenever he was hurt and angry. He asked only a few questions, which Pam couldn't decipher.

Do you know where they took him? How long ago? Has he called you? They brought her to your hospital? You talked to the mother?

When Eric hung up, he looked at Pam and said this one thing: "You were right, Pam. You were right all along."

He sat on the side of the bed and stared at the clock as one minute escaped into another.

Chapter 12

❧

*H*ilary sat halfway hunched in her chair in the dirty basement, staring at the toes of her shoes. If she stared at her shoes, she didn't have to see anything else. She didn't have to see the rows of WANTED posters. She didn't have to listen to the door that buzzed open and then latched shut with a sharp click. She didn't have to notice the phone ringing for hours because no one would answer. She didn't have to see the heavy traffic of detainees moving in and out of the door, their faces lined no matter how young they were, their eyes empty.

She didn't glance up until her ex-husband walked in the door. When he entered, she unfolded from her chair and stood. He stopped in front of her. "Hello, Eric." She saw his Adam's apple slide up, then down as he swallowed.

It seemed there was no proper way to greet each other now that his new wife wasn't there, now that Hilary had told him she needed him, now that their son was in trouble. She didn't open her arms. He didn't offer to hold her. They waited, only a breath's distance from each other, while each of them thought about the painful moments that had passed between them, none of them as painful as this one.

The jail had a reputation as one of the largest city jail in the country. As far as size as well as other things went, the *Sun-Times* likened it to a prison. It was overcrowded; there could be thousands of inmates on any one day. Who knew what sort of people Seth would be with in a holding cell? Murderers and armed robbers. Thugs of the worst kind. It hadn't taken Hilary long to understand that criminal charges were different from anything they'd ever experienced before.

"I called John Mulligan," she said.

"Is he on his way?"

"He's already been in to see Seth. He was here before I arrived."

The lawyer had been fast to take down the pertinent details—everything the officer had told her when he called, everything else she'd been able to glean about the accident from what Gina had told her, everything she'd seen at the hospital.

"Are there going to be charges against him?"

"I don't know. I just . . . wanted someone to be with Seth. I didn't want him to be alone."

Then Eric asked, "You called him before you called me, didn't you?"

"Well, you know. There are some people you can just *trust*." Hilary could have pinched herself for saying the words. It sounded awful the way they came out.

During the horrible months when Eric and

Hilary had been trying to keep their heads about their broken relationship, trying to come to some amicable means of dividing their property and their child and the wrenches in the garage and Gran's Christmas china, John Mulligan had seen the wounds of the war. He knew the worst in each of them, how helpless Hilary had been, how brutal and condemning she and Eric had been to each other. John had been instrumental in working out the initial court agreement to trade Seth back and forth according to a set schedule. And when Eric had married Pam and moved to California, he had forfeited that. Although it had disrupted Seth's two-a-days in the summer and his coaches had acted like Hilary had encouraged their star player to hold out on an NFL contract and robbed them of a team, Hilary made sure Seth made a trip to see Eric. And Seth had always been happy to visit his dad.

"I'm glad you called John. If we need him, he'll do a good job."

"I didn't know how you would feel about it. He was the only one I knew."

Eric nodded toward the cell phone she hadn't realized she still gripped in her hand. "He'll let us know what's going on?"

Hilary nodded.

"You know we were planning on leaving tomorrow. But maybe I shouldn't go back right now," Eric said. "Pam and the kids could go back, but I—I've got personal days coming at the office. I could use them to spend some time with Seth. I don't want to leave the two of you alone while you go through this."

Somewhere in the background, a buzzer sounded, the sound of a clanging gate. "I know what you want to say," he admitted when she stayed silent. "I know, and I deserve it. If I wanted to be there for Seth, I should have thought about it long ago."

Hilary glanced up and touched Eric's arm. She saw motion at the far end of the corridor. For a moment, she couldn't make out faces. All she could see was a battalion of uniforms, an entire battery of badges and sidearms and broad-chested men. They looked as grim as if they were escorting some notorious war criminal to the gallows. Then, as the group moved toward the security doors and the warden, who was sitting behind a tall spare desk, buzzed the doors open, an officer stepped aside and Hilary saw Seth.

Bloody scratches crosshatched one side of his jaw. A bruise bloomed on his chin. He looked so small and pale and disheveled that Hilary almost didn't recognize him. When had she started thinking that this boy was a grown man?

The escorting officers left Seth at the desk to be processed out. "You his parents?" the guard asked. "Which one of you is going to sign the release papers?"

They sprang from their seats. "Only need one of you." The guard opened a box that one of the officers had given him. Hilary walked forward and picked up the pen, which was attached to the desk with a beaded chain. Guess in this place you *really* had to worry about people stealing the pen. The guard marked where she needed to sign with a series of *x*'s. Hilary sifted through the wrinkled pages and scribbled her name.

Each of Seth's belongings had been identified with a yellow hangtag, and one by one the warden removed the tags and handed them over. Seth's smartphone. (Hilary had tried to call him. Had it been ringing and ringing in this box?) His wallet. The watch she had given him for graduation. A pack of Wrigley's spearmint. A handful of change.

Hilary was thinking, *What would it be like to be locked away for seventy years and, upon your departure, have the exact coins handed back to you? The ones that had been in your pocket a lifetime ago? The ones that had been there when you'd been a different person? The coins would be the same, but you wouldn't be.*

Seth sorted through his items and didn't pocket them right away. He picked up his smartphone and examined it as if it didn't belong to him anymore. He had to have dozens of messages. Hilary alone had left three of them.

Oh, Lord, she prayed. *What can I do to help my son?*

Seth picked up his wallet and thumbed through to make sure everything was there. Hilary could see that his thumb had been inked; they'd taken a mug shot and his fingerprints. Seth glanced over, saw his waiting father, and his face slammed shut.

Eric looked at Hilary. *I'll meet you at the house,* his eyes told her.

Hilary returned to the chairs where they'd been waiting, clutching her keys and her handbag. Her stomach was roiling. *Don't let him chase you away,* she wanted to say. *No matter how he acts, he doesn't want you to leave him.* Then, because they had nothing else left besides solidarity, she gripped Eric's hand.

Chapter 13

〜

"Don't you have Kleenex? A napkin? *Anything?*" Seth rifled through the glove compartment, shoving aside the insurance papers. "Does this ink come off? I've got to get this ink off my fingers." He dug out a wrinkled napkin and scrubbed his hands hard enough to take the skin off. Still the stain, the dark blotches etching the whorls and loops of his fingertips, remained.

His head hit the headrest again.

"Seth," his mother said.

"Laura's really messed up."

"Honey."

"It should have been me."

"No."

"I should be unconscious at that hospital."

"It was an accident. A freak accident, Seth. You couldn't have known."

"Yeah. Right. It would have happened anyway. She would have climbed that bluff by herself, even if I hadn't talked her into it. Even if I hadn't promised her that I wouldn't let anything happen to her." He slammed the dashboard with his fist. *"Stupid."*

"Seth. Don't."

"Mom. I can't do anything right. Not

anymore." He couldn't look at his mom. He didn't want to talk about it anymore. His anger and guilt felt strangely satisfying. All those years of living up to their expectations. All those years of being the "good boy." He felt like an animal inside him had been sprung free. He didn't have to pretend.

When they arrived home, Hilary elbowed her way in from the garage door. "Are you up, Mother? Where are you?" But she already knew the answer. The smell of strong coffee drifted from the kitchen.

"She's up," Pam said as Alva lifted a cup to her lips and slurped. "I phoned her." Pam stood in the kitchen with Hilary's cheese grater in one hand and a hunk of Monterey Jack in the other. "I thought she needed to know what was happening."

It was true, then. There was no magic time-out when your life started falling apart. Things didn't stop to let you grieve or let you blame yourself or let you pull yourself together. The realities kept shooting their relentless darts, the dishwasher that needed to be emptied, the bills that were overdue, the woman whom your husband had fallen for when he'd gotten tired of you. Pam seized the wooden spoon, tucked the bowl inside the crook of her arm, and whipped the eggs into a small cyclone.

When Seth walked in the room and saw Pam, his jaw clamped so tight he looked like he might break a tooth. He didn't ask the question, but everyone in the room could tell what he was thinking.

What's she doing here?

"Seth. Honey." Hilary reached for him.

"I'm going to my room," he announced.

At that moment, Pam seemed not to notice Seth's reaction at all. "In case you don't remember, we suggested you not let him go camping, Hilary." Pam's every accusation played in rhythm to the thumping spoon.

"*Seth* is a responsible adult." But, for the first time, Hilary wondered if she might be lying, to Seth, to herself. The video rewound in her head, the one of Seth being escorted toward her by the officers, the moment they'd stepped aside to reveal, not the young man she'd expected, but the broken, hurt little boy.

"This day would have been completely different if you had let him go with us last night."

"How did you get here, Pam? Taxi? Bus? Did my mother come to pick you up? What?"

Pam used the fork to stab a pat of butter and ring it around the pan. "That's just the problem. He *is* classified as an adult. An eighteen-year-old. The timing couldn't be worse for a kid getting in trouble with the law."

"This isn't the time."

"It never is." The butter sizzled and spattered as Pam poured egg into the pan.

"She took a taxi." Alva set her cup down hard in the saucer. "I wouldn't have gone to pick her up. Not this morning. Not like this."

Where had Eric gone? Hilary could hear the rhythmic *ping ping ping* of a basketball bouncing on pavement and she realized he must have gone to the side yard to keep the kids distracted.

Hilary remembered Gina saying what seemed a lifetime ago that Hilary needed to show Pam who was ahead in the cooking department. She grabbed a tomato, pierced its skin with a knife, and watched it hemorrhage onto the counter. "If we have anything to discuss at all, it's how to best support Seth after what's happened." Pam didn't step aside. Hilary reached across her to get the cutting board. "You have no idea how badly he's hurting." Hilary hewed the tomato into pieces, added basil.

"You see I was right about the party," Pam commented with false lightness. "You could have stopped this from happening. But you didn't."

Hilary sliced her finger. Blood oozed from the cut, mixed with the tomato.

"Seth is a part of our family, too," Pam said, and Hilary felt like the knife that had just cut her finger had also twisted in her heart.

Pam's accusations hit far too close to her own deep fear. *I was supposed to protect him. He was never supposed to know how it felt for his world to collapse.* Hilary stared at her gushing finger, her voice skating on the edge of panic. "You don't think this could have anything to do with you, too? You don't think this could have something to do with *all* of us?"

Eric wandered through the side door, herding the children. Pam snagged his attention. "Can you get them to wash their hands? It's time to eat." Eric tapped them on the bottom and they bounded away.

Hilary had no idea if Seth could overhear this conversation and, honestly, she didn't care. "I met Seth's English teacher at the florist shop the other day. Seth was supposed to write an essay about graduation and how his family was going to celebrate it."

"So," Pam asked, "did he write about the party that you told him he could go to?"

Eric was turning toward Pam, but Hilary made him stop. "No, Eric," she said. "You need to hear this, too."

"Did he write about us coming to visit?" Eric asked.

Hilary spared no details as she recounted the story of running into Seth's teacher at the flower shop. Seth's wishful thinking, unspoken. And even though she had never read the essay, she knew her son well enough! She knew how Seth would have described it. Eric and Hilary beneath sun so clear and sparkling that it burned through their resolve. A family float trip as if the divorce had never happened, the rapids boiling, the raft angling over river-slick boulders, fishermen's lines arcing in the breeze. "He's eighteen years old. And he made up a story that was pure fiction."

"Well," Eric said. "As long as he told them he'd made it up."

"He didn't, Eric. His teacher spoke to me after she'd read it. She complimented us for sacrificing for Seth's sake, for how well we parent together."

This made the second time I didn't know how to protect Seth from getting ripped to pieces.

"Seth doesn't like me," Pam started up again. "You should have seen his face when he walked in and saw me here."

To Eric's credit, he didn't tell her she was wrong. "Do you blame him? He can't help what he's feeling, Pam. Give him some time."

"He's had five years."

"And he's just made one of the worst mistakes he'll ever make in his life." Hilary recognized Eric's tone of voice, the same combination of anger and withdrawal that had made their divorce so difficult. He'd reached maximum input. In man terms, the War General had just sounded a massive retreat. "This isn't the time or place. I want you to just drop it."

At that Hilary expected Pam to explode. Only she didn't get the chance because Ben came out of the bathroom. "Mom, why won't Seth play with me today?" Then, "Mom? What's wrong?"

"Go find your sister," Pam said.

Eric and Pam went for a walk by the lakeshore that afternoon. They left their shoes on the boardwalk before they got to the sand. Ben and Lily skipped along in front of them. Lily was carefully picking up stones. Ben was being all boy, finding ropes of kelp that had washed ashore, saying it was a slimy green monster, and chasing Lily around with it.

"Ben!" Pam called to him. "Stop torturing your sister."

Pam and Eric watched for a while as the children ran zigzags in the sand, racing on sandpiper legs. Eric touched Pam's arm. "I have an important question to ask you."

"What?"

"Do you mind if I change my plane ticket and stay a little longer? I think it's important that I spend time with my son."

Pam strolled at his side, her toes digging in the sand. "I think we need to do whatever is right for him."

"You could take the kids back." Eric bent to pick up a flat stone. He sidearmed it and it skipped twice before sinking into the water. "Get them home and get them into their normal routine again."

Pam froze where she stood, her eyes troubled. "You don't want us to stay with you, Eric?"

He stopped, too. "You? Stay? Even the kids?"

"Yes."

"You would do that?"

"Of course I would. You know I care about Seth. He's your son. That makes him important to me, too."

"Pam, I know your heart. I know what you're thinking. But maybe it isn't the best idea."

"What do you mean, Eric? Don't you want me here?"

"It's the money issue. There's your job. And if you and the kids stay, we have to pay for the hotel another week."

"You could stay with your mom and dad," she suggested. "I guess you could do that if we didn't stay."

"Or I could even stay with Hilary."

Maybe it was the wrong thing to say. "Are you staying to help *Seth* through all of this, Eric? Or do you think it's Hilary who needs support?"

"I don't understand what you're so afraid of. What have I done to make you feel like this? Like you're trying to get the upper hand in some competition that doesn't exist?"

Pam had no answer for him. It was almost like she didn't hear. "What if Seth's done this to try to get you away from me? You heard what Hilary said about the paper he wrote. What if this is some trick he's pulling to get the two of you back together?"

"Are you kidding me?" Anger sharpened Eric's voice. "Why would you ask a question like that?" The waves of the lake slid up, curled onto themselves, and slipped back. "Trust me, Pam. Everything in life isn't about you. I know my son. He wouldn't pull something like this because of you. He wouldn't consciously hurt *anyone*. Not for *any* reason."

"We're your family," Pam said. "We want to stay with you. If it means another week at the hotel, so be it." But like sand that moves with the curve of the tide, something had slipped apart between them. The waves at their feet seemed to be asking questions, too.

Chapter 14

❧

*I*t had started to rain, one of those early-summer thunderstorms that took everyone by surprise. The Cubbies game in Wrigley Field would be rained out this afternoon. The high-school football stadium was a huge smudge on the horizon, a watercolor painting. Tires threw up rooster tails of spray as Hilary crossed an overpass. Lightning scribbled its name across the sky.

Hilary didn't know where she was headed. She hadn't thought anything through. She only knew she had to find a place to breathe, a place where she wasn't awash in other people's voices.

Landmarks passed without notice. The city streets gave way to mix-and-match blocks of suburbia, the chain stores and restaurants and movie complexes interchangeable with those of any other suburb in the country. She drove past the exit to the senior-party campground. She surprised herself when she didn't take the exit and turn into the park entry.

How hard would it be to disappear? She could buy L'Oréal Natural Black at a Wal-Mart and run her hair under a truck-stop faucet. She could abandon the car in a place it would never be found. She could start over as someone who'd never been Eric's wife, who'd never been called to the emergency room to be told an ambulance was coming in, that her son had gotten drunk and jeopardized a girl's life.

After Hilary had lost her father she'd awakened often in the night, her heart pounding, thinking it had been a lie. Her father wasn't gone at all. Hadn't she just seen him in a dream? And when she'd realize again that he had died, she'd weep again, awash in an ocean of pure pain, healing pain, pain that was sweet because she'd been entitled to it.

But this was a different sort of grief. It didn't help, wasn't working toward cleansing. She woke in the night and knew that she mustn't let anyone hear her sobs. It was a selfish sort of pain, because her son needed her to be strong.

Hilary knew where she would go, not to run from what frightened her most but to plunge to its very depths. She steered the car off at the next exit and turned toward the very place she probably shouldn't go. She headed toward the hospital.

She'd never actually signed out from her late-night shift. When Gina had told her about Seth, she'd grabbed her purse and her keys and had flown. Now the automatic doors slid soundlessly open so she could enter. The central waiting room bustled with activity. Families waited in petal-shaped chairs with their heads together, talking in low voices. A poster for cancer patients suggested:

FIND A POSITIVE MEANING AND INVEST IN HOPE. LIVE IN THE PRESENT. CELEBRATE MILESTONES AND SPECIAL OCCASIONS. SUPPORT YOUR SUPPORT SYSTEM. Fish slipped silently past in the glass aquarium.

Hilary stopped at the entrance to the PCU hallway and took a deep breath, steeling herself before she headed to the nurses' station. She closed her eyes, lifted her chin, and, when she opened her eyes again, found herself staring into the hospital chapel. It wasn't much bigger than the nurses' break room. For the size of this hospital, it ought to have been much larger. It was rosewood paneled and rich, with an ornate brass cross on the altar and walls lined with velvet curtains. Candles burned beside a bank of fresh flowers. A chalice sat to one side, gleaming in the candlelight, in case a priest or a pastor needed to make use of it.

Hilary couldn't keep from going in; the gentle atmosphere beckoned her. She stood staring at the cross as if she'd never seen it before, at the white dove and the likeness of Jesus etched in the blue and ruby glass window, and thought how just one week ago she, too, had been a normal churchgoer, one who always sidled ten minutes late into the seat that the usher knew was her favorite. Being a Christian had been more of a habit than a relationship. When her nursing schedule allowed, she attended a small women's group because she didn't want to lose touch with the latest Bible studies. During these last difficult days, she'd been quick to throw out a prayer for God to help, then just as quick to hurry forward with her own plans without expecting any answer.

Hilary knew from her years on staff here that this chapel had been a different sort of place. It had been a haven for those who had never trusted God before to utter their first desperate cries. It had been a place for those whose loved ones fell ill or who knew that their days were numbered or who had found out that they had lost a child. Between these walls had drifted accusations at God and gratitude for miracles and all the unanswerable faith questions that came when miracles didn't happen.

There had been a wedding here once. A pretty young bride, a leukemia patient, who'd been almost as pale and fragile as the lace on her dress. The nurses had watched from the doorway, wearing scrubs of every color and tissues poking out of their pockets along with their stethoscopes. *Well, what would* you *do if you didn't know whether you were going to make it to next week?* Hilary had overheard someone say. *The days you* don't *have can't subtract from the days you* do *have, can they?*

The last Hilary had heard, the woman had entered a clinical trial and gone into remission. Ten years had passed and she and the other members of the trial still stopped by on the anniversary to take their doctor out for dinner. The woman was still happily married and had a kid. Not bad. You never knew.

Hilary stepped forward and gripped the pew. How she longed to have the sort of faith that made her expect something beautiful to come from broken places. But she didn't think that could happen anymore. "What am I supposed to do?" she whispered to no one as she hung on to the pew the way that, when she'd been a girl, she'd hung on to a window ledge at a candy store, looking in. "Who am I supposed to be for all of them?"

She lost track of how long she waited there. Candle flames danced inside the glass. The roses in the arrangement shone dark as blood. As the sun moved over the sky, maybe it was only the moving shadow, but Hilary thought she could almost see the flowers opening. "Are you here, Lord?" she whispered. "Why won't you ever answer?"

There had been the patients she'd run out on this morning, the young woman learning to breast-feed, the girl struggling with asthma and a bad case of the flu, the man who'd gotten tangled between his dog and his bike who needed surgery for a tear in his ACL. As quiet as the pulse she might find in the crook of an arm, as urgent as breath, the message came. DON'T ASK ME WHO YOU'RE SUPPOSED TO BE, BELOVED. Words intermingling with the very beat of Hilary's heart. ASK ME WHO *I* AM.

But Hilary didn't hear the words, not this time. She was on her way to check patients' charts. She'd already left the chapel behind.

She told herself she'd returned because she hadn't finished the end-of-shift reports. But the minute she stepped into the elevator, Hilary understood something she hadn't admitted to herself. She'd come for a different reason. She wanted to keep vigil, too.

The Intensive Care Unit waiting room had a different feel from the gathering space downstairs. This room wasn't nearly so broad and welcoming. The patients weren't allowed visits from anyone except immediate family. The chairs sat like clenched fists facing one another. Everywhere you looked were boxes of tissue.

Usually somber and silent, today this room was a circus. The senior class of Jefferson High had started arriving not long after the ambulance had careened into the bay. As Hilary edged toward the desk, she saw knots of sobbing girls hugging one another. Emily's mother stood with her arm roped around her daughter. In spite of signs with red circles and slashes over drawings of phones, kids babbled on their cells anyway.

The bank of gifts had grown to monstrous proportions. It must have started on a table beneath the television and grown toward the west wall. Balloons bobbed from their strings, their glinting Mylar belying the gravity of Laura's condition: GET WELL SOON and THINKING OF YOU. Someone had brought in candles although hospital rules forbade them to be lit on an oxygen floor. The stuffed animals came in all shapes and sizes, some of them new, with tags, others dilapidated. Single-stem flowers had already started to wilt in their paper skins. Makeshift posters, in all different styles and colors, proclaimed: LAURA, WE LOVE YOU!!!!!

The boys had bunched around each other, their knees locked, their jaws squared, an army of grim-faced soldiers. Against the back wall, Hilary saw Remy wipe his face with the hem of his T-shirt. T.J. slid down the wall until he landed on his rump, his eyes never leaving his iPod screen. Ian stared at the fluorescents overhead. Chase and Michael stood quietly talking, their fists shoved inside the pockets of their baggy jeans.

Don't forget Seth, Hilary wanted to say to them. *There's someone else who's dying here, too. You have another friend who needs you.* But even as she thought it, Hilary knew she was wrong. She would do what she could to support her son, but she couldn't save him. Seth had taken it out of her hands.

Gina had just signed off doctors' orders and was entering them into the computer. She squinted from screen to paperwork to screen, her fingers sailing over the keys.

"It's a madhouse up here." Hilary found the color-coded file and opened it.

"Tell me about it." Gina didn't miss a beat. "Seven of my own patients to see, two admits, three moving downstairs, and the phone keeps ringing. I haven't gotten away from this desk for an hour."

Hilary kept her voice light. "I ran out of here so fast, I didn't get my reports done."

"That isn't surprising. Hilary, it's okay."

"I couldn't finish my charting."

Although Gina's gaze never left the screen, her lifted eyebrows indicated the milling throng of kids. "You know we're bending every rule in the book to let them stay."

"I know." Hilary had helped herself to a pen from a can beside the telephone. All three lights were blinking. Gina had everyone on hold.

"They needed a place. They needed to be together."

Hilary ran the pen down the column of I & O numbers, working the math in her head. She got to the bottom, scribbled a figure, and initialed the form. There she froze, unable to go further. If her eyes could have burned a hole in the page, they would have. She wasn't fooling anyone.

Wordlessly Gina slid a Kardex out that had been resting near the bottom of the pile. She moved it in Hilary's direction in one economic motion. Her eyes never left the computer screen.

"This is what you came for even though you won't admit it. This is what you wanted to see, isn't it?"

"No, Gina. I—" But even though she protested, Hilary couldn't keep from being drawn to the printed grid, the doctor's almost illegible assessment: "Patient: Moore, Laura. Age: 17."

Here were the vital signs taken during the past hours, the crushed parts of her they'd tried to repair, the punctured lung, the bleeding on the brain, the low blood pressure, the drug-induced coma. The evaluations made no sense on the page. When someone hissed Seth's name, Hilary didn't notice. When she glanced up and found eyes on her, it didn't register that she'd been recognized. Only this one thought clanged in her ears louder than if someone shouted it: The girl was fighting for her life. She'd be lucky to make it through the day.

Chapter 15

୰

$\mathcal{T}$he shower was still running behind the bathroom door when Hilary went to check on Seth. She knocked tentatively, hoping Seth would hear her. When he didn't respond within a half minute or so, she opened the door a crack. She asked in her cheeriest voice, "Hey? You there?"

Seth stood in the shower, the water pouring over his head. He didn't move. He didn't turn off the shower. Hilary could tell, by the lack of steam in the room, that the water wasn't hot anymore.

"Seth," Hilary said through the door. "Do you think you could eat anything?"

For a long time, he didn't answer.

"Seth," Hilary said. "I love you."

His voice, when he spoke, was ragged and angry. "Mom. Don't."

"Honey."

"I don't want to talk about it."

"You don't have to do this by yourself. We're here for you."

But here came a lightning burst of grief again, Seth's voice that sounded like it was suffocating in air, like a fish gasping after it had been yanked up on land. "Please. Go. Leave me alone."

• • •

Two days after Laura Moore had been admitted to the hospital, the eighteen-year-olds who had been caught at the senior-class party were brought back to the courthouse for an en masse arraignment hearing. All had been charged with willful trespassing, for violating an Illinois state statute for being in a state park after sundown without a camping permit. Those who had been caught drinking, whose field sobriety tests had come back positive and could be proven admissible in court, had also been charged with Consumption of Alcohol by a Minor.

Hilary had left the hospital halfway through a shift. Seth had driven over with his father. George and Ruth Wynn met them inside the front foyer. Hilary's hands shook as she tugged off her bracelet and stepped out of her shoes. She watched her purse as it jostled along the conveyor at the security checkpoint. Behind her, Seth and Eric unfastened their belts and emptied their pockets.

When they made it through security, John Mulligan was waiting for them at the courtroom door. Other lawyers for some of the other kids were waiting for their clients, too. It had been a characteristically hectic weekend for the precinct police, John told Hilary, and the judge was moving cases through at about the same speed an agent runs kids through a Disney audition. It was almost Seth's turn.

Mulligan greeted Eric with an extended hand and a fierce handshake. "I'll do the best job I can for your son."

"Thank you."

John Mulligan shook Seth's hand, too. He told Seth he had secured an interview booth so they could rehash the charges and discuss Seth's plea. "You ready to get this under way, buddy?" Mulligan slapped Seth on the back with more joviality than any of them felt. Just before the lawyer walked away, he spoke quietly and competently: "The District Attorney knows you're attending the hearing with Seth. I've slipped him a note. With everything that could happen, we want the DA to know that your son has plenty of support."

"What do you mean?" Eric asked. "With everything that could happen?"

The lawyer leveled his eyes on the three of them. "If anything should happen to Laura."

Eric's hand rested against Hilary's shoulder blade as he escorted her into the hall. It had never occurred to her that people they knew would come to Seth's hearing. At first she thought everyone was here to support individual families, individual students. But when Hilary walked in and recognized familiar faces, her world began to shift. A couple of girls from the hospital were there, their eyes smoldering with compassion. Ruth and George Wynn found a place to sit beside their neighbors on the second row. Kim Draper from Spilling the Beans was down the aisle, sending her a nod that, in spite of everything, made Hilary nod, too.

Another hearing was under way. A defendant wearing a jail uniform, what looked like wrinkled khaki scrubs, stood with his hands shackled in front of the judge's bench. As Hilary glanced at her friends from Spilling the Beans, she was trying to let them see that she was grateful. Ever since they'd identified the passenger in the incoming ambulance, ever since she'd found out Laura had been injured because of Seth's actions, Hilary's emotions had been locked in solitary confinement.

"I'm so sorry," said Clyde Pope, a middle-school teacher. "I know Seth and Laura are good friends. It's a terrible thing to happen."

"Oh, Hilary," Emily's mother said. "There aren't words, are there? I'm so sorry for all of them. I'm praying for Laura's recovery, and I'm praying for your family, too."

Every hand that landed on Hilary's shoulder she wanted to grab hold of and never let go. As Jane was pulling away, Hilary actually did it. "Jane, how's Emily?"

"She's frantic to talk to Seth, but he won't call her."

"Seth hasn't been talking to anyone."

Jane shook her head. "Emily's doing all right.

She's a very sad girl, but she'll work her way through it. The family is giving everyone updates. But, well, you work in the hospital. You know if it's ICU, they won't let anyone in."

"And how's . . . how's Abigail?"

This time Jane's words didn't come so quickly. She shook her head. She and Hilary were both perilously close to tears.

"You've seen her?"

Jane nodded.

"If you get the chance," Hilary said, already realizing how inadequate her words were, "please tell her how sorry we are."

"Oh," Jane said much too quickly. "I'm sure she already knows."

Julie Rogers, the younger woman whom Hilary had counseled at Spilling the Beans, was the last to approach. Hilary quietly introduced her to Eric and squeezed her arm. "You'll never know what it means to have you here."

"You've been such a mentor to me, Hilary." Julie hugged her. "I wanted to be here." Then Julie told them about an impromptu service that had taken place at their church yesterday. Hilary asked, floored, "They had a *service?*" Why hadn't Seth known?

"A prayer service," Julie said. "Pastor Greg invited them to the church if they needed a place to gather. So many of them came!"

"Those poor kids," Hilary said.

"There weren't microphones and nobody was leading it or anything. The kids just stood up and talked about Laura and cried together and prayed. They prayed for Abigail and Rudy and then they prayed for Seth."

Hilary thought it might be wrong of her, but she had to force a smile. "I'm glad they prayed for my son," she said.

Up front, the judge was standing to take a break. "All rise," the bailiff said. The spectators rose in one motion.

"God used it, Hilary. Those teenagers were *praying* for Laura. God took something awful and he's going to make something good of it, I know."

"That's nice." Hilary said the words by rote as Julie returned to her seat. It just hurt too much to go to that place in her head. She was standing there considering the simple, easy answer, that God could use Seth's mistake and make something good come from it. But suddenly, out of nowhere, the anger hit her like a blow. She was so furious at Julie for oversimplifying things, she was ready to detonate.

Or maybe she was furious at herself. Or Seth. Or God. Or at Laura for falling, for being stupid enough to do what Seth told her in the first place. The girl could have said no. Why didn't she? *Why didn't she?* Why hadn't someone seen what was happening and stopped them?

Maybe in a few hundred years Hilary would be

able to look back and see something good in this. For now, Julie's "Kids are praying at church, so that makes it a good thing," was too pat an answer.

Lord, why couldn't it have been somebody else? Why did it have to be my son?

Eric and Hilary sat side by side, their elbows touching, their spines as straight as Chicago's Sears Tower, on a wooden pew that was hard enough to make them count every knob of their vertebrae.

The arraignment was a dry, short procedure that didn't veer off-course. Mulligan nodded as the District Attorney read a statement that the People of the State of Illinois intended to use to prosecute this case. He listened without reaction as the DA read a short recitation of the events that led to the trespass and MUI charges that were being leveled against Seth.

When the judge asked, "Mr. Mulligan, how does your client plead?" the lawyer's answer was almost cordial.

"Not guilty, Your Honor."

The judge asked the District Attorney for a recommendation on whether Seth should be released on his own recognizance and John Mulligan said, "I'd like a sidebar. May I approach the bench, Your Honor?"

"Certainly. Come on up, John," the judge said. "What do you have in mind?"

After a quiet conversation, it was over. "Seth

Warren Wynn released on his own recognizance." The gavel fell. The bailiff called the next case.

During an impromptu conference in the corner, Mulligan explained that he was working toward Seth's participation in a diversion program, which would include community service and counseling. If the judge agreed, it would mean that the charges would be erased from Seth's record.

"Looks like the entire senior class may be vying for community service projects this summer," Mulligan said.

Hilary couldn't get out of there fast enough. But before they could exit, they had to speak with the acquaintances who'd driven this far to be with them, who were siphoning out the door in a stream of mumbled condolences and promises of support. Clyde Pope introduced himself to Eric and shook his hand. Jane stood close by, watching with a sad smile the boy her daughter had been dating. Hilary heard the woman warn Seth quietly, "People can't help taking sides."

As Hilary stood in the midst of the motion and the words, her own sense of nothingness made her dizzy. She watched Seth in the crowd as he was being pulled away for another conference with Mulligan. She loved Seth so much that her body ached. She felt like she was going to be sick, she was so scared for him, for all of them. And she couldn't help wondering if Pam, given the chance, would have done a better job of raising Seth.

Hilary couldn't help wondering if, had their roles been different, Pam might have kept him out of this.

If this blew over, someday Eric might tell his son about his own brush with the law. He'd been fifteen, into Van Halen, Brooke Shields, and being the voice of rebellion. The hockey game with Glenwood South had ended and Eric and his friends were looking for an evening's entertainment.

Nothing said fun like the electric security gate at the bus barn and the girls' basketball team coming back from Monroe. The boys had been standing around the chain-link fence, scuffing the dust with their Nikes, trying to figure out how to sneak inside. Then, like a Houdini trick, the gate shuddered, squeaked, and started to open.

The returning basketball bus had already disgorged the girls with their pillows and duffel bags in front of the school. Now it was rounding the corner, a lumbering beast with two wavering headlights that hadn't quite focused in the boys' direction yet. "Come on!" someone shouted, and, doubled over to avoid the lights, they'd darted through.

Just their luck to get a driver who wasn't in a hurry to head home. With their stomachs rumbling and sneezes coming on, they hid behind a maintenance tractor while the guy whistled and walked the circumference of the bus, checking the windows, examining something in the vicinity of the tailpipe. "Come on, mister," one of the boys had urged through his teeth. It was getting cold out there.

Eric had always wanted to drive a bus. He'd always wanted to drive a car, too, for that matter. And now, with his learner's permit in his wallet and at least two hours of practice with his grandfather, Eric felt like an old hand.

Floodlights bathed the yard. No sooner had the driver shouldered his bag and keyed in the code to slide the gate into place, than they bolted.

One shove on the hinge and the door accordioned open. He'd left it unlocked. They tramped up the stairs, falling against the hand railing and the steps with laughter.

"Think you can hot-wire this thing, Raymond?"

The kid didn't answer. He was already jimmying the ignition with a knife.

Dane stared at the gearshift. "Wynn, you know how to drive a stick?"

When the engine started up, Dane flipped on the public-address system and held the microphone to his face. The machine emitted an earsplitting wail until he pulled it away. "Our tour of Rome has been rescheduled. Today, ladies and gentlemen, you'll be pleased to know that we'll be taking you on an all-expense-paid, death-defying trip to Addison Street, where you will see—"

Eric had stomped on the clutch and tried to find reverse. He found the gas pedal instead and the bus lurched forward. They fell on top of one another. Eric shifted again, a horrible grinding noise that sounded like the transmission was eating itself. The bus leapfrogged forward, clipping off the bumper of the Handi-Van in front of it and impaling its nose in the fence. "Evacuate!" someone shouted, and, leaving the engine running, they leaped, ducked through the hole the bus had torn through the fence, and ran.

Even though the school district had pressed charges and they'd gotten suspended for two weeks, even though Eric had taken a 0 on a test and it brought his grade down to a C, even though he'd missed the first track meet because he'd had to get in a certain number of practices before he could run with them again, his friends hadn't ostracized him. Even his own father had told the story, years later, with a twinkle in his eye. But there hadn't been a life at stake. When they'd made it back to class, they'd been treated like heroes.

Eric's BlackBerry indicated he had a message. That's all it took, the vibration in his palm, to return Eric to the present. There wasn't a need to check who'd sent the text. He already knew.

He weighed the small device in his hand for a moment, just let it balance there, and thought how easy it would be to let it fall through his fingers. His whole life, captured inside the small screen and a narrow case. By any investigator in the know Eric's every call could be retrieved, a jumble of information from acquaintances who'd communicated only once, family and friends he cared about whom he talked to a half-dozen times a day. In his palm, he held Pam and the kids' itinerary for their return flight to LAX. He held the photo of Ben hugging his best friend, Charlie. He held the complete sequence of Lily's life, starting with that first fuzzy shot of his daughter in the pink hospital cap all the way to the U5 soccer game last week, with Lily's shin guards almost bigger than she was. His second life encapsulated on a PDA.

Yet Eric still caught himself thinking about Hilary. She'd always been exhausted from juggling Seth with her long days at the hospital. She'd been distraught over a patient they'd lost. She'd been busy making Seth a costume or going to Bible study or having coffee with the girls. She'd always found some excuse to be distant, and he'd always found some excuse to let her stay that way. He'd let it happen. He'd blamed it on everyone but himself. He'd fallen for Pam. The days had passed and they'd been swept into an irreversible current. Even now he'd argue that it hadn't been a mistake. It had just been *life*. And *life* made everything more complicated.

Can a man live the same story twice with a different cast of characters? Could he blame Seth for his abrupt pulling away when he had been the one who'd taught his son how to do it?

There was more than one way for a man to fall off a cliff.

Chapter 16

❧

*E*mily stared at her phone, willing it to ring. She shouldn't even have it on. Cell phones were prohibited in the hospital. She'd sent Seth about a dozen messages, but he wouldn't answer. *Come on,* she thought, aching. *Don't do this to yourself.*

Don't do this to us.

It was a horrible feeling, wanting to save him, wanting to tell him that nothing was going to happen to Laura, wanting everything to be okay for him, when she really didn't know.

She should have guessed it would happen this way. When it came down to it, people sided with the injured one. When the police had come to the hospital to question Seth's friends, Emily didn't think anyone had actually told the whole story. Not because they wanted to protect Seth from anything but because they wanted to protect themselves from getting into trouble. Rumors were running rampant on the Internet: Seth had been drunk and had dared Laura to the climb. Or they'd been up there fighting about something. Or maybe he'd even pushed her. People could be so stupid.

Nothing could move as slowly as the hours at the hospital. Most of the kids in the senior class had stopped coming by now. There wasn't anything anyone could do. One of Laura's mom's friends had set up an account on CaringBridge and was sending an updated report every few hours. It had been three days and no one could get in to see Laura except family, so only a few of her closest friends still kept watch. Now people were talking. Texting. Blaming. Covering their tracks.

At least *most* people were texting. Seth wasn't.

Down the hospital hall Emily saw Laura's mom shut the door to Laura's room. When the woman glanced up and saw Emily waiting, she offered a faint smile. "Oh, honey. You're still here."

Emily nodded.

Laura's mom held out her arms for an embrace. Emily buried her face against the woman's sweater.

"There's not anything else you can do here, Em," Abigail Moore said. "You ought to go home and get some rest."

"I'm so sorry," Emily whispered. "It's my fault, Mrs. Moore. She wouldn't have done it if not for me."

"Emily. You can't say that. I'm sure you didn't have anything to do with it."

"I *did*. I don't want to leave until she's better. Please don't make me go."

Abigail held Emily away so she could see her face. "The nurse says that the last sense people lose is their hearing," Laura's mom said. "If she can hear, Emily, she knows you're here. I've told her many times."

"She knows it's my fault. I'm the one who told her it would be okay." How could Emily make Laura's mom understand that it hadn't only been Seth, it had been her, too? Emily had told Laura she could climb it, there wouldn't be any problems if she went with Seth. When the police had come to ask questions, Emily had stood in a corner with her throat sealed shut, like she was trying to swallow a mistake she'd never be able to change.

Abigail touched Emily's shoulder. "Would you like to go in? I could convince the nurse to let you see Laura. Now that the crowd has thinned out, I don't think anyone will mind."

"You'd let me do that?"

"It would be good for you to talk to her."

"I . . . I don't know what to say."

"Yes, you do."

"I—"

"Tell her you're glad to see her. Remind her of the fun things you do together. Hold her hand if you'd like. Tell her things that will make her want to fight to come back."

Emily followed Laura's mom up the hall. When the heavy door swung open, Emily hung back, not knowing what to expect. Her eyes took several seconds to adjust to the darkened room. The small, draped figure on the bed didn't look like anyone Emily knew. The shape might have been a mannequin onstage, a strange pale thing used for a prop, its head wrapped with dressings, skin as pale as wax. An array of hoses hung at the bedside, the clear tubes dangling from the IV station, delivering coma-inducing drugs. The plastic tubing that carried oxygen and the flex trach tube attached to the ventilator. The shape in the bed didn't have hair; it must have been shaved. Laura's hair had been long and thick, dark strands that just last week Emily had braided.

Just when Emily thought she could pretend this person wasn't anyone she knew at all, just when Emily thought that this must be some terrible error, this wasn't Laura here at all, she recognized the feet poking out the end of the blanket. She saw the long second toe that Emily had always teased Laura over, the cracked nail that had happened when Laura had stubbed her toe. They'd been dancing to a Taylor Swift song.

Emily couldn't hold back another sob. Other than the chest rising and falling with the ventilator, her friend lay motionless. Emily lifted Laura's hand and used her other hand to close Laura's thumb over her own. "I'm here," she whispered. "I've been here lots. Did you know that? Your mom said she told you."

No response. Emily glanced at Laura's mom for reassurance.

Abigail nodded. *Go ahead,* she mouthed.

"You know how we planned to go shopping for our dorm rooms together?" Emily asked. "There's a bedspread at Urban Outfitters I really like. I can't wait to show it to you."

A long pause, then, "We can go to the thrift shop and find old chairs we can paint to match. I watched a TV show about how to refurbish old chairs."

Another pause. "I miss you. You've got to get better." Here the tears started again while Abigail came up from behind to hug her. Emily had lost count of how many times she'd cried. "You've got so many stuffed animals and flowers and balloons in the waiting room. You should see it all."

Then, "You've got to keep fighting, okay? We just want you to get better."

Laura's mom's fingers tightened on Emily's shoulder.

After Emily left the hospital she tried once more to reach Seth. *Hi, you've reached Seth's phone. Leave a message. I'll get back to you.*

Leave.

She left a voice message when he didn't pick up. She punched in a text message, which he didn't return.

She waited, but the screen stayed dark. Emily shoved the phone inside her purse as she climbed the steps to the L. She pitched her backpack onto the bench as the train lurched forward. Her body went boneless as she slumped onto the seat and buried her face in her hands.

Hilary dropped the tangle of towels on the kitchen table and began to fold one, her hands smoothing the terry cloth into thirds. Across the room, she watched as Seth sat slumped on the sofa, his albatross arms draped across the entire width of the couch. Perched on his small knees, his feet tucked under, Ben had settled in beside Seth, his face upturned toward his stepbrother's. The question, innocent and troubled, left Hilary's throat knotted.

"How come you don't like the truck we gave you?"

"Man." Seth must not have realized his mom was anywhere within hearing distance. "You're wrong about that. It's the hottest truck *ever*." Hilary stopped, gingerly laid the towel on top of the pile, raised her head.

"Really?" Ben asked.

"Of *course*. Are you kidding?"

The boy's eyes grew round, expectant. "Then why won't you drive it?"

Seth drew in a sharp breath. He untangled his long arms and rocked forward. He rubbed his thumb against the bridge of his nose as if trying to make a headache go away.

"Why?" Ben asked again. "I don't understand."

Hilary stood her ground that Eric and Pam should have talked to her before they showed up with a Ford F-150. It's true they ought to have conferred with her as they'd kicked around the idea of a *truck*. But she'd let that woman bait her into returning hostility and bringing herself down to Pam's own level. And because of that, Hilary had let Seth see beyond the poker face she ought to have been wearing and, like the day he'd tried to knock-knock-joke her back to sanity when he'd been eight, he'd gone and done what he thought he needed to do to make Hilary feel better.

Which you were perfectly willing to let him do, she reminded herself. *You were perfectly willing to walk away and let him carry the weight of all that, the way you've been willing to let him carry the weight ever since Eric left home.*

Seth said, "I guess some things are hard to explain."

Apparently Seth's noncommittal answer was enough to satisfy Ben. The little boy shifted subjects with the same deft speed he used when he shifted to go after a rebound.

"We've got pictures on our camera. You want to see pictures?"

"Sure."

With their heads together like that, even with one dark and the other light, it was hard to see where one boy ended and the other began. Ben launched into a travelogue of the adventures of the Wynn-children-exploring-Chicago-with-their mom, which he accompanied frame by slow frame from the viewfinder of the digital camera. They'd visited the Children's Museum and spent a great deal of time in the schooner exhibit, he told Seth, with Lily checking out the fish and Ben scaling the schooner riggings. They bought a kite in the museum shop and Pam had to find an open spot so she could teach them to fly it.

Then, just like that, Ben's conversation changed course again. "Seth, if you ever drive your new truck, can Lily sit in your lap and hold the steering wheel? She really wants to."

"Of course she can."

Whatever the boys had been watching on television ended. Music played, then gave way to a toothpaste commercial. "Seth?" Ben asked.

"Yeah."

And when Hilary heard his words, her heart felt too big for her chest. "You know what I'm going to do if you get put in jail, Seth? You don't have to worry. I'll come rescue you. I'll figure something out. I'll break you out of there."

John R. Mulligan, Esquire, was grateful for business. No matter that the economy had tanked on Wall Street, no matter that people were going hungry on Main Street, litigable conflicts didn't go away.

Sure, divorce numbers had fallen. Not as many folks could afford a breakup these days. But when it came to knife altercations between neighbors, brothers threatening each other over the selling of land, colleagues accusing each other of blackmail and conspiracy, the trade kept getting better and better. Let people call him idealistic if they wanted. He liked to think of himself as representing the poor, the injured, the ignored, the forgotten.

If he liked civil cases, he liked pro bono criminal cases better. Still, he didn't take a case unless he was sure he could win it. He'd told this to Hilary Myers, the former Hilary Wynn, the first time she'd appeared in his office. John was a modest attorney who had never lost a criminal case as either a prosecutor or a defense attorney. He was best known for his powerful courtroom victories. He hadn't lost a civil case since 1983.

He had his tricks; this was easier than it sounded. He kept the odds in his favor by declining cases he couldn't win, no matter what he believed about the guilt or innocence of his client. He liked mounting wins without any intervening losses. Selective maneuvering. That's what he called it.

So why take a case that might blemish his record now?

When Hilary Wynn had stepped into his office, when she had told him her husband had filed for divorce, Mulligan knew the moment he looked into her face that her world had been overturned. But she didn't rant or cry when she'd told him the details. She sat in the chair across his desk with her hands folded and her chin raised. Her eyes, steel gray with determination, hadn't wavered from his. "I know you're the best," she'd said. "I don't trust my husband and I don't trust myself through this. Can I trust you?"

"There are others you could trust, Mrs. Wynn." But something about her reminded him of himself—the resolution in her eyes, the way she'd asked for an appointment in person instead of relaying those first details over the phone. Until John saw Hilary, he hadn't realized how much of himself had been carved away by his dead wife's absence.

Hearing Hilary's story—ironically—brought back the physical symptoms of grief that he'd experienced after his own wife's death, the speechless immobility, the shaking knees. After that, each small triumph in Hilary's case had felt like a conquest for John, too. She'd given her case a boost by being present in it, bringing him new details in a measured voice that neither condemned her husband nor released him from his responsibility.

During a lunch meeting she had leaned across the table and had told John how she admired the man she had married in spite of what he'd done to her. After that, in one brief phone call, she'd suggested a formula for sorting out their financial differences, something she'd come up with on her own, that John still used with other clients.

Yes, they would think he had done it because of Hilary.

Others would say he did it because he had a soft heart, because he understood the boy's emotional upheaval. John knew what sort of damage could be done when a father exited his son's life.

But no matter how people speculated, they wouldn't come up with the correct answer. Because John didn't think anyone, not even Hilary, had noticed what he'd seen when he'd visited with Seth the day the entire senior class had an arraignment hearing. John had seen the bright surge of anger in Seth's eyes.

John R. Mulligan, Esquire, knew how to analyze potential clients. No matter what had happened to one girl climbing a rock, like the ice that coated limbs and power lines whenever bitter cold struck Chicago, John sensed the boy had been on the verge, ready to shatter to pieces.

Who am I? I don't know who I am, the boy might as well have been shouting. *What have they done with Seth Wynn?* The truth be told, John Mulligan had accepted this case because he'd made a snap judgment, and he would stick by it.

Perhaps finding out what the boy wasn't telling would be worth going down in defeat.

Pam's body had always revolted with pregnancy. It wasn't fair how some women could carry a child with as much ease as they would attend a tea party while others, like Pam, felt overcome. She felt like she'd been attacked by a marauding intruder, like carrying a child was an affliction instead of a normal occurrence. How could one tiny living thing in your uterus make you sick enough to turn your stomach inside out? How could a normal biological function make you feel so tired and antisocial that you wanted to turn your face to the wall?

Ben had made her run to the bathroom each morning for weeks, but she'd handled it, the same way she'd handled everything else going on in the marriage that her father had approved. At that point it had been hard but fine. She'd hoped having a baby would make things better between her and her then-husband; the nausea had been a relief, a sure signal of success.

It had been the onslaught of Lily that had altered Pam's world, the first tinge of queasiness that she'd thought was the flu, the morning she'd canceled a design appointment because she just didn't have the energy to talk to anyone, the hours she'd spent perched on the edge of the bed trying to make her stomach settle so she could do *anything*.

She'd waited a week to tell Eric, which she had known was too long, but she'd needed time to get used to the idea before she could announce the news without a question in her eyes. She had no idea how he would react. She and Eric hadn't talked about this. She knew how to arrange rooms that pleased people, how to place paintings, rugs, and pillows to create focal points and balance, how to entice someone's eye with form, texture, and color. If only her life with Eric could have been arranged with such ease! An affair could be an uncomfortable, messy thing. Even after such a wait, a ripple of terror had gone through her as she sat across the table from him. His face had been unreadable. "We'll get this figured out," he'd said.

"I didn't want this to be something we had to figure out," she'd said. "I wanted this to be something we'd be excited about."

"Will it be hard for you to take time off from working?" This whole conversation had been like a labor pain, squeezing them, shooting them forward. Pam had shaken her head. No. It wouldn't be hard. But it might not be easy.

"It *is* something to be excited about, Pam. Something I've wanted a long time."

"But you have Seth."

"It's something I've wanted with *you*."

Chapter 17

❧

*E*mily had discovered a secret about graduating from high school. You walked around your senior year and everybody thought you were the most important thing on earth. They envied you because you'd almost made it to the end. There was a whole big world out there and you were about to walk to the end of the high-diving board and jump off into it.

But what people didn't know was that no matter how boring high school could be, no matter how tired you got of seeing the same people, there was something comfortable there that you missed when it was gone.

Gone. Finished.

Every end was also a new beginning.

That is, unless you died.

If anyone had told her she would be sorry that school had ended, she would have called that person certifiably crazy.

It was the routine she missed, mostly. Graduation always happened the third week of May. The other three classes stayed in school until finals the first week of June. During May, the underclassmen looked at you like you were royalty. They skittered away and gazed at you, starry-eyed, from afar. Emily would have given anything to rewind the clock to last week. She wanted a do-over.

Today Emily had gone to say hi to her teachers. Three days after graduation and, instead of treating her like she belonged, they treated her like a guest. The principal had even made her backtrack to the front office and sign in to get a *visitor's* pass.

One blink, one breath. Like that, everything changes.

Emily's hands were shaking as she parked her car beside the curb at Seth's house. Walking up Seth's front steps, she felt like her feet were heavier than steel. She didn't think Seth was her boyfriend anymore. He wouldn't talk to her. He wasn't returning her texts or her calls. Emily had heard about girls who got broken up with via text message or Facebook. You'd think Seth would at least talk to her long enough to break up with her!

Emily paused at the front door. She wanted to turn and walk away. Instead she took a deep breath and steeled herself. She knocked on the door and waited. Knocking seemed so much less intrusive than ringing the doorbell.

It was too late now. Emily could hear Seth's stepsister, Lily, shouting, "There's somebody at the door! Somebody get it!"

No one must have heard her. Either that or they were all too busy thinking about their own problems. Everyone ignored the little girl.

Emily knocked again. "Isn't anybody going to *get* that?" Lily called.

Just as Emily was about to give up and go back to the car, the door started to open. "Lily, are you sure there's someone out here?" It was Seth's mom. It took Seth's mom a long moment of staring before she recognized her, which Emily thought was probably a bad sign. "Emily? Sweetie? Oh, honey. It's *you*."

"I came to see Seth." Her voice croaked. "Is he here?"

"He's here." Seth's mom hesitated before she opened the door. "But I don't know if he'll talk to you."

Emily stood her ground. It was too late to retreat now. "Maybe it isn't fair. But do you think you could convince him? Would you try?"

Seth's mother threw open the door. "Of course I can try, Emily. Honey, I'll see what I can do."

"Thank you." Emily stepped inside. "Thank you so much."

"Em," his mom said. "If he'll talk to anybody, I know it will be you."

Emily listened, her throat bone-dry, while his mom went down the hall and gave three light raps on Seth's door. "Seth. There's someone here to see you. You have a guest."

The mattress creaked, which meant he'd been stretched out on the bed staring at the ceiling.

Seth's mom nodded at Emily, as if they were making progress. A creaking mattress meant that he was sitting up, maybe considering it. When Emily had called the house, Seth's mom had apologetically said the only people who'd been able to roust him out of his cave had been Lily and Ben. "Who? Who's here?"

"It's Emily."

A beat. Then, "I don't want to see anybody."

"Are you sure? She's standing right here."

"We have nothing to talk about."

"She says she's been texting you and you won't answer."

"Well," Seth growled through the door. "Tell her to get an idea. When a boy stops calling a girl . . . you know what that means. I have nothing to say."

"Seth." Hilary leaned her forehead against the door. "There's been a lot of hurt already. Is that a reason to cause more?"

"It's *every* reason."

"Seth." His mom's voice was starting to sound a little frantic. "You know me. You know I respect your privacy. You know I respect your opinions. I wouldn't push you to do this. But I'm worried about you."

A sound came from Seth's room that sounded like something between a chair thumping sideways and a sigh of regret. "Tell her to wait up. I'll be out in a minute."

By the time Seth emerged, Emily had been

waiting a good fifteen minutes. From the direction of Seth's bathroom, they heard the Oral-B buzzing and the water rushing and the electric razor going where it had begun to look like no razor had gone before. Even after all that extra grooming, when Seth emerged he still looked stricken.

"Hi," she said.

"Hi," he said. "You came over."

She let her bodily presence answer that one.

"You shouldn't be here."

Before Seth could say anything else to push her away, Emily handed him a teddy bear. "Somebody bought this for Laura. The waiting room at the hospital is full of them."

"My mom said."

Tears started to well in Emily's eyes. "She's getting so much stuff that they asked the Moores if they could give it away to other people."

Seth scrubbed his face with his T-shirt as if trying to wipe his face clear of any emotion.

"I thought you might like to have it instead."

He was moved by the gesture, Emily could tell. He clamped the bear between two monstrous hands like he was clamping a football before a pass.

"It isn't much, but I—I wanted you to have something."

He gripped the bear again, examining its face. "Emily. Why are you here?"

"I guess." She shrugged and clapped her hands, trying to be casual. "I guess you could put it on your bed or something."

"Yeah," he said. "I started that not long ago. Putting animals on my bed. Been looking for another"—he surveyed the plush toy without smiling—"bear to add to the pile."

That little shrug again. "Thought you'd be the one to give it a good home."

"You didn't answer my question," he said.

"Maybe I don't know why I'm here," she told him, the frustration curling in her voice. "I just thought it would be fair to, you know, *talk* this *out*."

As they stood talking, Lily bounced up and down on the sofa. She was so small that the toes of her Cinderella sneakers barely touched the floor. He grabbed Emily's arm roughly. "Come with me."

When they got to his room, Emily lifted her eyes to Seth's. The entire conversation was a façade, mindless words they were murmuring while they avoided the huge, unspoken entity that stood between them. That Emily felt as guilty as Seth. Because she was the one who had told Laura it would be okay. She was the one who had told Laura that if she did what Seth told her to do, everything would be okay. And it hadn't been.

"Seth, why won't you talk to me?"

He lifted his chin in surprise. The way he kept fidgeting, the way he kept squeezing and gripping the bear in his hand, Emily expected its head to pop off and stuffing to fly.

"Why didn't you answer my text messages?"

Seth set the slightly misshapen bear on his bed and turned toward her. "There's no way to make up for what I've done. She's your best friend."

"Seth."

"You don't want to be with a loser like me."

"Please," she said quietly. "Don't push me away."

"What else am I supposed to do?" His voice was a high wire of tension. "You know I'm no good for you."

"Look," she said. "Break up with me because you're tired of me. Break up because you want to date other girls now that summer's here. Break up because you don't want to have a girlfriend anymore. But don't give me the pity party about you not being good enough." She felt her face flaming with anger. "Don't you sit in your room and think you're the only one who's hurting, Seth Wynn, because you're *not*."

He looked like he'd been broadaxed.

"You give yourself way too much credit, don't you think? Don't you think you're the only one responsible for what happened to Laura, because you're *not*. The whole senior class planned that party, not just *you*."

"You seem to forget," he said, his teeth clenched, his features a tangle of pain. "I'm the one who let your best friend fall off a cliff."

She wanted to hit him. "And I'm the one who told her to go with you!"

Seth stopped. He eyed his girlfriend, if that's what she was anymore. Maybe he could see her point.

"Everybody's pulling for you, Seth," she said. "But you have to pull for yourself."

He looked at her like she had grown three heads and six arms, a total alien.

"You don't believe me?" she asked. "You don't?"

"No."

"Then look on the Internet."

"What?"

"I *said* look on the Internet."

"I know what'll be on the Internet. There'll be stories about Laura. There will be people saying I should be shot. There will be people saying I should never have been let out of jail. That I'm a criminal. And I am."

"Go to your Facebook page, silly. You may be able to shut yourself away from everybody who cares about you at your house, but you can't get them off of the computer."

He stared at her like she was speaking a foreign language.

"Do it," he said. And because they'd been dating

almost a year, because she'd sat beside him at his desk for hours while they'd researched a project on the human heart for Life Sciences class, she knew how to log on. She did it for him.

"Look," she said. "Go ahead."

Seth lowered himself into his chair and stared at the screen.

"Read," she ordered him.

"I'm reading," he said.

The sentiments were all there for him to see. Seth couldn't believe it. Names. Times. Faces. Hearts.

"Keep your head up, Wynn," Remy had written. "We're all in this together."

"I can't even imagine what you're going through, Seth. Stay strong, hon!" from one of Laura's friends.

"You're one solid kid. Keep the faith," from Seth's football coach.

The messages trailed all the way down two pages and onto another:

You and Laura and both your families are in my prayers.

There's no doubt in my mind that you're feeling bad right now, but remember you are one awesome person, Seth.

All you who know Seth W. know how big his heart is. He'd give you the shirt

off his back. Seth and Laura are friends. This has got to be tough.

Stay strong, S.W. We're behind you. You're going to get through this.

Seth read to the end of the messages. He stared at the screen.

"See? I told you." From behind his chair, Emily wrapped her arms around his shoulders and held on. She felt him sag at last. She felt his breath on the curve of her ear.

Chapter 18

✍

$\mathcal{T}$here were eight people in the house, including Emily, and being a teenager's mom, Hilary was programmed to provide entertainment. That was how they ended up crammed around the coffee table with the Cranium game spread in front of them. Pam, Ben, and Emily were lined along the couch. Seth was on the floor next to Emily; Eric was perched on the leather ottoman, with Lily, who was much too young to be playing according to the box, on one knee, helping move her token to a green space and decide which card to pick. Alva had dragged in a dining-room chair so she could oversee the rest of them.

Lily selected a card and handed it to her mother. Pam and Ben conferred. They'd gotten a "humdinger." How to hum a tune so Eric and Lily could guess it? Ben didn't know what the song was at first, but Pam said she could absolutely hum it so Eric could get it. And she did. It was a bit ragged at first, terribly off-key, then the flash of recognition dawned on Eric's face as he whispered the answer to Lily.

" 'Hotel Cawifornia'!" she shrieked. Her team cheered for her. They got to roll again.

When the other team finally got a chance to

play, it was Emily's turn. Emily tossed the dice and watched as they tumbled across the cardboard. All the time she was moving her game piece, Hilary kept thinking, *Lord, bless her heart.* Because Emily had been the one who'd saved their lives these past few days. She'd been the one who hadn't given up on Seth. She hadn't let him push her away the way he'd done with all his other friends. She'd been the one who'd convinced Seth to turn on his computer and check out his Facebook page. She'd been the one who'd made him read and reread his messages, including the dozens of new ones coming in every day.

Hilary had noticed a slight difference in him. A faint light had returned to his eyes. He'd begun to return phone calls, to yank his phone out of his pocket every few minutes to check for texts the way he had before. And she prayed, oh, how she prayed, that he was taking a break from mentally flogging himself.

Emily landed on red and Seth selected the card for her. Their team had to answer a trivia question. "On what television series did Leo DiCaprio have his first regular role?"

While the three of them were considering the possibilities given, Pam leaned toward Seth and spoke as an aside: "So many people wrote to say they supported you." Then louder, a proclamation: "I'm glad so many people wrote to tell you that they supported you. I'm especially glad someone posted on your site that they'd be praying for you, Seth. I'm impressed with any teenager who's brave enough to tell you he's praying for you."

Hilary couldn't help but glance sharply at Pam. Hilary, who'd always been the one at a loss for words when it came to confrontation, felt the perfect comment lying on her tongue like candy: *Why would you talk about prayer, Pam? How can you act holier-than-thou when you're the one who committed adultery with my husband?*

Gina would be proud.

But Hilary managed to keep her mouth shut. And as the lozenge of bitterness melted away, Hilary saw that she'd been mistaken. Pam hadn't been making the statement in judgment, to remind Seth how he'd done wrong. She'd been making a comment because as much as the situation had surprised Seth, it had surprised Pam, too. Still, this wasn't the time.

"We're playing a game here," Hilary growled out instead. "Don't you see that we're all fighting to keep this light?"

But no. Pam had to bring it up again. "I'm just surprised that a teenager would post about praying. Praying is a private thing. I don't always . . ." Pam faded out.

Well, Hilary wanted to say. *Me, too.* She just didn't have the energy to do any more than what she was doing. She didn't have time alone to get to her Bible. She didn't have anything eloquent or smart to say to the Heavenly Father during those hours when she lay awake in a bed that felt about as populated and warm as an Arctic ice slab floating offshore. Her prayers, if you could call them that, had been something resembling a drowning cat: *Help. Help me. Oh, help, help, help.* The last thing she felt like doing was matching Pam's jousts with her own, giving lip service to her faith. She'd probably rather do something like muck stalls at Lincoln Park Zoo instead of talk about prayer or homeschooling or church programs with her husband's new wife. With Pam in her house, Hilary felt like she had to trust Jesus just to *breathe*.

"The answer is 'b. *Growing Pains*,' " Emily told them. Seth looked at her like he had absolutely no idea what she was talking about. "The answer is *Growing Pains*."

"What?" Hilary asked.

"That's the show where Leo DiCaprio got his start."

"Oh." Seth remembered the game before Hilary did. Oh yes. How could she have forgotten herself? This was supposed to be *fun*.

"Here, Pam." Hilary handed her the die after they'd answered two or three more questions and made considerable progress toward regaining the peaceful atmosphere. "Why don't you roll? See how well you do?"

Alva, overtaken by nostalgia now that Emily

had come to visit, chose this moment to launch into the story of how she and Hilary's father played canasta every Saturday afternoon while they were dating. The story she told was one Hilary had heard about a thousand times, how her dad wasn't supposed to visit when her parents weren't home, but she got away with it by hiding him in the closet. Emily and Seth grinned at each other, which made Hilary somewhat nervous.

Because they'd had this conversation before, Hilary knew where Alva was headed. Before Hilary had the chance to head her off, Alva started sharing tales about the first Christmas Hilary brought Eric home to meet the family, how Eric had bombed the neighbor kids with snowballs, how he'd built a snowman and dressed it in Hilary's beach clothes, how he'd given Hilary her Christmas present wrapped inside a roll of toilet paper—which meant she'd had to unwind about four hundred 2-ply squares before she got to the pearl earrings.

"Mother," Hilary said, shooting Alva a wide-eyed admonition that Alva didn't pick up on. "Maybe this isn't the time."

"Oh no," Seth said. "Go on. I love hearing this stuff about Mom and Dad. It's so funny."

There were so many reasons why talking about Eric and Hilary together was a horrible idea. Hilary didn't want to think of these things again, didn't want to feel sad. As quick as that, Alva's story edited out the past twenty years of life footage and cut them, without warning, to that punched-in-the-gut time when Eric and Hilary's relationship had been green, fresh, raw, that time before they'd fallen apart, that time before they'd devastated each other.

The second terrible reason was Pam. Was Alva doing this because of the competition she'd sensed when Hilary had walked in from the jail and Pam had been in the kitchen? Was she doing it because Pam had accosted Seth during this game? Shouldn't Eric be the one to stand up for his son? Or would they always be like this, families trying to compete with each other? Was Alva being passive-aggressive for her grandson's sake or just innocently nostalgic? Hilary could just hear what Pam would say to her friends back home. Rolling her eyes, *Oh, we had a* lovely *time in Chicago with Eric's family. I got to sit with Eric's first mother-in-law and hear all* sorts *of stories about what he did while he was dating his ex. I heard he gave her pearl earrings for their first Christmas. It was* great.

Hilary wouldn't inflict that sort of torture on anybody.

None of that seemed to matter, because Alva had her audience. The children were delighted to hear how Eric dressed the snowman, how he recruited Hilary's mom to get her bikini out of the drawer, how he got it wet and stuffed the cups with snow and froze it in the refrigerator so it would retain its proper shape in the front yard.

"Did the bathing suit go all the way around the snowman?" Lily asked, wide-eyed.

"It wasn't a snowman, silly," Ben said. "It was a snow *girl*."

"It didn't go all the way around," Seth told them while Emily giggled. "Grandma talked about it all the time. He just sort of *pasted* it on the front. So the neighbors would get the *idea*."

Pam said, "Oh, good heavens, Eric. How ridiculous. You'd think you could come up with some better way to spend your time than that."

"Hey," he said. "You can listen to all the old stories you want, Pam. But you know that you are still the star in my sky."

Hilary's heart dropped to her knees. In spite of family all around them, when he spoke to his new wife he had gentled his voice in a way that transported Hilary a dozen years into the past. No matter if Eric was just trying to placate his wife. *Once, long ago, Eric said those sorts of things to me.*

If there had been a way to seize those moments and make them last, those rare times Eric had been able to express himself in the high fever of love, would the two of them still be married? But like the fireflies that sparked beneath the trees in the evenings at Austin Park, those words had always only seemed touchable when they were just out of reach. The moment Hilary would try to catch one, the glimmer would go out and she felt like she was grasping empty air.

Hilary had lost count of the nights she woke up alone, always alone, and smothering. It started with the prickle of adrenaline beneath her skin. Next, her heartbeat quickened. She knew if she didn't throw the comforter onto the floor and expose her limbs, she'd be terrified and gasping. She'd be wide awake for hours, trying to swallow the choking panic.

Tonight as Hilary lay uncovered on the mattress, willing her heart to slow and her lungs to fill, she was suddenly struck by the darkness outside the window. A faint street lamp burned on the corner. Beyond that vague, artificial light, the world had gone pitch-black.

She padded barefooted to the window and peered through the blinds. For a good twenty seconds she couldn't see beyond the elm tree just outside the window. Her eyes adjusted and she could barely make out the outline of the concrete cherub that stood in the neighbor's garden.

She found the moon, and gasped.

Just as quickly as she could wriggle her toes into her slippers and knot the belt around her robe, Hilary hurried to Seth's room. He was snoring slightly as Hilary pushed open the door. In spite of everything, his snoring made Hilary smile. "Hey." She shook his shoulder. "Wake up."

"Hm-m-mmm."

There was no telling whether he was responding to her or that was just another deep sigh. "Wake up, sleepyhead," Hilary tried again. "I've got something to show you."

For the moment, Seth just slept there with Hilary's fingers trailing across her son's temple. Then he jolted awake, rolling toward her with a tightly clenched fist. He shot up to his elbow, guardlike. One minute he was in a dead sleep and the next he was surveying the room.

"It's okay," Hilary told him. "Seth, nothing's wrong."

"What is it? Mom, what are you doing in here?"

"There's something you have to see. If you don't come now, you'll miss it."

"What?"

"Put on your shoes first. And maybe a sweatshirt. We're going outside."

"We are? Why?" Seth asked her.

"Don't ask questions. Just come on."

And so he did. Within minutes they were tiptoeing out the door. They stood side by side in grass that felt like thick lace beneath their feet. Even though it wasn't too chilly for three in the morning, Hilary hugged herself tightly with her own arms. Ah, nighttime. As still as glass yet with its own loving, healing song.

No shadows lay at their feet. They had quite the show overhead. "How come I didn't know this was going on?" Seth asked. "How come I didn't hear about it?"

"I didn't know, either," Hilary told him. But the answer to his question was simple. Their minds had been way too occupied to think about things like this. They hadn't been thinking of anything as inconsequential as the movement of the planets through the heavens.

Overhead, the full moon was obliterated by the mammoth shadow the Earth was casting. They were in the middle of a lunar eclipse. When Hilary had discovered it outside her bedroom window minutes ago, it had only been beginning. Which meant that no matter how fast the universe was moving, they'd been given plenty of time.

Seth and Hilary caught the eclipse at the moment the two orbs merged in perfect alignment. The sky became darker; the stars throbbed so full of light that they seemed to vibrate. Fleeting, threadbare clouds reflected a soft wash of illumination from the land below, nothing from above. The faint halo around the moon, all that was visible of the astronomical body that circled the Earth, was a thin ice-blue outline.

"If you hadn't come to get me, I would have missed this," Seth said.

Hilary gave a sad laugh. "I guess it's good I couldn't sleep. It was so dark that I got up and looked outside. It was an accident that I found it."

Seth searched his mother's face in the pale light. "Accidents. Is there really such a thing as accidents?"

Even here, even tonight, with the heavens cavorting overhead as if only for them, they couldn't escape what had happened at the campsite. "Why don't you think about that?" Hilary asked her son. "Why don't you tell me?"

Seth turned back to the sky. A pale rim of light was beginning to appear, glowing like a big cosmic fingernail. He watched it grow larger before he draped his arm around Hilary's shoulder and pulled her close. The moon was half-visible by then. She waited for what he would say, holding her breath as the light swelled in the sky, as they began to cast shadows.

"I love you, Mom."

After everything, why was it that which finally made her cry?

Chapter 19

❧

*W*hen the telephone rang, Seth had gone with Emily to the bank to deposit the money gifts they'd gotten for graduation. Hilary tucked the receiver under her chin. "Hello?"

The man introduced himself as a representative of the Stuart Foundation. It took a beat, two beats, to understand the significance of this call. The Stuart Foundation was the community group that had interviewed Seth and awarded him his largest scholarship to Emhurst.

Hilary's stomach plummeted when she finally recognized the name. "Seth's gone out for a little while," she said, trying to keep her voice even. "I'm sure you're calling to talk to him."

"Under the circumstances we think it would be best, Ms. Myers, if I had this conversation with you."

"We?" Hilary didn't know about the "we" he was referring to.

"The board of directors," he explained. "The community group that awarded Seth their annual scholarship. They thought it would be best if I spoke for all of them."

The whole time he talked, Hilary's ears rang. She heard parts of his speech, only parts, and it

234

seemed like he didn't once stop the explanation to allow her to reply. "In view of the circumstances . . . doesn't measure up to the board's expectations . . . someone who we feel might better represent our mission."

When Hilary had been a little girl growing up in Indiana, one of the Myerses' neighbors had cut a maze in his cornfield. He took such pride in letting the local kids go out and pretend to get lost. Hilary used to spend hours shrieking and running and trying to find her way out of Pete Walker's field. But once, she couldn't remember how old she'd been, she got turned around. No matter how hard she searched, she couldn't find a way out.

She could hear her friends' voices, but she didn't know how to get to them. When they laughed, she knew they were laughing at her. Everywhere she turned, she'd run into another dead end. Even now, she couldn't have told you which was worse, her arms' itching like fire from the cornstalks or the fear she couldn't find her way out.

As the man's voice droned on, Hilary was lost in that field again. She was making her way through an emotional maze, every blind corner leading her to a passage that stopped and went nowhere. Only it was worse because she wasn't searching for a way out for herself but for her son.

She should have listened to Pam and Eric. She should have been strict with Seth; she should have stopped him from going to the party. *How could I have let him get harmed this way? How could I have let it happen?* Added to that, she felt a cold fury at anyone who tried to touch them, anyone who threatened to take anything else away. She heard this gentleman saying words like "in light of what happened," "while we certainly *support* Seth," and "the decision wasn't unanimous." All the time he was speaking, Hilary was thinking, *How can I tell Seth?*

Even before she hung up the telephone, she knew Pam was standing right behind her. Hilary stared at the wall, unwilling to turn around.

"He's lost his scholarship, hasn't he?"

"Yes."

"I've always known something like this was going to happen."

"Pam," Hilary begged her, "please don't make something of this. It just hurts too much. *Please* don't talk to me right now."

"You don't need to worry. He'll still go to college, Hilary. Eric and I have set money aside for Seth."

Hold my tongue, Father. Don't let me speak. Don't let me make things worse than they already are.

The only thing she could choke out was this: "Eric never told me anything about that."

"Well, it was my idea from the beginning," Pam said.

"What?"

"You shouldn't be upset. Together we can take care of this. Eric and I are capable of paying Seth's college tuition. We've already talked about this."

But this wasn't just about *Hilary* anymore. She was devastated for Seth. Each disappointment seemed worse than the last. Yes, he'd made a terrible choice. Yes, it had ended in a deplorable accident that could have been avoided. This was the most difficult of everything for her, standing by and watching the blows begin to pound away at him in succession.

"But you don't understand." This time, when she tried to explain it to Pam, she honestly felt like her heart was breaking. "We've done everything *right*. Seth *earned* that scholarship."

"We want to help, Hilary."

"It was something he could be proud of. Heaven knows he needs something to be proud of right now."

Pam was holding one of Ben's shirts. It looked so perfect and small dangling between her hands. Hilary remembered when Seth had worn shirts like that, when she could dress him exactly the way she wanted. She'd have to catch him in the crook of her arm as he ran past; she'd have to make him stand still at the sink. She thought of brandishing the comb, the sweat-sweet smell as she wet his hair, the tiny, perfect line of scalp she could see. Pam still got to do those things. She still had time left with her children. *Is that why this is so hard, Lord? Am I the one who's jealous?* Hilary was suddenly so jealous of Pam holding that little shirt, suddenly so jealous that she had all this time left with her children. It was a fierce, ugly sensation. Hilary couldn't escape it.

But that wasn't what Pam had been saying, was it? Wasn't she only saying that she and Eric were offering to help? That they'd talked about it?

In the keepsake box under Hilary's bed she kept Seth's precious Christmas ornaments he'd made in Sunday school. An old video of Seth performing a song in elementary choir. The letters he'd sent home from camp. She could prove she'd been a dedicated, involved mom when Seth had been in elementary school. But Hilary's pain kept urging her to throw punches. "You think you know so much, Pam, but you haven't even been initiated yet. You have no idea what it's like raising a teenager."

That one quiet truth broke through her anger, reminded Hilary that the words Pam needed to hear were the very ones she needed to take to heart herself. Seth was older now and she was parenting him differently than she'd parented him before. And that was okay.

"Please." This was the only thing Hilary knew to do. She could only beg Pam not to make it so hard on both of them. "Don't provoke me anymore. Please. It's too rough on both of us."

At last Hilary was able to sort through the whirlwind of conflict within her. On the inside, she was a roaring tigress, claiming her own territory. On the outside, her words were measured, as level and strong as the Michigan Avenue Bridge.

"Pam, you are welcome to visit us here. I know that Eric needs his family. But you aren't welcome here if you're going to treat me like this."

Pam took one look at Hilary's face and knew she meant it. "I don't want any of this to hurt Eric. You know how much I love Eric, Hilary."

"Of course," Hilary said. "I do."

The only things Pam had ever gotten for herself she'd gotten by outperforming others. Playing hardball, her father used to call it as the five sisters sat around the supper table and he quizzed them about their extra-credit projects, their advancing to first chair in orchestra, their extra visits to the small private colleges up and down the California coast when it came time to be interviewed for scholarships.

Hardball is for making candy, Pam's mom had always reminded him, *not for making girls.*

But no matter how her mother put it, Pam had grown up in a family seething with competition. The first girl to the bathroom had long enough to complete her beauty routine; the others didn't. The first ones to the breakfast table got the fruit left in the bowl and the milk in the pitcher; the others didn't. The first girl asked to a dance was allowed to shop for a new dress; the others had to borrow from friends or find something in the "dress closet," where most things already had sleeves removed or waists altered or their hems cut off.

Pam only half-jokingly had told Eric how growing up in that house had been like playing musical chairs all the time. There had always been one less chair to sit in than the number of people who needed one.

If she had to put her finger on it, she'd tell you that she'd disappointed her father the most when she'd decided against law school. He'd been furious that she would turn it down after she'd worked so hard for the opportunity. *Interior design?* he'd scoffed. *How are you going to change the world working in interior design?* Pam had two sisters who'd become doctors, one who'd become a lawyer, another who'd moved with her husband to northern Virginia because they both commuted to Washington, D.C., every day and worked in some capacity at the Pentagon.

Pam's first marriage had been to a man her father had wanted her to marry. A man who'd spent years in law school and was working in environmental law in San Diego. *If you didn't make it yourself,* Harvey Kloister had whispered in his daughter's ear as he'd escorted her up the aisle, with the church full of the social select of Southern California, the Reagans included, *at least you've latched on to someone who did.*

But the problem with her husband, she soon discovered, was that he didn't rely on his valuable law education when it came to his family. He liked to hit. She'd planned on leaving; she had money socked away in a ziplock bag in the bottom drawer of the freezer beneath the bag of tropical fruit she used to make smoothies. She'd stay until she figured out how to make her father accept the inevitable. But then her husband had gone after Ben.

Ben had been so little, his tiny legs as spindly as willow twigs, when he'd dragged over a bucket in the garage and climbed up to reach a tray of nails. Pam had been in her home office, using a gigantic square of grid paper to piece together a conference room for a client, when she'd heard the commotion: The raindrop patter of a thousand pieces falling. Ben's wail. The roar of a grown man's anger.

She'd raced to the garage to find Ben crouched on the cement floor, nails pressed into his knees. "He's staying there until he picks up every last one of those," her husband bellowed as he'd tugged his belt through its loops again. "That'll teach him to bother my belongings."

Pam had shrieked, "But he's *three!*" Only it hadn't mattered whether he was three or thirteen or thirty. No human was going to treat her child that way.

She marched straight to the kitchen, found the ziplock in the freezer, that contained emergency cash, shouldered her Dolce & Gabbana purse, and marched out to grab her child. She picked nails out where they'd been embedded so deep that they made purple *t*'s in his skin. "We aren't going to do this anymore," she'd said. With quaking hands, she'd latched Ben into his car seat. She'd driven ten blocks, terrified she was being followed. And when she'd finally pulled over in a neighborhood miles from her own, she'd thrown on the parking brake and run to the backseat to gather her son against her. She'd kissed the welts on his calves. She'd nuzzled him, stroked his back. "Mama's here," she'd said over and over again. "Mama's here." Even then, he'd still been crying.

She'd given herself three years after that to build her design business into something she could market on the Internet. The travel had been grueling, but her mother had agreed to take care of Ben. It had been horrible being away from him so much, almost like losing him every time she left for the airport, every time she kissed him good-bye.

But it wasn't going to last forever. She had a goal in mind. Once she'd proven to her father that she could build her business into something that would rival her sisters' careers, she would set about building a family that would rival her sisters', too.

Somewhere during the middle of that was when she went to Chicago.

Somewhere during the middle of that was when she'd met Eric.

Ever since Eric had first introduced her to Seth, Pam had been trying to connect with Eric's son.

Maybe she struggled because she'd grown up with girls. Maybe because she'd been so busy trying to prove herself to her father that she'd missed being a teenager. Maybe Seth resented her; maybe he was the one who kept putting up the walls. For whatever reason, Seth walked into the room and Pam felt like she might as well be trying to make friends with a fence post.

I really admire you, Seth, she'd said to him once when he'd come to visit, hoping to get him started talking. *You're doing so well.* She could have asked, *What kind of music do you like?* but it sounded like she was fishing. *You want me to take you shopping?* but that sounded like she was trying to buy him out. And every time she tried, whenever they were alone without Eric, Seth barely grunted a reply.

Pam felt drawn to Seth. It went beyond loving Eric. She saw Seth caught in the middle of something and she wanted to rescue him the way she'd once rescued Ben. But Eric didn't seem to think there was anything wrong. And no matter what she felt, she wasn't Seth's mother.

Chapter 20

❧

*H*ilary didn't know why she expected her friends at Spilling the Beans not to meet the following Tuesday. Alva had left yesterday amidst hugs and well wishes. Hilary figured that everyone would be in the same shape as she was in, recuperating from having a houseful of relatives. Hilary expected they'd all decide to take the day off and get a massage or clean out the refrigerator or collapse in bed. When Fay got her on the phone and said, "Oh, Hilary. We're still planning on getting together. You're not going to wimp out on us, are you?" Hilary couldn't have been more surprised.

"Well, no," she said, slightly offended. "I'll be there."

So here they sat in their corner booth, with June slanting in through the window and café umbrellas fluttering in the breeze on the patio. As they were jostling for position (Julie liked to sit to the left of Donna because Julie was left-handed, and Gina liked the head of the table for obvious reasons), the proprietor of the place beckoned from where he was refilling an iced-tea cooler. "Back again, I see? You ladies come around often enough, we'll have to put a brass plaque on that table with your name on it."

Of course, the idea of a brass plaque pleased Gina. "Here? You want me to write the name down for you?" She waved a pen and a napkin at him.

"We've added lemon bars to the menu since you were here. You get settled; I'll bring you a couple of them to try. You ladies sample them for me and tell me whether you think they're a good addition."

This gave them something safe to discuss for about four minutes. They'd been selected to be his taste testers! They oohed and ahed when the plate was brought out. Kim bit into hers and exclaimed, "Oh, they're a good addition, all right." Donna moaned and made one bite-sized piece last through about five nibbles. "Delicious." Hilary didn't have one; she wasn't hungry. But she realized this was what Mr. Spilling the Beans was after all along, all these ladies in the corner making suggestive noises over his newest dessert pastry.

"My grandmother's recipe," he admitted loud enough for the nearest patrons to overhear. "Only I made a few tweaks."

As soon as he removed the plate and disappeared into the kitchen, the table went silent. Gina scraped the floor as she moved her chair. Lynn was suddenly fascinated by the zipper on her purse. Donna was picking a crumb out of the seat stitches. Julie arranged packets of sweetener according to size while Fay read the list of ingredients on the ketchup bottle.

The sucker punch came when Hilary understood they had all talked to one another. About *her*. *Without* her. They had been on the phone, or maybe they'd been sending group e-mails, careful that her name wasn't on the address list. "What can we do to help Hilary? What can we say? Let's try Spilling the Beans. Let's get together."

"I thought we were supposed to be meeting in the Bahamas," Hilary said. "I wanted to buy a new bathing suit."

By the way they laughed, this was the funniest thing Hilary had said since the boys were in eighth grade and they'd been roasting the football coach and Hilary had made some offhanded comment that the coach's bald scalp sweated like a mozzarella. It had been one of those things where she could be on her deathbed and Seth *still* wouldn't forgive her.

"I'll get you a sandwich." Kim sprang from her chair. "Egg-white salad on rye. That's the way you like it? Right?"

"It's fine, Kim. I'm fine, really. It's okay. You don't have to take care of me."

"But the sandwich—"

"I really haven't been all that hungry anyway." Not until the words were out of her mouth did she realize that it had been the wrong thing to say.

"How long has it been since you've eaten?" Gina asked.

"Breakfast," Hilary lied.

Actually, it was hard to remember. She'd been cooking for everyone else. She would get all those plates on the table and then she'd remember what was happening. That's when she would think of Laura Moore and Seth. That's when she would feel something alive and squirming in her stomach. Just like that, she'd feel sick again, like she'd been pitching around for hours in a car.

"Get her a turkey with pesto and cranberry smear and a large fry on the side," Gina instructed Kim. "And get one of those oatmeal raisin cookies. The girl needs *calories*."

"Gina," Hilary asked, "how are things at the hospital?" Their silence was all the answer she needed.

The nausea came again. Hilary didn't think she could work her way through a sandwich. But her friends had ganged up against her, which meant they were going to win anyway. Kim had already lurched toward the counter and pulled out her wallet. At the table, they all went quiet again.

"Stop it, you guys," Hilary said. "I know you're trying to help, but maybe I shouldn't have come."

In an attempt to rescue them all, Lynn launched into a convoluted story about cooking turkey for her in-laws this past weekend. She had the bird in the pan and she'd followed the recipe from

Gourmet magazine where you slip lemon slices and rosemary beneath the skin. "All I was doing was cooking this turkey," she said. "Joe's mother walked in and said, 'Oh, good heavens. You're not *stuffing* that, are you? You'll give us all botulism.' "

They shrieked with laughter. Hilary had forgotten how good it felt just to hear something funny again.

Lynn lifted her hands to indicate that she was speechless. "I just told her, 'I've been doing turkey for twenty years for this family and we haven't lost anyone yet.' "

Donna said, "My father spent the whole weekend telling us why we're wasting our money on cable. He said, 'I have Channel Two and I have Channel Four and when the weather's good I get Channel Eleven and that gives me everything I need to watch.' "

To which Hilary couldn't resist chiming in, "My mother told Pam stories about Eric and me dating each other. She told our dating stories to Eric's new *wife,*" she said. Which set all seven of them to shrieking again.

A server retrieved their number and plopped Hilary's baguette in front of her. Because they were all watching, she forced herself to take a bite.

"How was that?" At first, Hilary thought Fay was talking about the sandwich. But then she realized that Fay had been asking about Pam instead.

Hilary wondered if Fay noticed she had a hard time swallowing. Hilary covered her mouth with her hand.

Oh, Fay noticed all right. "That bad?" she asked.

It was Hilary's fault for bringing it up. How easy it would have been to fall in line with the earlier thread of conversation. How easy it would have been to moan and let them assume the worst, and even then they wouldn't understand how difficult things had been with Pam.

But just this morning, Hilary had come across the old "Love your enemies" passage in Luke. "Bless those who curse you, pray for those who mistreat you." As surely as she swallowed a hunk of bread and turkey that tasted like sand, something told her to swallow the words she wanted to say, too. The truth suddenly appeared in her hand like a pearl. No matter how provoked Pam made her feel, she'd never be able to get over the hurt if she kept reopening the wound.

Now that the subject of Pam had been broached, it seemed like everyone at the table wanted to weigh in on Hilary's other circumstances: ". . . already so weak when they took her in for the second surgery . . . ," ". . . could have happened to any of those kids. It *could* have."

"I'm so sorry," Donna said. "It must be so hard."

What was Hilary supposed to say? "It's hard,"

she agreed. "I love my son. This weekend was supposed to be so happy."

"To have all this happen when your husband's wife has come to visit. I can't imagine what she thinks. I can't imagine what she's been *saying*."

And so, just like that, they'd gotten back to Pam. "You don't want to talk about Pam, do you?" Gina asked. She must have read the resolve in Hilary's face. "Your mouth looks tight."

"It's the sandwich," Hilary said, trying to get them off the subject. "I told everyone I didn't want this sandwich."

"Have fries then," Kim told her, dipping one in ketchup. "Here. Ketchup has lycopene in it. Eat healthy."

Gina knew too much from being at the hospital. She had seen the grieving kids, the doctors who were doing their best to work a miracle, the visits from the police. She laid a comforting hand on Hilary's knee. "It's good you haven't had shifts the past couple of days." She paused. "I didn't think it could get worse than it is already. But Pam's made it worse, hasn't she?"

"I don't want to talk about it."

"Hilary?"

There was a moth behind Gina's head, beating its dusty gray wings against the window. Even in the crowded café, with the conversations flowing at the other tables, the cash register chiming each time a patron made a purchase, Hilary heard its wings drumming the glass. She watched it for the longest time because she didn't dare meet Gina's eyes. If she did, Gina would know the answer to her question.

Seth and Hilary finally got the chance to square off alone on the opposite sides of their garage foosball table. He maneuvered the handles, working the red players. Hilary was on the opposite side, working the black. For the third time since they'd started, Seth took a shot on a goal that about took his mom's hand off.

The plastic ball ricocheted off the sidewall and careened right back to him. His shots were so angry, Hilary didn't need her goalie to fend off his attack. He was wild, all over the game table. With each jab and yank of the handle, Hilary expected Seth to make some hotheaded comment about the Stuart Foundation and the lost scholarship.

I don't care if those people took my scholarship away. I'll stay home and get a job.

A trick shot to the left between Hilary's defending midfielders.

I'll show them. I'll show them I wasn't supposed to go to college in the first place.

A bullet to the outside, which bounced off the side of the field.

Dad should have thought about helping me before he decided to leave our family. Why would he think I'd let him and Pam help me now?

But Seth never said a word. He just got the serve over and over again, took aim, and slammed it. After all, Hilary reminded herself, he was yet another member of the human male species.

Seth way outclassed his mom in the fine-tuned-motor-skills department. He had a strategy going where he abandoned his attack players and controlled the ball from the rear line. Every time Hilary was finally able to get hold of a ball and volley it back, she shot with as much frustration as he did.

Laura was the huge presence in the room that stood between them, the thing neither of them dared speak about.

Seth made a spinning shot to the right that narrowly missed the goalkeeper. Hilary countered with a curve ball that went nowhere. Seth shook his head at her attempt and sent it blasting back.

Hilary returned the shot straight. The ball rebounded off the corner and dropped into the goal.

Seth was stunned. "You scored."

Hilary held out her hand for the ball.

"I can't believe you scored on me."

When he placed the ball in Hilary's palm, her fist curved around and she caught hold of her son's fingers, too. He looked at her. They both knew they had to talk about this. His entire bearing changed. He literally drooped in front of Hilary's eyes. He turned into someone who looked so forlorn and lost, he might as well have been eight years old again. Suddenly they weren't talking about foosball anymore.

"I know you thought you could trust me, Mom."

"Yes," she said. "I did."

Hilary went to make her serve on the game table. Seth gripped the foosball handles as if he were going after her, only he didn't move. The ball did the quick-bounce thing until it came to a dead stop, out of play.

"They said it could have happened to anybody, Seth. They say it was just an accident. But you *knew better.*"

His chin jerked to attention. He looked at his mother. "I did know better, okay? You talked to me about it all the time." He took the ball and handed it to her. Hilary dropped the ball onto the table and took a shot that might have landed in the next yard if Seth hadn't blocked it and sent it flying in her direction again.

"I trusted you for the wrong thing, Seth. I trusted you to prove that I was right to everyone. No kid should have to do that, Seth. I expected you to be inhuman. So strong that you could carry the burden for both of us."

"Mom."

The ball came to a standstill again. Hilary gripped the foosball handles with both hands, staring at the painted men, their pointed black shoes, their team colors, their faceless heads. At last she let go, wrapped her arms around herself as if she were trying to hold in her whole heart. "It was wrong of me to trust you so much, Seth. It was wrong of me to trust you with my whole happiness. My entire sense of self-worth."

"You think that, Mom?" When Hilary moved to embrace him, he shrugged her off, looking astonished. "You think you're wrong about that?"

"I do." She shook her head sadly. "I just don't know how to do it any other way."

Late the next afternoon, when Hilary arrived home after running errands, Seth wasn't home. "Seth?" she called. "Are you here?"

Only the silent house echoed back at her.

"Seth?"

There was an inlet that snaked in from the lake about three blocks away from Hilary's neighborhood. It followed a route that was nothing more than swamp fifty years ago and ended in a sort of flat-ended gully where Seth and his friends used to play pirates and catch minnows when they were young.

Whenever Hilary couldn't find him, whenever she was looking for him and the house turned up empty, she knew that's where he would be. She walked up the street, watching the sunset gold over the housetops. Everywhere she looked there were families in their yards, a man pruning his bushes, a woman shouting for someone to come to supper, a passel of boys playing softball in the street. She rounded the corner and saw Seth in the distance, a solitary figure against a darkening sky. She felt her breath catch in her throat.

He was skipping rocks. She could tell by the way he was searching the ground. He found a stone and side-armed it toward the water.

"Hey," Hilary whispered as she came up behind him.

"Hey."

"I came to see if you were okay."

Seth pitched a rock and only got two skips before it sank underwater. He immediately searched for a better stone. "Yeah, I'm okay."

"Then I'm okay, too." Which was all Hilary needed to say. She didn't need to teach him more lessons. *Life is going to do that without me, thank you very much.*

Hilary considered joining him, but she didn't. She considered stepping up beside him and helping him scrounge for just the right rock, but she sensed that would be intruding in his personal space.

"I'm going back to the house," Hilary told him. "But I was thinking about going to a movie later or something."

Her feet crunched over stones as she climbed toward the road. She was halfway to the sidewalk when he called her back. "Mom?"

"Yeah?"

"Thanks."

"For what?"

"For coming to find me. For playing foosball. For standing on the other side of the table and taking my shots."

"You're welcome."

Then he was beside her. "You shouldn't walk home alone in the dark."

"You don't have to come if you don't want to. I'm perfectly fine on my own."

"I know. I'll come, though."

It made no difference that she had been walking alone in the dark along these streets for the past twenty years. Hilary had never been so happy to have an escort. And she could tell something was different between them; the wall had come down. Seth chatted easily at her side.

Or maybe "chatted easily" would give the wrong idea. It wasn't like conversing back and forth.

In all of Hilary's experience with the kids who parked themselves at the house, this was the way she knew it happened. She'd learned to keep her ears peeled for clues. She'd learned to be a sort of respectful amateur detective. She'd gleaned info about what was going on in their lives when it accidentally presented itself. And she'd learned whenever one of them got ready to talk she'd better step back and get ready. Seth didn't converse. He started to talk and he just spouted.

His subjects were all over the board. He let

Hilary in on the little-known fact that Laura flirted with him behind Emily's back, which really freaked him out. He told Hilary he didn't know what was going to happen between him and Emily after they parted in the fall. He admitted he'd like to know what it was like to date people he didn't know growing up and he told Hilary he thought Em would like to try it, too.

Hilary peppered his musings with thoughts of her own. "You're still so young," she told him. "Anything can still happen. You don't want to tie yourself down yet if you don't have to."

"I like talking about girls with you, Mom," he said in a burst of warmth. "You know so much."

"Yeah, I know so much," Hilary reminded him. "I *am* one."

He laughed like he thought that was funny and Hilary gripped his arm. *"Seth."*

"If I *do* go off to school, I'll probably call and tell you what's going on. I'll probably ask your advice all the time."

"You think so?" Hilary teased him. "If you don't, I might have to drive wherever you are and stalk you. You know, the helicopter mom that can't let go. Always hovering."

"I'll probably call you as much as I call Em."

"Well, that's something."

"Emily has been so great these past few days. It's hard to imagine a time in my life when I won't care about her."

"There won't ever be a time like that," Hilary said.

He stopped in his tracks and caught his mom's elbow. "You think so? You really mean that?"

"Sure I do." Hilary went off on a long-winded explanation about how once a relationship happened, it was always going to be a part of your life. How it existed even after it ended because it formed a part of who you were.

It didn't mean that you were still mooning over someone, Hilary continued in her philosopher's voice, and Seth interrupted her. "Mooning, Mom? Are you sure you want to use the word 'mooning'? That's like from the fifties or something."

"Yes. I want to use the word 'mooning.' It's my word. A good word."

"Make me a promise. Will you be careful who you say this stuff to? Where I come from that means something totally different."

Hilary realized where he was taking her regarding the word "mooning," and things didn't seem quite so serious anymore.

"Look. This is what I'm trying to tell you." Hilary pretended to be exasperated with him even though she wasn't. He'd gotten her stuck on the vision of someone mooning someone, and so help her, if she didn't keep a straight face, she'd do something ridiculous and let him know she thought he was funny.

"You think about people in your past sometimes. You wonder about them. You wonder how they're doing, what's going on in their lives. You don't go calling them up or looking for them on Facebook or anything." Which was a slight exaggeration, because she *had* spent one red-eyed night checking out a few members of her graduating class to see how certain young gentlemen had fared. "You just send a prayer their way. A bright thought of gratitude. Wish them happiness. You've got your own life now and it's good. So you go on."

"So that's what it's like," Seth said, "now that it's over between you and Dad?"

Hilary had thought they were talking about Emily. She hadn't realized she had been leading the conversation in exactly this direction. "Yes," she said in a tentative tone that let Seth know she was just now deciding the answer. "Yes. I think it is."

Chapter 21

❧

*H*ilary's cell registered a voice message when she checked it the next morning, and when she flipped open the screen John Mulligan's name appeared. She listened to the lawyer ask if she'd be willing to meet him, doing her best to keep her expression bland.

"What's wrong?" Seth asked as she clicked the phone closed. "What is it?"

"Oh, I'm sure it's nothing," Hilary said.

But Hilary *wasn't* sure. There had been something in John Mulligan's voice that she didn't like. The way he'd asked her to join him at a spot away from his office. The way he'd asked her not to speak to Seth about it before they had a chance to talk.

"What are you doing today?" Hilary asked. "You got plans with Remy? You and Emily going to do anything?"

But Seth shook his head. "Remy starts his new job at the fish market this afternoon. Emily's going downtown to find some new shoes."

"You don't want to go shoe shopping?" Hilary teased.

Seth grinned, gave a resounding "Noooo."

Hilary gestured toward the window at the shiny

black Ford F-150 that hadn't moved since Eric had abandoned it in the driveway. "How about it? Just suppose you take that new truck out for a spin. What do you think?"

"Mom?"

Hilary grabbed the keys and pitched them in his direction. Seth caught the keys in midair. "Come on. You know you want to drive it."

"But I didn't think you wanted me to have it. I thought you were angry at Dad for that. And now you want me to drive it?" Seth held his palms toward Hilary. "You don't mind?"

"Of course I mind," Hilary told him. "Your dad comes in with his beautiful wife and great kids. The two of them can afford to buy you a truck for graduation, so they do it without consulting me. They make a big show in front of the whole school so everyone else will see how cool you are and how great they are and I'm left in the background. Of course I mind. I mind that I'm not the one who could afford to do it. Now go get your derriere in that thing. Stop feeling guilty about it for my sake and take it for a drive!"

Seth turned back. "Where should I go?"

"Well." Hilary made a big production of trying to figure something out. "You could drop over by the hotel and spend time with your dad. You could thank them for your graduation gift. You could thank them for staying here when I'm sure Pam has a very busy work schedule waiting for her and they're choosing to be with you instead."

"I could do that."

"I'm sure the hotel is boring, but there's a Y over there on Sixth. Something tells me Ben would love to shoot hoops with the local kids. Or you know, there's that waterslide at the pool."

He didn't move, which surprised Hilary.

"Well?" she asked. "What are you doing standing here?"

"Mom? Do you really want me to go spend time with her? With *Pam?*"

Would Hilary say this if she weren't trying to shepherd him out the door? If she weren't going to meet John Mulligan? Maybe not.

"I do."

John Mulligan had asked Hilary to meet him in Wicker Park, which was a good way from their neighborhood but only three blocks from his law firm in trendy Bucktown. Hilary rode the L to the nearest stop, then walked the rest of the distance. It was a lovely block in which to window-shop; there were boutiques on both sides of the street. Sparrows skittered along the sidewalk. The sun reflected off the display in a store that sold nothing but silver ticking clocks.

Hilary arrived at the park and expected to spy John Mulligan straightaway. In her mind, he'd be wearing some sort of intriguing trench coat. She knew it was June, but sometimes imagination didn't allow for the weather. Ever since she'd sent Seth on his way in the truck, she couldn't help feeling lighthearted. By one more degree she'd been able to let go of her son, one more way she'd been fair. But a tinge of fear kept niggling at her. What had John not wanted to tell her over the phone?

When she opened the gate, it sang on its iron hinges and she realized the meeting wasn't going the way she'd pictured at all. John had picked a place where they wouldn't be so easily found. He'd picked a place they'd both be surrounded by people.

Shrieking toddlers padded across wet ground inside the water playground. Elderly men argued politics around a concrete table. A woman stooped over a community garden where the hydrangea blossoms were as big around as bowling balls.

The benches were occupied, but not one of them was occupied by John Mulligan. Hilary wandered a bit, growing more confused and a little angry, until she finally spotted him chatting with a troop of police officers taking a break, their bikes leaning against the Wicker Park fountain.

Hilary stood within eyesight for a while, watching, waiting for him to glance up and see her. Contrary to the picture she'd carried in her mind, the lawyer was jacketless, his blue shirtsleeves rolled to his elbows in homage to the sunlit day. His hair lifted in the breeze as he laughed at a joke one of the officers made. And Hilary couldn't help feeling somewhat relieved at John's demeanor. His news for her couldn't be too dire or maybe he wouldn't be quite so casual. But Hilary saw it when he glanced in her direction. "Oh, there you are!" he said, and right away, as he excused himself from his buddies and approached her, she was worried again because his eyes filled with compassion when he saw her. "Sorry. You caught me catching up with friends. Those lucky precinct buggers out on bikes in this weather. Of course they'll also be out in January, but we won't talk about that." He looked a little longingly back at them.

"What do we need to talk about, John?"

"Why don't you come with me over here?" John touched Hilary's shoulder and guided her to the table that had been recently abandoned by the political analysts. They'd left crumbs. John had to shoo away a pigeon before he could stake their claim.

"John? What is this about?"

He didn't answer right away. "You took the L?" he asked instead.

"Yes."

"I'll drive you home, okay? You won't want to be out in public after—" He stopped himself.

Hilary's eyes shot to his. "After what, John? What did I come here for you to tell me?" But

264

maybe she didn't need to ask. Maybe that was when she already knew.

"Laura's gone, Hilary. They lost her this morning."

That's when Hilary understood why she had to come alone and why Seth couldn't know where she was going and why John wanted them to meet in a public place, so she wouldn't scream and disrupt things in his office.

It was so *warm* in the park. Bees hummed among the roses. Children were romping in the fountain.

Somewhere inside the cavern of her mind, she heard John Mulligan telling her that Laura's family had asked the hospital not to release information yet because they needed the privacy to grieve. From Hilary's remote, solitary place she heard that the sheriff's office had already been in touch with Mulligan's firm, that the state had responded, that the stakes were now considerably higher, that the DA was considering filing charges against Seth for involuntary manslaughter. And then, somewhere, echoing as if in a cave, Hilary heard the lawyer's voice saying how Laura's death actually occurred in the wee hours of the morning, that this much had been helpful, that the timing of the string of events had bought them some time.

"Manslaughter." Hilary had seen that term a thousand times in newspapers, heard it on the news. But had she *looked* at that word? Felt it in her mouth? "Manslaughter." Just saying the word made her mouth taste like blood.

John had to physically help Hilary stand and escort her to his vehicle. A few days ago, Hilary had made the decision to be steady and strong if something like this ever happened. Seth *needed* her to be steady. She buckled herself in the front seat of the lawyer's Escalade before the questions started to flow. "How do I tell him?" She was thinking, *John's a lawyer. He's gone through years of schooling and he's passed the bar exam, probably had to study for it two or three times, so he ought to know how to word things better than I do.* "I don't know what to say."

"You're the one who knows Seth better than anyone, Hilary," John said. "This is going to be tough news for him to swallow. And I don't know the best way."

When they turned the corner to the house, Hilary was terrified that Seth was already going to be back, that the new truck would be nosed up against the garage and the television would be on. But, thank goodness, the driveway was still empty and the house was still locked. John hurried around the front of the SUV, and when he opened the door for her and she climbed out he asked, "Do you want me to stay with you, Hilary? Do you want me to be here with you when you tell him?"

She shook her head. "No."

"I'll need to see you both in my office as soon as possible. Phone me as soon as the two of you are able and I'll rearrange my schedule. We have some regrouping to do."

Hilary was halfway to the door before she thought to glance back and thank John for the way he'd chosen to convey this news, the way he'd chosen to support her. He'd driven her all this way so she wouldn't have to face people until she was ready. He'd chosen a place with police officers on bicycles and groups of young people reading on the grass. He'd picked a place with so much life to tell her that Laura had died.

Hilary heard Seth coming home a good three minutes before he hit the front screen. Hip-hop blared from his truck. She could name the song before he rounded the corner five houses down.

On any normal day she'd meet him in the front yard and tell him in no uncertain terms that he had to turn down his sound system. That he'd better have respect for the Smiths and the Hendersons and the Hartmans; *they* didn't want to listen to his music selections.

But today wasn't any normal day. Hilary stood at the sink with her head raised, waiting. She knew what Seth was doing out there. He was fiddling with the sound system, adjusting the rearview mirrors for the umpteenth time, making a complete inspection of the truck's paint job to make sure there weren't any nicks.

And then, here he came, bounding into the kitchen with a broad grin on his face, anxious to recount the adventures of his truck's maiden voyage. "Oh, Mom. It was so great. You should have seen me on the interstate. I was blowing people away."

Outside, Hilary could hear the sparrows chortling in the trees as if they were mocking. Somewhere in the distance, a dog was barking. "And I took Dad out and he showed me how to get it in four-wheel drive when the weather's bad."

"Seth." She shook water off her hands and reached for the tea towel. "I need you to sit down, buddy. There's something we need to talk about."

As if Seth knew her biggest fear, he set his smartphone on the counter beside her, right where she could see it if it started to ring. He was still so excited about driving his new graduation gift, he hadn't even heard what Hilary had said. And then Hilary realized there was more to it. It was obvious he had had a great time with Eric, Pam, and the kids.

"You should have seen us at the Y," he was telling her. "Ben jumped off the high-diving board. It took him forever to get brave enough, but then I waited for him on the ladder and he did it!"

"Seth."

"Lily's the cutest thing. She got out and she was

so cold that she was shivering and her lips were all blue and I made up this game called towel monster and started chasing her around with her towel and then she wasn't cold anymore."

"Honey, we have to talk."

But Seth was bursting with more news, too. "Mom, you won't believe what I found out. I have something to tell *you* first."

Hilary saw a man jogging past, not a neighbor or anyone she knew, just someone from a few blocks away who was out for an early-afternoon run. All she wanted to do, at that moment, was throw open the window and shout, *Wait! Wait for me!* She wanted to run away from this, from what she had to tell Seth.

"Lily and Ben told me. Did Pam and Dad tell you they're having another baby?"

"What?"

"You know. Pam's pregnant again."

With everything else on her mind this news shouldn't have fazed her. But here in this place, on this day, under these circumstances, it had the opposite effect. Hilary felt ashamed, but this piece of information, small as it might be, was the very thing that finally pushed her over the edge. The news reduced her to tears. She couldn't bear it. *Oh, Father. Please. Nothing more.* Seth was watching her, thinking he knew why she was crying. "Mom. I know you don't want me to like her."

She couldn't give Seth the news about Laura now that her composure had crumpled. She had to find a tissue and mop up her face. Now.

"Mom. I know you and Pam don't get along. But I want those guys to be a part of my life. I have a brother and a sister."

Hilary yanked a good number of tissues from the box in the bathroom. She was so distraught that she went through the whole handful before she could even think about speaking again.

"If I don't let them be a part of me, I'll feel like I'm pushing half of my life away."

"But I'm the other half," Hilary choked out. She held her hand to her chest. "Make sure you don't lose *me*."

"But with you, Mom, I always feel like I have to choose between one life or the other," he said. "Now, what were you going to tell me when I came in?"

If she only had to tell him about the new charge that might be filed against him, this wouldn't be so difficult. But it was the news about Laura that would devastate him. She couldn't tell him Laura was gone. Not now. Not this way. She'd failed Seth in so many ways and maybe she was wrong, maybe she was failing him again by doing this, but she couldn't break the news to him this way.

Hilary shook her head. "It'll keep. I'll tell you later."

"Really?"

"Yeah."

Seth didn't even push her. He was on to the next thing. He headed into the den to find the remote and turn on the television.

Just as he did, Seth's phone, still beside Hilary on the counter, gave out a short ping. It wasn't a call coming in, which launched his cell into about a dozen different gyrations and a bar or two of a hip-hop song. The short sound meant he had a text message coming in.

Hilary checked the screen. It didn't give any hints, but she'd bet it was Emily.

Oh, Father. I'm not going to be able to protect Seth much longer.

Help me know what to say to him. Help me know when the time is right.

Hilary slipped his phone off the kitchen counter into her pocket. Once it was inside her apron, she found the right button and powered it off.

Seth was flipping through the TV channels in the other room. Hilary was suddenly terrified that he'd happen across some news station that was reporting the story. What if the news had already been leaked to the media? What if he skimmed past a channel and saw Laura's face?

To Hilary's relief, he paused on a channel that was broadcasting baseball. There was a St. Louis game on, and the announcer made some comment about the White Sox playing in an hour.

Which gave Hilary the idea she'd been searching for.

"Hey," she said. "The White Sox play this afternoon. You want to go? Just you and me?"

The TV remote paused in midair. "Nah. You're kidding. No way we could still get tickets this late."

"I'll bet we can," she said.

"No way we could make it all the way to the South Side in that length of time."

"Well. We could try."

"You're kidding me."

"We'll never know if we don't give it a try, will we?"

Seth was considering it. She could tell by the way he was staring off into nothing with that half smile on his face.

"But Mom," he asked, "why?"

"Don't ask me a question like that! Aren't I allowed to do anything spontaneous anymore? Aren't I allowed to just treat you to something when I get in the mood?"

He shrugged.

"Go get your glove." Hilary hooked the apron over the pantry door, and when she did she was well aware of the dangling weight, the phone she'd hidden in the pocket. She removed Seth's phone from the apron and slipped it into her waiting purse. "Come on. What do you say?"

Chapter 22

❧

*T*hey were only a few minutes late by the time they got to New Comiskey Park, which made it easy to find a parking lot that still had a few spaces. Luckily, the throng of fans along 35th Street and Shields Avenue had dispersed, everyone had already gone inside, and so they didn't have to wait long at the ticket window.

It was still the top of the first against the Phillies and Bobby Jenks was pitching. Thanks to the afternoon schedule and Hilary's willingness to fling around the credit card, she and Seth managed to snag two pretty decent seats. They were in left field just past third base, prime foul-ball territory. The guy sitting beside them was keeping the stats on his smartphone.

Seth watched the game with his hat brim pulled low to shade his eyes. The hot-dog vendor climbed up and down the aisles, clanging the lid to his steamer. "Hey." Seth elbowed Hilary in the ribs. "You want one, Mom? I'm buying."

Hilary couldn't eat, not with everything on her mind, but Seth was already signaling for the vendor before she could stop him. By the time the exchange was finished and everyone had helped pass the little packets of condiments down the row, Hilary was juggling two buns-with-wieners wrapped in foil and Seth was trying to find places for three more.

"Seth." Hilary was shaking her head at him. "Really."

"It's okay if you can't eat any, Mom. I can take care of all five."

"Oh." Which, in spite of the weight in Hilary's heart, made her smile. Of course. What had she been worried about?

If they made something in a packet to put on a hot dog, Seth used it. It took him the entire third inning to apply those onions, the pickle relish, and ketchup *and* mustard. On the field, Vizquel had singled to right, the next player had singled to left (which moved Vizquel to second), and Hilary would have given anything to be able to enjoy the game with her son and not have this anguish hanging over the two of them. Seth was totally involved with the play on the field as Konerko struck out swinging and the next player hit a fly ball out to center. Hilary was so grateful for the moment, for this day, for the seats at a baseball game, for Seth's moments of being carefree and happy.

Ramirez hit a homer to center and the crowd went crazy. The lady in front of them gave Hilary a high five and Seth jabbed his fist in the air as three runs went up on the scoreboard just like that. Everything was delirium. Everyone was happy and wanting to share it with them. The bittersweet of it didn't escape Hilary. They were celebrating with total strangers while the people they knew were hurting, ready to condemn. Seth and Hilary looked at each other for an instant, shook their heads, and Seth swept his mom into a giant bear hug.

Oh, if Hilary could hold this hour in the palm of her hand! If she could only keep it as a treasure in a box and pull it out to examine it at her whim! But, just like that, Seth said, "I've got to call Emily and tell her about this. A Ramirez three-run homer! She didn't even know we were going to be at the game." He fished in his jeans pocket, looking for his cell, and Hilary felt a deep spasm of fear.

"Did you see my phone, Mom? I think I must have left it at home. I don't remember bringing it."

Hilary found something interesting on the JumboTron and, with her heart hammering, pretended not to hear.

"I think I left it on the kitchen counter. I think I remember putting it there when I first came in."

A picture of a cute little kid flashed up on the huge digital screen. "Oh, look. Seth. Isn't he cute? Look at the White Sox hat."

"I don't know why I wouldn't have picked my phone back up."

It was the perfect time for Hilary to say, *I don't,*

either. But she couldn't do that. For a moment, she was terrified he'd be able to borrow a phone from someone else. She was terrified he'd search for his phone by calling it and, the minute his voice answered after one ring he'd know someone had sabotaged him and turned the thing off.

But, "Do you have yours with you, Mom? Emily's got to hear about this! I've got to call and tell her."

Hilary promised she didn't orchestrate it this way. She promised she didn't even have enough time to think it through. But after she'd gotten home from the meeting with John Mulligan, her battery had been almost completely drained. She'd plugged it into the wall charger and hadn't given it another thought. Which meant, thank heavens, she didn't have to lie to Seth. Because hadn't she already done enough?

As the innings progressed, her heart felt about as light as an armored bulldozer. Who knew that a baseball game could end that fast? And as they wandered out onto Shields Avenue amid a horde of rowdy, delighted fans, who were either waiting in line to buy more White Sox paraphernalia or leading people along the sidewalk in impromptu victory chants, Hilary turned to her son and suggested, "Let's don't go home yet." He looked at her like she'd finally crossed the line and gone nuts. "Let's go get something to eat."

"Mom. I just ate *five* hot dogs."

"What? You can't eat more?"

"No."

"Are you kidding me?"

"No."

"Well, that's a first."

"It is *not*."

"Oh yeah? Go tell that to somebody who hasn't been buying you groceries for the past eighteen years."

It took a great deal of time to find the parking lot where they'd left Seth's truck. They'd been in such a hurry when they'd arrived, neither of them had happened to note the landmarks as they'd raced toward the ballpark. Finding the truck actually involved a serious discussion, pointing in opposite directions, and fifteen minutes of sheepish looking around. Once they'd found the truck, it took another good while to edge their way into the line of idling vehicles and wait for a chance to enter the freeway. They were almost there when Hilary saw the ramp backed up and had another idea. "Turn left instead," she told Seth. "Let's see what this baby will do. Let's take the back roads home."

"This baby? Did you just call my truck a *baby?*"

"Cut it out with the old-lady vocabulary lessons," Hilary said. "Just do what I say."

Which led them straight from the South Side up toward the lakeshore. The afternoon had dissipated into dusk by the time they broke out of the neighborhoods and on to the water. What light was left was reflected in tiny copper coins that swelled and waned along the waves of the lake.

Boats swayed in their slips as Hilary and Seth passed the marina. Lamps had begun to flicker in some of the vessels. Out a little farther, the party barges had begun their nightly voyages, creeping along the length of the shore so revelers could have their perfect view of the Chicago skyline awash in a brush of evening watercolor. Hilary imagined the music, the food. She imagined the happy, untroubled passengers inside. The barges' illuminated windows laid down streams of candlelight as they passed.

That's when Hilary noticed the sign for the sailboat charter company. White incandescent bulbs encircled the sign. AFTERNOON, SUNSET AND EVENING CRUISES AVAILABLE.

If the sailboat hadn't been just sitting there bobbing, tied up and moored and waiting for them, Hilary might have been able to resist. But here was the boat, a beautiful four-masted topsail schooner.

"Hey," Hilary said. "Let's go out."

"What?"

"Park the truck somewhere. I want to take you out on that boat."

"Now? Tonight? Mom, it's getting *dark*."

Hilary gestured toward the sign. "It's the best time to see the city. You know that."

"Mom. I've seen the city. I was born here."

This was no tourist-trap putt-putt boat with a set-course schedule, Hilary could tell. The schooner would go where the wind would take her. She was a gaff schooner, she carried a traditional square rig, and Hilary counted at least a dozen ropes on her. She probably looked like a trading ship from the eighteenth century when she was under full sail.

Seth swung to the side of the road, turned off the ignition, and looked at Hilary like he'd never seen her before.

"Come on," Hilary said. "Let's go sailing."

"Are you kidding me? We're really going?"

Hilary took off for the wharf. "You wanted to go floating around with your family for graduation? You wrote a story about it, I heard. Well, let's go do it."

Seth followed her, although he was still somewhat dubious, she could tell. "Mom, this isn't exactly what I had in mind."

Hilary was amazed that there was a crew waiting to take the boat out. But it must always happen that way. The brochure stated it explicitly: For any hour-and-a-half skyline cruise, reservations weren't accepted. Anyone who got the notion could have a trip.

She paid their fare and they hopped aboard. They just *went*.

The captain instructed them how to help raise

and trim the sails once they'd gotten away from the dock and he'd turned the engine off. He said that each of them could even take a turn at the wheel if they liked. But as the motor shut off and, one by one, the sails snapped as they unfurled, Seth and Hilary stood elbow-to-elbow on the leeward deck as the city's silhouette slipped past.

The breeze caught the boat and brought them around. Instantly she picked up speed. The sails filled. Whitecaps danced along the hull. Seth draped his arm around his mother's shoulders.

"I don't ever want you to doubt this," he told his mom, as much in awe of this experience as his mother was. "No matter what happens, I'm really glad you're my mom."

Hilary drank in his words the same way she was soaking up the solitude, the silence out there. And she was thinking, *Oh, Seth. Oh, Seth. I* hope *so. Because I'm going to have to rely on what you say now. You won't be saying it later.*

When a crew member asked Seth if he'd like to learn how to trim the sails, Seth took him up on the offer. Hilary strolled forward and stood with her hair whipping her face. She pulled strands of it from her eyes. They sailed on, soundlessly, heading nowhere. Lake Michigan was a dark mirror being silently sliced beneath their prow. When Hilary started to cry, she couldn't tell where her tears had come from—the peacefulness of the evening, or the streaming wind, or the hopelessness in her heart.

Hilary scrounged through her purse and found Seth's phone. When she powered it up, it made a great deal of noise. The screen told Hilary her son had seven voice messages and double that many texts. And so the bad news must be out. Everyone was looking for them.

For two beats, maybe three, Hilary balanced the offending cell against her fingers, felt the warmth and the weight of it. Then she clutched it inside her fist and hurled it as hard as she could, out into the depths of the lake. She might as well be Matt Thornton throwing for the White Sox, she slung it so hard. As Seth's phone sailed end over end in slow motion out toward the waves, Hilary felt like she was watching her soul disappear with it. She was reduced to only this. One ardent, heartbroken prayer.

Oh, Father. Her soul was in so much distress, she couldn't help letting God have it by the bucketful. There was so much she wanted. There was so much God could give her if he would only look upon her with favor. *Remember your daughter, Lord. I'm so sick and tired of being afflicted with this.*

Hilary lost all sense of time; she didn't know how late it was or even how long they'd been on the water. She might as well have been standing at the door of the tabernacle. She only knew that she wanted this one thing with complete desperation, with complete fervor. Her mouth might be moving, but she wasn't speaking aloud. She was just asking over and over again for this one particular thing, the one special good thing that she most needed and desired. And maybe this was what God had always wanted from her. Maybe this was the place he'd always wanted to bring her. She was reaching for him with every bone of her body, with every pore of her skin.

I promise I'll let Seth go if you'll just help him through this. I promise I'll give him up to you.

From out of nowhere the boat's captain clutched her shoulder. Hilary started; she hadn't known there was anyone else around. But this burly weather-beaten man was in command and he was watching her with hard censure. His fingers felt like a vise on her collarbone.

"Lady, in this day and age, believe me, I end up with my share of drunk women stumbling around my deck. But I've got strict rules for the passengers who board my ship. I can't allow any drunken or disorderly conduct aboard this vessel."

Hilary stared at him. Was that what he thought of her? That she was drunk?

"Do you know what my insurance company would do to me if I let somebody fall overboard? Could lose my whole business because of it. I'm taking you back to shore."

Which left Hilary wiping her face with her

shirtsleeve, desperately embarrassed. "Don't take us to shore. Not now. Not yet."

"Maybe you should have thought about that before you started sampling all those bottles of wine, what do you say?"

"Please. It isn't what you think."

"Is that so?" He took a solid step back and watched Hilary. She wouldn't be surprised if he started in on the sobriety tests next: *Ma'am, follow my finger, please,* while he examined her pupils and how steadily they tracked. *Ma'am, walk this straight line for me, why don't you,* while he waited for her to totter.

There wasn't any other reason why she would share such intimate information with a stranger. But he was wrong about her drinking, and being here, praying like this, was so important to her. She didn't want him to put her and Seth off.

Even as she was denying the captain's charges, he was leaning in to have a good look at Hilary's face, his brows knit in disbelief.

"Please, Captain," she said. "You have to believe me." She told him softly because she would never make a show of this. "It's very important. But I'm only *praying.*" *I'm a woman of sorrowful spirit. I have poured out my soul before the Lord.*

Maybe it was her sheer discomfiture that convinced the man. "Well, lady. All I can say is, that must be *some* prayer."

Hilary mopped her face with her sleeve again, trying to regain her composure. "I didn't mean to make a nuisance of myself."

But he wasn't acting like she'd bothered him anymore. He gripped the railing and peered out in the distance toward the hills of Indiana. "You want something as bad as all that, lady, I'd think God would be willing to give it to you."

Hilary leaned over the railing, too. "Maybe."

It surprised her that this man didn't act affronted after she'd shown him he was wrong about her. She hadn't put him out of humor. On the contrary, he encouraged her.

"You know, I talk to God a bit myself. There's something about all the time I spend out here on the water. Something about the way the wind fills the sails that convinces me."

Lights had begun to sparkle into view all over the city. Hilary had never seen the skyline look so pretty.

"Being a sailing captain makes you understand certain things," he said. "Makes you understand how even though you can't always see the wind, it's still there to propel you forward with power."

The stars seemed to swirl overhead in a sky that was fading from velvet blue to black. The captain's words resonated somewhere deep in Hilary's spirit. She kept thinking how, all this time, she'd been praising God and praying to him in some desperate attempt to feel something, a desperate attempt just to know that he was here with her. She *worked* to make God come to her because she forgot that he was already always there.

"I figure, when a person asks for something the way it looks like *you're* asking for it, God can't *help* but listen," the captain told her. "I don't know what you want so bad, lady, but let me add my hearty 'Amen' to it. I'll be praying right along beside you for whatever it is. How about that?"

Hilary could hardly speak. How long had it been since a stranger had stood beside her and offered to pray for her this freely? Without having to know a complete lineup of details? Without first having to decide what side of the fence they ought to be standing on?

"I don't know what to say."

The captain gave her a wise weather-beaten grin that she'd never forget. "Now I'd best get back to those sails and my crew. We'll be changing direction here soon."

Not many hours later, seagulls would be flashing their wings overhead, dodging and wheeling and fighting for bits of food, hoping the sailboat's draft might churn up some breakfast. But for now, the sky had gone totally dark around them. The darkness wasn't frightening. It warmed and calmed her, like a hug that lingered.

A magnificent sense of peace surrounded Hilary. For here, beneath this sky, atop this water, she was suddenly made aware of how small her problems were in the big scheme of things, and how deeply she was loved. Gone was her melancholy and her discontent. The King of the Universe was orchestrating everything for her benefit. She believed it, discovered it, knew it to be true, deep in her spirit. Oh, what a discovery!

The schooner's captain was halfway to the wheel when he turned to tell Hilary one last thing.

"Lady?"

"Yes?"

He tipped his cap. "May the God of Israel grant you what you've asked of him. You just wait," he told her. "Things are going to be okay."

God's will is my counsel; his presence is my joy, even when I can't feel him nearby.

Hilary watched after this man for a long time. She heard him call, "Man the mainstay!" And as the ship began to veer and come around to starboard, she was satisfied. She sensed the Holy Spirit in the broad, creaking shift of the schooner beneath her feet. She sensed him in the way the sails overflowed and the vessel began to surge in the opposite direction.

She had never been alone.

Hilary knew she had to confess to Seth about the phone. The first thing she told him as they sat in the front seat of his truck in their driveway was that she'd stolen his phone, she'd launched it into the depths of Lake Michigan. Then, as a cloud of summer bugs swarmed and clicked against his headlights, she made him look at her. She gripped his arm to hold him steady. She told him about Laura.

Seth's body arched with physical pain. His arms and his spine went taut with the news. He asked every angry question that came to mind. He flung accusations. *Was this why they'd spent the day together? Had she kept him busy because she didn't want him to find out?*

How long had she known? How many hours had she kept it from him?

Hilary couldn't help being frightened while his rage took charge. "How could it happen?" He pummeled the steering wheel with clenched fists. "How could it happen?" He flopped forward in his seat, slammed his torso back again. "What have I done?" he cried as he clubbed the air with his arms and the butt of his hand slapped Hilary's headrest.

"Listen," Hilary whispered. "Listen." But she didn't mean she wanted him to listen to her. She meant that she wanted him to listen to his own heart, to let his grief win out over his anger. His anger at himself. His anger at her.

Which, eventually, it did.

Seth's angular body went as slack as unused rope. His shoulders slumped; his arms fell helpless at his sides. There was only so much fury that one human body could contain before it broke apart. Hilary had been longing to hold him for so many days, to make him into the young child he had once been, to fold him inside her arms and take some of the burden. But Seth would walk a road for this and none of them could walk it for him. Hilary's instinct said he'd jerk away if she offered so much as a reassuring hand. So she sat beside him, didn't express the slightest discomfort at his explosion of anger. She waited until this new ache became ingrained in Seth's soul. And still, she waited more. She was thinking how dangerous it could be to press sharply against life the way the kids did at the party that night. Because life likes to shove and throw punches and press sharply back.

Chapter 23

❧

$\mathcal{H}$ilary didn't leave Seth alone for very long at a time in the days following Laura's passing. She gave her son his space, but she was always in the house, a room away from him, in case he should need her. Every time another of Seth's friends showed up, Hilary breathed another silent prayer of gratitude. Remy haunted the door and so did Ian. Emily spent quiet hours with Seth when he needed to cry. Chase stopped by to play Xbox.

Laura's funeral wouldn't be until next week. The Moore family had decided to wait longer than the ordinary few days before they held the memorial service for their daughter. Hilary had heard that the Moores' church didn't have a room large enough to accommodate the number of families expected to attend, so they'd decided to move it to a different church on the outside of town. She'd heard that Abigail wanted the kids to take part in Laura's service; she wanted to give them time to grieve and, at the same time, give them a chance to come up with a meaningful way for them to memorialize their friend. It made sense putting it off a bit.

It was Seth himself who convinced Hilary that

she didn't need to shadow him every moment. Eric and Pam had driven over for a visit. Lily had been beside herself, telling how she and her mom had reservations for a *Braids and Bows* event at American Girl Place in Water Tower Place the next day.

"Braids and Bows," Hilary said. "Do you have one of those dolls, Lily?"

"No. But Mom says I can get one tomorrow. I'm going to get Ivy. She'll be the first one in my collection."

"For years I've been hearing about that place," Hilary said in all innocence. "But you have to have a girl. I couldn't have gotten Seth within miles of that place."

"I'm a girl!" Lily exclaimed. "You should go with us!"

"Oh, I couldn't do that," Hilary backpedaled. She glanced at Pam, who had said nothing. "Your mom has it all planned for just the two of you."

"You should go with them, Mom," Seth said. "I'm tired of you shadowing me. You don't mind if she goes with you, do you, Pam?"

"Seth."

"You don't need to worry. I'm going to handle this. I'm not going to off myself."

If anyone noticed a strain between the two, no one mentioned it. "It starts at eleven a.m. tomorrow." Pam's eyes were dark as pitch. "You don't mind meeting us downtown, do you?"

"Absolutely not," Hilary said with more conviction than she felt.

The doll store, or, as Hilary decided later, the doll *city,* had all sorts of activities to keep little girls busy with their dolls: Making memory boxes. Attending high tea. Learning how to make "Dazzling Doll 'Dos" for fancy occasions. As Lily's small fingers fumbled with what the doll stylist called "a ponytail veil hairdo," Hilary tried her best to disappear into the crowd. But Lily always managed to find her. "Do you like the yellow flowers or the pink crown?" Lily would ask.

"They're both pretty," Hilary would defer, not wanting to step on anyone's toes.

"You have to tell me which one you *like,*" Lily said. "Otherwise I won't put a decoration in her hair."

"I like the yellow flowers," Pam said.

"But I want to know what *Hilary* thinks," Lily pressed.

"Yellow flowers," Hilary said too fast. "Definitely yellow flowers."

Next, when Pam gave Lily the choice between a horseback-riding outfit and a skiing outfit with a cast and a matching crutch, she asked, "Do you like to ski, Hilary?"

"I do," Hilary said.

Lily said, "Then that's the outfit Ivy wants, too."

After Ivy got fixed up with a final touch-and-spray from the salon stylist and Lily was handed a goodie bag, Hilary made some offhanded remark as they waited in line, something about how Pam spent more money on Lily's doll than some mothers spend on clothes for their children for the entire first year.

"I don't know why money is such a big issue with you," Pam snapped. "Are you looking for ways to criticize me, Hilary? I don't need your opinion. I can spend whatever I like on my daughter."

Two days ago Pam's haughty comment would have started Hilary's confidence falling down around her. Her words would have left Hilary questioning herself, broken, her spirit nothing but a pile of rubble.

This morning, Hilary's face wasn't flaming. She oozed with self-control, something that felt so foreign! She simply refused to be rattled by Pam. She refused to be hurt by this woman or to let Pam inflict pain. Ordinarily Hilary would have given in and let Pam have the last word. But after the boat ride, the talk with the captain, the days Hilary had spent with Seth, today wasn't any ordinary day. She had important duties.

"I've had a lovely morning with you and your daughter," Hilary said. Feeling the protection of God's insurmountable love, she had no need to get defensive. "Lily was the sweetest thing to include me. If I've offended you in any way, I hope you know I didn't mean it."

Just as John Mulligan had known to select Wicker Park as the place to tell Hilary the momentous news of Laura, the lawyer became a lifeline to the three of them as they moved through the next week of a complex and intricate legal maze. John had suggested Seth turn himself in and request a meeting with the District Attorney, a move that Mulligan said he hoped would impress the judge with not only Seth's compliance to the law but also his willingness to be accountable for his actions should manslaughter charges be filed.

"I made the choice," Seth told John. "I'm the one who chose to drink at the party. Nobody forced me."

"Yes," Mulligan said, looking somber. "But we're already dealing with those separate charges. This time it isn't about you drinking."

Even though Seth wasn't scheduled to meet with the DA until after ten, Hilary, Eric, and their son arrived at the Superior Courthouse an hour early. Eric, who'd driven Hilary's car, hadn't been sure how hard it might be to get through the morning Chicago traffic. They had no reason to leave their seats after Eric turned off the ignition.

Hilary was in the backseat so Seth could sit up front with his dad. She knew her son. If he hadn't been so worried and distracted, he would have bowled her over trying to call shotgun.

It was the first time the three of them had been in the car together since the vacation they'd taken to Michigan, to a little town called Lake Buffalo. Eric had thought it might be educational for Seth if they took a weeklong drive along Lake Michigan's shore to meet people who lived in the small towns there. Each lake town touted a dairy that made the best ice cream along the Gold Coast, and they'd set out to find out who might be telling the truth and who might be exaggerating a little. Hilary had gained seven pounds that trip.

"Hey," she said as they sat in the silent car, waiting. "Remember maple fudge ripple?"

The question was out of the blue. She didn't expect either of them to answer. Neither of them did.

Then finally Eric said, "I still dream about that ice cream sometimes." He pushed the radio knob and fiddled with the scanner. Seth made no comment.

The radio landed on a station that was giving a rundown of the day's forecast. "Look for Rockford to top ninety-six this afternoon, which matches a record set back in 1953 for that city. On the North Side, we'll be looking at sunny skies and—"

But then Seth said, "I can't make myself feel anything."

Eric glanced sideways at his son again. "What?"

"Everything that happened with Laura." It was the first time he'd spoken of it since the ride home from the jail. "It's like it happened to someone else. It isn't real. She's not gone."

Hilary laid her hand on the shoulder of Seth's suit jacket.

"It won't come out. I can't let myself feel anything. Because there are so many things inside of me that if I start letting it out, I might never be able to make it stop."

"Expect gorgeous weather on the lakeshore today with scattered clouds early. It'll be a good day to leave the office early and enjoy summertime in the Windy City."

"You made a mistake, Son. Sometimes you do things without thinking. You just don't realize who it's going to hurt until later."

Or sometimes, the thought popped into Hilary's head, *you do.*

Once the weather report ended, pop music started playing on the radio, jarring and surreal. Thankfully, Eric turned it off. The three of them sat without speaking for so long that Seth's shoulder warmed beneath her hand. There hadn't been an obvious moment to move her hand. Hilary waited. Then, uncomfortable, she rubbed his shoulder hard and let him go.

Eric checked his watch. "What time is Mulligan meeting us here?"

"Nine thirty," Hilary said. A flock of pigeons had invaded the courthouse lawn. Most of them were pecking at the grass or checking out the pavement with their bright yellow eyes. One waddled toward the car, its head bobbing perfectly to the gait of its legs, reminding Hilary of a toddler's pull toy. "We should go in," Hilary said.

As they entered the superior court, the front foyer stood empty. Today wasn't a scheduled court date. No bailiff stood at the courtroom. No other families stood in clusters, their faces twisted with worry. Eric's, Hilary's, and Seth's voices echoed in the empty lobby as a single security officer directed them to empty their pockets for the x-ray machine and step through the metal detector.

"Manslaughter." Ever since Mulligan had first introduced it, the lead weight of the word had been as heavy on Hilary's tongue as a stone. In legal terms, if the DA decided to file manslaughter charges against Seth, it meant that the state's prosecution team felt they could prove that what had happened at the campsite had been an unlawful killing of a human being without malice or premeditation, either express or implied, distinguished from murder, which requires malicious intent. Malice doesn't have to be present for a manslaughter charge. Manslaughter is voluntary, when it happens in a sudden heat; or involuntary, when it takes place at fault in the commission of some unlawful act. The legal definition made it sound so clinical. A simple summary of a tragedy that was too complex in its reach for mere words.

The words rattled in Hilary's head like a broken strand of pearls. *"Without malice." "Involuntary." "Commission of some unlawful act." "At fault."* Seth's drinking had been unlawful. But so had Laura's. And so had about two hundred of their closest friends'. Where were those other words, the ones Hilary had been singing out like a battle cry, the ones she'd been applying to her son's wound at frequent intervals like comfrey? "Accident." "Mistake." When Seth had taken Laura's hand, when he'd led her toward the hill and said, *You can do this. Don't be afraid.* And Laura had followed because Seth had pressed. *It was an accident. You made a mistake. It wasn't your fault.* When you thought you were doing the right thing, could it be unlawful to make someone follow?

Mulligan had forewarned them about the meeting. It would be informal, held in the DA's office, no imposing robes or judge's chambers, no packed courtroom, no rows of spectators to encourage Seth, no onlookers to hiss behind their hands that someone had to be punished. It would be a conversation. The DA had the right to question Seth as long as he deemed necessary, but Seth couldn't be held in jail without the filing of formal charges.

If the DA decided he could make a manslaughter charge stick, another arraignment would be scheduled, bail would be considered again, and, depending on what amount a judge decided, Eric and Hilary would know whether they had to hire a bail bondsman or Eric would be able to post bail using stock certificates.

When Eric had picked them up, Hilary had left the house not knowing if Seth would be returning to his own room at the end of the day. Or they might have to wait over a week to find out what might be decided. John Mulligan had prepared them for anything.

Hilary had been so afraid and angry at Seth's first hearing, she'd been ill. But this time her heart kept its pendulum balance of determination and peace. She wasn't alone. She was treasured, loved. Inside, she kept praying, *Father. Please. I know how close you are. I know you are there for Seth. Hold what will happen in this office in the palm of your hand.*

The elevator yawned open on the third floor, and when the three of them stepped out John Mulligan flanked them. "Good timing," the lawyer said. "He'll be ready for us in about five minutes." Mulligan offered his big club of a hand to Seth. "Wow. Anyone ever told you that you clean up well?"

"Yeah," Seth said. "My mom."

Hilary nodded. She couldn't help but be proud of the way Seth looked in his suit. He'd wet-combed his unruly hair until it lay flat. The tie he wore, the one that had taken him three tries this morning to knot beneath his chin, had been a Christmas gift from Alva. He'd worn it only once before, when he'd gone for his scholarship interview at Emhurst.

John was holding the door open to a small reception area, beckoning them to enter, when he looked hard at Hilary. "Hey," he said. "What gives?"

"What do you mean?" Hilary honestly had no idea what he was talking about.

"You."

"What?"

"You seem different. Like something's changed."

"Maybe that's due to the fact that I've actually been getting sleep these past few nights."

"Maybe that's it. But—" He surveyed her face. "You look so peaceful, Hilary. Beautiful. Calm."

He flustered her, saying things like that. But honesty got the best of her. "Something *has* changed for me, John."

That's all Hilary got to say before the door swung open and a male assistant said, "Daniel Vignaroli will see you now."

They all four stood rooted to the spot, not one of them wanting to be the first to step forward.

"Hey," Mulligan said to break the ice. "After all this is over, how about we head around the corner for lunch? There's a great little place I know of. Amazing Irish stew."

Seth walked in first and shook the attorney's hand. "I'm here if you want to press charges. My lawyer and I thought this would be the best thing to do. I want to take responsibility for my actions, Mr. Vignaroli."

The first thing Hilary noticed about the office was that it looked like it belonged to someone who might actually be human. A photo with a lineup of baseball players in throbbing red uniforms hung on the far wall. It was mixed in with the framed Doctor of Law degrees, a membership in the Trial Lawyers Hall of Fame, a Bar Register of Preeminent Lawyers, an Honorary Law and Letters Decree from the American Academy of Achievement, and a picture of two blond-haired boys hugging a sleek hound dog. "My grandsons," Vignaroli said, following Hilary's gaze. "The boys. Not the dog. I don't lay any claim on that dog. He's no relation to me."

"Good to see you, Daniel." Mulligan shook his hand.

"Have a seat." Vignaroli gestured toward a sofa along the wall. "Seth. You sit right here." He indicated a chair beside his desk. "Let's talk about this."

Daniel Vignaroli slid a pair of bifocals up his

nose and thumbed through his notes. After he'd finished, he leaned forward and braided his fingers together. The line of questioning he pursued with Seth was more than harmless conversation. Vignaroli was pointedly gathering evidence that could be used against their son. "Tell me about this party," he asked over steepled fingers as Hilary shot a look of concern at their lawyer. "How long ago did everyone start making plans?"

"I didn't make any plans at first," Seth said. "The party gets inherited every year from the class before it."

Mulligan gave a slight nod. *It's okay,* his eyes seemed to say. *This is best, letting Seth talk it out. I have weighed the odds.*

"So there wasn't, say, a certain individual who came up with the plan?"

Seth shook his head.

The majority of criminal convictions, Mulligan had told Hilary over the phone, resulted from suspects who provided evidence against themselves. The lawyer had said, "There is no worse enemy of the suspect than the suspect himself."

"Then why are we letting him do this?" she'd asked.

"Because Seth has nothing to hide."

For the good part of an hour, Vignaroli posed questions. In answer after answer, Seth summarized the incident. He talked about the hours that had led up to the party. He recounted his conversation with Laura, outlined his relationship with most of the people there. As the DA furiously scribbled notes on a yellow legal pad, his glasses slid down his nose and he shoved them up again. He took them off once and polished them on his sleeve.

When the DA asked Seth why he had promised Laura that nothing would happen to her, Seth said, "I didn't know she would look down." When Vignaroli asked Seth who else had watched the events unfold, Seth said, "Emily. My girlfriend. Laura's best friend. That's all. Emily was down at the bottom, trying to keep her from being afraid. I didn't think either of them should drive. I was so sure I was doing the right thing." When Vignaroli asked Seth what he'd said when Laura had been afraid, Seth had to think a minute. He tried hard to remember. And Hilary thought how people could remember things different ways, how sometimes facts could become fiction and fiction could become facts, and how people thought some stories could be true when they weren't, like Seth's essay about the Grand Canyon.

"I reached for her. I told her to *move*."

"You did?" Hilary asked.

Eric gripped Hilary's hand.

"I told her she had to hurry. The rock was breaking. I told her to *move*."

"You see why I wanted you to hear this for yourself, Daniel." John rose halfway from the couch, a finger pointing toward the last few words Vignaroli had jotted.

"Sit down, Mulligan." The old, seasoned DA frowned on the interruption. "If I want to hear you speak about your client, it will be because I've scheduled a hearing before the judge in the courtroom. Or it will be because I am calling you to ask more questions. Right now, I'm listening to Seth. Do you understand?"

"He's turning himself in, if that's what you deem appropriate."

"No more interruptions, Mulligan."

John allowed his voice to fade out. But not before he'd squeezed in one last punch: "This boy never made a conscious choice to hurt anyone."

"Manslaughter isn't always about conscious choices, Mulligan. I'm sure you're aware of that."

Vignaroli read over his notes one last time. He tilted his head so he could view them with his other eye, as if they might look different to him then. Satisfied, he polished his glasses again and laid them carefully atop the pad where he'd been writing.

"Well, considering all the circumstances, all I can say is this: There are several people in this occurrence who made grave mistakes. You are one of them, Seth."

"I know that, sir."

"It seems this young lady, Laura, made several mistakes as well. One was to drink, which caused her to be impaired in her decision-making as well as her ability to drive herself home. The second mistake she made was to climb a rock with you. The third mistake she made was *not* to do as you said when she got into trouble. You offered her help. No matter how quickly it happened, she chose not to react when you needed her to."

"I see that, too," Seth said.

"There will be news tomorrow," Vignaroli said.

Mulligan asked, "You will make your decision tomorrow?"

"No," Vignaroli said. "I've made my decision today. But the news will be out tomorrow in the *Sun-Times*. The story will say that the DA has found no just cause to proceed. It will say that there are no additional charges filed."

"What do you mean?" Seth asked. "I don't understand."

The DA lifted his brows just high enough so that he could peer at the boy over the top rims of his glasses. "It means, young man, that I hope you can salvage what's left of your summer. It means that you are free to go."

Chapter 24

❧

$\mathcal{P}$am couldn't help being exhausted. Even though she hadn't gone with Eric to the DA meeting, she'd spent hours downtown in a city she didn't know very well trying to keep the kids occupied. The outcome had been better than expected, but the emotional toll of the day had been punishing. Everyone needed a break. She and Eric had decided to entertain themselves at the hotel tonight.

Ben and Lily had been swimming in the hotel before supper. They'd made friends with other kids and played about a hundred rounds of Marco Polo before Pam called them out of the water. Lily looked like she was about to fall asleep standing up as Pam dried her off with a towel. Pam held her daughter just a little longer than it took to pat her dry. Ben's eyes were so red from the chlorine, Pam felt ashamed she'd forgotten to pack his goggles.

As Pam rinsed out their bathing suits in the sink, she felt like she was the one being squeezed and twisted. She wrung out the suits and hung them to dry on the retractable clothesline over the tub.

The kids were hungry from swimming, although

Pam knew if she tried to eat anything, it would taste like sand.

"How about the room service menu?" Eric asked. "Did you look at that?"

Pam shook her head. "Order whatever you think. I don't care."

"We could just get the kids some fries."

"That's fine, Eric. Whatever."

The argument between Pam and Eric started simply enough. While they'd been waiting for the French fries, Pam had wandered down to the front desk to see if the hotel had any games or videos that would keep the kids occupied until they were ready for bed. The concierge had dug out a shredded Monopoly box that looked like it had been stacked beneath a row of books for at least a quarter century.

"You brought Monopoly!" Ben said when Pam carried the box into the room.

"Does this look like a good idea?"

Lily eyed the box dubiously. "I thought I was too little to play that game."

"You and I can be partners," Pam told her.

It took them fifteen minutes to organize the money and elect Eric banker. After they unfolded the game board, Lily found the houses and hotels and became immediately obsessed. She set out building a large town on the patterned bedspread.

"I'm taking the car," Ben announced as he dug the little steel sportster out of the box.

"Something tells me that's not going to be the last time we hear him say that," Pam said, laughing.

But Eric didn't catch the humor. He was examining Ben's eyes. "Ben? Gosh, your eyes are red. Do they hurt?" Then, to Pam, "Maybe you shouldn't have let him stay in the pool so long."

"His goggles," Pam said. "I forgot to put them in the suitcase." It had been an aside for Eric, a quick comment when he'd noticed the boy's bloodshot eyeballs. But Pam couldn't shake the feeling that she'd been judged in some way. She was tired, she told herself. Shake it off. It had been a long day. But some of the fun had gone out of the game as Eric let Lily roll the dice.

It wasn't long before Ben had managed to wheedle his way into three of the four railroads and the matching set of Mediterranean and Baltic avenues. He began to peel off hundred-dollar bills, improving his properties house by house. Lily, who had been drifting off to sleep in Eric's lap, sprang awake to protect the town she'd built on the bed. "It's just *two,* Lily," Ben tried to explain. "It's how you play Monopoly. I'm moving them from your town to my town. The same way Eric did when he married Mom."

The most horrifying thing of all, Lily understood the analogy. Very seriously, she selected two plastic houses, not two sitting beside each other but one from one side of her arrangement, one from the other, and handed them to her brother.

Pam landed on Baltic Avenue the next time she passed "go." Ben proudly read aloud the rental charge as Pam clucked at her son, pretending to be annoyed at the fee. Eric bought St. James Place and let Lily hold the card. Pam landed on Water Works. "You want to buy it, Mom?" Ben asked. "If you don't, I do."

When Eric made the fateful comment, he'd thrown a 10 and was already headed toward jail. "It's good we'll be headed home in a couple of days."

"I know," Pam said. "It's been tough. I'm ready to have our lives back to ourselves."

Eric could have said *anything* here. *Anything.* He could have said, *I know it'll feel great to get to your office, Pam.* He could have said, *I want you to take care of yourself. I'm glad you'll be able to keep your checkups with your OB-GYN.* He could have said something, *anything,* to give his wife the idea that he was out to protect her. But, instead, Eric said, "You being here this long has been too hard on Hilary."

Pam's eyes darkened. "What did you say?"

Eric paused with the metal shoe in his hand. Regret briefly flickered across his features. Too late, he'd realized what he'd started.

"Why does it always have to be about Hilary, Eric? I don't understand."

Ben found something interesting in the corner of his thumbnail. Lily climbed down from her dad's lap and huddled next to Ben. She started to count her brother's five-hundred-dollar bills with one hand while she sucked on a knuckle.

"Pam," Eric said. "Not now. Not here."

"Why *not* here?" Pam asked. "You started it here. Why can't we finish it here?"

Without speaking, Eric looked pointedly at the two children.

"Outside then," Pam said, defying him. "You want to have this friendly family discussion out in the hall?"

Eric took Pam's shoulder and propelled her out the door. "We'll be back," he said over his shoulder.

They squared off in the hallway with industrial carpet that looked like it had been designed by someone colorblind and a row of doors that seemed to stretch into oblivion. Two doors down, a DO NOT DISTURB card had been propped inside the lock.

"I meant what I said, Eric." Pam crossed her arms. "Why does it always have to be about *her?*"

"Why does it make you so angry when I talk about her? Why can't you understand that she's a part of my life, that she always will be because of Seth?"

"I'm trying, Eric. Can't you see that? I'm here because I'm supporting you. But it's not my fault that it isn't the best time hanging out with your ex-wife."

"It's your fault that you just keep harping on her about Seth going to that party. You have to stop. I just want a little *unity*."

"So it's *you* we have to please!" Pam lifted her chin. "And *harping?* Did you really use that word?"

Eric propped an elbow against the wall, leaning against it resolutely. "Look, Hilary's the one who's being hurt here. I don't like to see her this run-down by all this with Seth. It's my duty to support—"

"You don't make it look like that, Eric. You don't make it look like *duty*. You make it look like you care about her more than me."

"That's just *you*, Pam. It's how your dad pushed you when you were a girl. It doesn't always have to be about who gets top prize."

"You should have seen Lily with her at the doll place the other day. Even *Lily* likes her better than me."

"You can't be serious to think that. Lily was being kind. You're Lily's *mother*."

"Do you know what it's been like being married to you? Ever since the beginning? From the minute we first met each other, you started telling me about Hilary."

"I don't do that."

" 'Hilary would do it this way.' You say it all the

time; are you aware of that, Eric? 'Hilary doesn't grill chicken like that.' Or, 'Hilary always helped Seth do his homework right after he got home from school.'"

"Not true."

"You take every occasion to make sure *I* think it's true."

"Is that what all this is about? I'm a guy, Pam. Sometimes I say insensitive things. You want me to measure every word that comes out of my mouth?"

"You could try."

"I'm trying to balance two lives."

"Oh?" Her fists knotted at her sides. "So that makes you a hero?"

The door with the DO NOT DISTURB sign opened a crack. A muffled voice asked, "Do you mind? Everyone can hear you."

Inside the adjoining rooms, it took forever to get all the money and the game pieces stuffed back into the box. Ben sorted everything by color and stacked the bills into their proper compartments, pretending he couldn't hear. Lily lined the tiny hotels in a row on the floor. She kept at that as long as her parents' dull voices volleyed outside the door. Until she told her brother that the town she was building was a stupid town, that she didn't like it anymore, and she swept the pile of buildings away with her hand.

• • •

Laura Moore's funeral was as pretty and bittersweet as a summertime funeral can be. Thirty minutes before the service, the church that the Moores had selected had already filled. Since then, people had started parking on the grass. A guest book was open on a table outside the heavy double doors. Lines of solemn attendees waited to sign.

It seemed the order of the day not to speak. Church visitors recognized one another, met one another's eyes grimly, and nodded. A few whispered and hugged; others saved seats or milled around the foyer. Most had already saved a pew in the overflowing sanctuary. The sound system played a quiet worship song. Pictures of Laura when she was a little girl, some the very same shots that the boys had used in the senior video, faded in and out on an overhead screen. Members of the senior class each carried a yellow daisy, tied with a blue ribbon.

It had been Emily who'd convinced Seth he needed to be there, Emily who had been with Seth since early morning, repeating the same words that encouraged him when they appeared on the Web site this week: "Keep your head up. We're in this together. Stay strong."

Emily said, "We both have to let her go, Seth. We have to tell her good-bye."

"I can't," he said, his voice tortured.

"You don't have any choice." Tears leaked from Emily's eyes. "Neither of us do."

"You know, Em," Seth said with the voice of someone who'd finally lost patience with a young, pesky child. "I wish you'd stop telling me what you think I should do. I already have a perfectly good mother."

"Seth." The tears started rolling down Emily's face. "I have these dreams, you know? Sometimes they're daydreams and sometimes I'm asleep. I see Laura standing in front of me with those leaves in her hair."

"It's okay," he said, fishing in his pocket for a tissue. He'd jammed a whole wad in there when he'd gone into the bathroom. "You go ahead and cry."

"She looks at me with this smile on her face. Like we never went camping that night, like she never fell. But still, there are all those *leaves* in her hair. She's just standing there."

"How do you feel when you wake up?"

"I don't know. Not scared really. Just . . . breathless. Because I wake up thinking she's here. And then I remember she isn't. It's like she's playing a joke on me."

Seth knew what he had to say next. "Em. I was such a jerk. I had to go away from everybody. And that meant going away from you, too. I had to figure out on my own how to come to terms with it."

She sniffed and blew her nose. For a long time, she stared at the shredded tissue as she folded and unfolded it in her hand.

"Sometimes I think you were lucky because you got to go back to the courthouse. Because they had to talk about what happened and if they were going to charge you. And then they didn't."

"Maybe you're right," he said.

"Do you think about that sometimes? Now, when you try to blame yourself, do you realize that they didn't?"

"Yeah," he told her. "I guess I do."

"Well," Emily said. "I didn't have that."

He gripped her shoulders. "Em."

"You know that when I tell you what to do, when I tell you to grieve, when I tell you not to worry, that you have to do things, it's because it's easier to tell you, Seth. It's easier to tell you than it is to tell myself."

"You were just doing what you and Laura always do. You were encouraging her. You were telling her everything would be okay."

"But it wasn't okay."

"But Emily, of course you thought it would be okay. It's always been okay. Always." He found another tissue in his pocket. He dabbed at a tear that had frozen on her cheek.

"I was at our favorite shop yesterday. I found a skirt on the sale rack Laura would have really liked. It *looked* like her, blue and white striped, the turquoise blue that matched her eyes. I pulled it off the rack. I turned around with it in my hand. I was going to turn around and show her."

Seth pulled her against his chest.

"The color of the ribbons on the daisies," she said, sobbing. "That was the color of that skirt."

"Em."

"We have to be there for each other, Seth. Even after we break up at the end of summer. We share this. I need to know you're there."

"I'm here, Emily," he said.

Seth knew he couldn't hide anymore. He needed to be there to support the Moores. Who knew how many times he and Emily would need to talk before they could go forward with their lives? Who knew?

Chapter 25

❦

$\mathcal{L}$aura Moore's memorial service lasted over an hour. Many of the girl's classmates stood and spoke. Various aunts, uncles, and cousins had anecdotes to tell. A family friend read a eulogy. Laura's senior picture was framed, displayed on an easel at the altar. Roses, daylilies, and ferns stood in featherlike fans in their vases. With a few variations, everyone repeated the same thing: "Such a lovely young woman. Such a loss." Emily reached across Seth's leg and grabbed his hand. Their fingers braided together. Seth was bouncing his knee and his jaw was clenched and he didn't move. Tears dripped from his chin.

Eric and Pam sat on the other side of Emily. The concierge at the hotel had found a babysitter for them, so they could be here for Seth. After the service ended, the minister invited everyone to gather in the fellowship hall for a meal. And Hilary did what she always did when she found herself in a big crowd and she wasn't in the mood to talk to anyone. She headed straight to the kitchen and asked what she could do to help.

"Oh, thank you!" a dear frazzled lady said, then promptly sent Hilary on her way with two huge salads for the buffet table. After that, she restocked dinner rolls and those little gold packets of sweet-cream butter, which were being kept cool in a bowl of ice. She gathered up used glasses on a tray. She had never been much of a dishwasher; she'd managed to skip that particular duty during her odd-job college days. Someone who was more familiar with the industrial kitchen showed her how to organize the glasses in the rack.

As Hilary removed glassware from the machine, steam enveloped her face. She shoved her hair from her eyes and looked around for a spare towel. That's when Hilary noticed Pam doing very much the same thing that Hilary was doing. Pam was carrying dirty plates to the counter and setting them beside the sink. Hilary glanced at her, made herself glance away.

Hilary found a towel and began to polish glasses. She wiped stray water droplets from them and loaded them on the cart. Just as she pushed the cart toward the double doors, another kitchen volunteer shoved her way past. She balanced two empty platters on one hand and headed for the stove.

She opened the oven door and yanked out a pan of fried chicken. The pan clattered to the counter. She slammed the oven shut. "I can't believe that boy has the guts to show up here," she said as she brandished a pair of tongs. As she reloaded the platters with chicken, she was so angry that her hands were shaking. "If that *boy* hadn't talked her into it, if that drunk kid hadn't dragged her up the rocks, Laura would still be making plans to go off to college. She'd still be thinking about decorating her dorm room. She'd still be making plans for her future instead of *this*."

Ice coursed through Hilary's veins. Across the way, she saw Pam raise her head. Of course, Hilary knew people were out there saying things like that. But here they were in a church, seeking grace. Here they were remembering Laura, trying to heal.

"Let me tell you, you couldn't punish that kid enough for what he did."

Hilary's hand spun the rag inside the glass. The only thing she could do was stare at her fist twisting inside the goblet. Across the room, Hilary knew Pam had heard what the woman said because Pam started scouring plates so hard that lettuce fluttered in every direction. Beans flew into the trash can. Pam dashed the dishes into the sink, making a horrible racket. When she aimed the heavy commercial sprayer at the plates and let the water surge, Hilary wasn't sure what she expected from Eric's other wife. Pam was hanging on to that sprayer like she was about to turn it on somebody. Hilary was just waiting for Pam to aim the water across the room at the volunteer and shout, *Don't you know that's his mother over there? You can't blame Seth for this because* she *could have stopped him! You have to blame* her. If

Hilary knew anything about Pam at all, it was that she didn't do well controlling her emotions.

The woman hoisted the two platters of chicken and balanced them precariously on two hands. Just as she was about to shove her way out through the double doors, Pam whirled and asked, "How can you resent Seth being here?" She dropped the sprayer in the sink. "How can you talk about punishment when that boy's already in so much pain?"

Chicken Lady went pale. Apparently she hadn't expected anyone to challenge her idle gossip. The platters bobbled in her hands. She looked for a place to set them down but couldn't find anywhere to leave them.

"What happened up there that night was an accident," Pam said. "That poor boy is devastated. And I admire him a great deal for wanting to be here."

The woman held the doors open with her behind. "Look," she said. "This chicken needs to go out on the table."

"We've already lost one kid over this," Pam said. "If you make Seth Wynn go through more than he's already going through, then we're going to lose another. Is that what you want?"

The kitchen volunteers had stopped working to listen. Hilary stood with her eyes closed, her hand over her heart. How could this be Pam? Standing up for Hilary's son! Her knees went weak, she was so grateful to Pam for supporting him. It would have been so easy for Pam to grab another victory here, to make sure that Hilary had been the one nailed with defeat.

Pam said, "You mustn't single him out like he was the only cause of what happened. At least three dozen kids out there happened to be at that party. It could have been any of them, *any* of them."

Chicken Lady figured it out. "Of course you'd say that. You're his stepmother, aren't you?"

Hilary joined in. "He is a young man who has to live with this the rest of his life. Maybe Seth was at the wrong place doing the wrong thing, but so were a lot of others."

"I'm sorry," the lady said. "I didn't realize you were family."

"Everyone out there in this community is family," Pam said. "When there's a young man out there and he's taking this so hard, how *dare* you make it worse for him?"

When Hilary left the cart and glasses behind and went in search of Seth, she couldn't find him. He wasn't anywhere around. She tried the sanctuary again, where she thought she might find him sitting, staring at Laura's picture. She tried the patio outside where the teens had gathered. Remy greeted her. Ian waved. Several of the girls offered hugs and said they were glad she was there. "No," they said in unison when she asked. They didn't know where to find Seth. They hadn't seen him in a while.

As Hilary climbed the stairs and squinted down the length of a dark, deserted hallway, she called, "Seth? You here?"

She considered the likelihood that he'd fled after Pam's tirade in the kitchen. She was thinking, yes, Seth needed protection, but it wasn't the sort of flailing, offended defense Pam had been offering. And it wasn't the misdirected duty Eric wanted to heap upon the two of them as parents. The only thing Seth and Hilary could rely on was the quiet, strong safeguard of the Lord. The Heavenly Father would be there for them, however they needed him.

Hilary's voice echoed down the empty corridor. She tried dozens of doors lining the hallway. She searched each room that wasn't locked. She asked everyone she knew if they'd run into Seth since the service.

Downstairs she found Emily huddled among a group of girlfriends, with hands shoved into sweater pockets and mascara smudged beneath her eyes like two bruises. She was biting her bottom lip and jiggling her knees and Hilary knew, even from this far away, that she was only pretending to be a part of the conversation. She stood there with her head bowed, her weight balanced on the balls of her feet, sort of bouncing her knees to keep from crying.

Hilary had no choice but to break into the circle. She gripped Emily's shoulders. "Em? Honey, have you seen Seth?"

Emily looked at Hilary like she was holding her breath underwater. It was Hilary's question that broke through to the surface, forced Emily to take a gasp of air. "He isn't here."

Hilary froze. *Emily knew something.* Hilary's chest knifed with fear. "Did he leave? Where did he go?"

But Emily was shaking her head.

"Did he tell you?"

Emily bit her lip so hard that Hilary saw flecks of blood oozing to the surface.

"Em, how long has he been gone?"

Emily shook her head, helpless, didn't speak.

"Emily, please. You've got to tell me, sweetie. For Seth's sake."

She opened her mouth to answer and, as quick as that, she was bawling, huge swallows of air—that sort of jagged hoarse weeping that, when you see it, makes you wonder if someone can even breathe.

"He . . . made me . . . promise."

By now all the young women, Class of 2011, had realized they had another friend in trouble. They were quick to surround Emily, to place a reassuring hand on her elbow, to draw the circle closed around her.

"Something he . . . had . . . to . . . do."

Hilary had a wad of Kleenex in her pocket. She handed the girl several. Emily clutched them inside her fist as if she didn't have any idea what to do with them.

"He made you promise, Emily? What did he make you promise?"

Emily gripped her arm. "He wanted to go out *there* again. I told him . . . it was . . . crazy."

"Where, Emily? Where did he go?"

"That awful place—"

"The—" Hilary felt like she'd just been hit in the chest with a club. *Seth was on his way to the campsite.*

"I don't know why he—"

"Is that where he's gone, Emily?" Hilary was frantic. "Has he gone to the place where Laura fell?"

Emily nodded.

Hilary wheeled for the door. Emily grabbed her by the arm. "I want to go with you." Just as they were leaving, Eric and Pam came into the room.

"Eric?" Hilary asked. "Have you seen Seth?"

"No. I haven't. Isn't he here?"

"Emily thinks he's left. That this was—" Hilary didn't say the rest: *Too much for him.*

"Is the truck still in the parking lot?" Pam asked. "Have you looked?"

"It isn't there," Emily said, tears pooling in her eyes. "I was already out there looking for him. I wanted to talk to him and tell him not to go. To make sure he was okay. But I remember where he parked it this morning. He's gone."

"I'll get my purse," Pam said.

"I'll drive," Eric said.

Hilary still had her sleeves rolled up from helping in the church kitchen. She took a deep breath and started to run. Together they steeled themselves for whatever would come next.

Emily knew how to get to the campsite and so did Hilary, because she'd driven past the turnoff only days before. The whole time they were headed toward the state park, they were driving farther into the thornbush, weaving through stands of water-worn limestone and billows of shrubs, Hilary stared out the window without seeing anything. *I committed my case to you that night on the schooner; I've left it with you. I don't have to ask anything more of you. Seth belongs to you; he's in your hands.*

Emily was giving them quiet directions: "Take a left up here." "It's the second right." "After you pass this next sign, it's three miles to the camping area." The left-turn signal clicked off after Eric made the turn. He braked as they approached the sign. Emily was leaning forward, pointing toward the curve in the road. "Once we veer to the right, we ought to be able to see the bluff."

The parkway changed course and the scrub brush thickened. Rising above the brushwood was a precipice that resembled a giant rotund troll crouching over the horizon. The butte was not all crags and sharp outcroppings as Hilary had expected. It was a gathering of mammoth, once-undetached stones fraught with fissures and crevices, separated by rock faces that had been worn smooth as baby bottoms by some ancient sea. The closer they got, the higher the ridge towered overhead.

Seth had left his truck at the entrance. Only it wasn't like he had parked, exactly. The truck had been left in a spot with its windows rolled down and its tires cocked into the turn, as if Seth had leaped from the seat in a panic, trying to escape something.

Eric was the first out. "Seth!" He shaded his eyes. His own voice, calling his son's name, echoed back at him from the far distance.

"Seth!

"Seth!"

Pam clutched Eric's forearm. "Do you see him?"

"Where do I even look? How big is that thing? I had no idea."

Emily stood beside the fence and pointed. She knew the route. "That's where they started up last time."

"Seth!" Eric hollered again.

And just like that, Hilary caught herself telling her ex-husband, "Don't shout. Don't distract him." Because she saw a dark asterisk against the slick rock face and knew it was her son.

He was climbing without any rope or harness. With arms outstretched, he moved sideways and melted into grainy shadow. Seth had found a break in the cliff, an ungainly scar where he could stand.

Eric rushed to the wall and searched in vain for a handhold. He set his foot into a notch and started to follow Seth. He slid down after three steps. He jumped the rest of the way to the ground. "How did they do that?"

"Don't try it," Hilary said. "You can't rescue him, Eric. He's got to do this on his own."

"I ought to be able to help him," Eric said. "I'm his father."

"But you can't," Pam said. "Not with this."

Eric and Hilary held each other's hands as Seth checked his footing and continued. Once, Seth slipped and Hilary gasped. He landed in a tangle of roots and brambles, two-thirds of the way up. It seemed forever before he screwed up the courage to start heading vertical again.

Pam said, "I don't know how to do anything except compete with people. My sisters and I, we were verbally sparring all the time. We were always after each other. I never wanted to compete with you, Hilary."

Hilary couldn't tell how long they stood there, helpless, as they watched Seth climb again. "It's hurting Seth," Hilary said. "It hurt him when his father left. It's hurting him because I won't let go of my bitterness."

"I know that," Pam said.

"He *is* a part of your family. He *wants* to be."

Pam touched Hilary's arm, was silent.

Hilary didn't flinch away. "He was angry at Eric for leaving. He was angry for a long time. But he adores your kids. It would make him happy to be comfortable with you, Pam. But he hasn't been willing to do it because he's been protecting me."

Seth moved hand over hand and searched, often in vain, for footholds. From where she watched, Hilary knew he must be fighting frustration as his muscles grew weak. He lost his grip again and, this time, Hilary, Eric, Pam, and Emily scurried backward as loose scree and pebbles bounded toward their heads. Seth didn't notice. That was when Hilary sensed Seth's herculean focus. With grim determination, he moved horizontally across the rock. His every motion had become firm and able. He wasn't going to fall.

Each time his hand found a hold, the motion was sure and swift. Each time Seth's knee angled or his leg swung sideways, he made his move with elegance. The steep-sided precipice might be Seth's enemy, but he was clinging to it however he could, each groping step and each slight swivel of balance another small defeat of the hill.

"I was already pregnant with Lily when Eric left you." Pam watched Seth, strong and proud, as he conquered the final slope. "There have been times I think he's regretted your divorce, Hilary. And my whole life, I'll have to wonder whether he left you because he loved me more, or because I was having a baby."

"You can't go forward while you're looking backward," Hilary said. "You have to trust what the next step will bring."

Emily, who had been standing separate from them, wrapped her arms around Hilary. Hilary draped an arm around Emily and drew the girl close.

Pam said, "I've tried to do everything I could to feel more sure of myself around you."

Hilary let out a wry laugh. "Don't you think it should have been the other way around?"

"Maybe." Pam shrugged. "But who's to say how pain manifests itself between two women who have loved the same man?" Pam smiled at Emily. "You know how to do this so well, Hilary. You have all these special young people in your life. That's another thing to make me envious."

Hilary said, "We're hurting Seth unless we can come to some truce between us. We ought to try to do that."

Seth reached the top and disappeared from view for three maddening seconds. Briefly he stood beneath the tree that was on top of the ledge, and then he glanced over and spotted them. Hilary could see his shoulders heaving. He sat down, and he was satisfied. His feet dangled in empty air.

Chapter 26

❧

Maybe it was fitting that Pam and Hilary found themselves standing beneath the Picasso they both loved, the much-maligned gift from the master artist. It stood in Daley Plaza, the piece of work that some Chi-Town residents, even all these years after it had been presented to the city, would never quite comprehend.

Hilary felt Pam's eyes on her. Hilary crossed her arms and trained her gaze on the metal statue. "I lost Seth in a swimming pool once. He almost drowned. He was scared to go down the waterslide. I told him I would hold him in my lap and he would be safe. He thought I would drop him, but I told him I'd hang on for dear life, that there was no way he would get away from me."

Pam met Hilary's gaze.

"I promised him I wouldn't let go. I told him that, as long as he was with me, he'd be okay. But we hit that current at the bottom and he flew out of my arms. All that water was rushing out of the tube and pushing me under and I couldn't find him. The lifeguard had to jump in and pull him out."

Pam said, "I don't know what I'm going to do with another baby." She shook her head. "When

Lily got potty-trained, I thought I was finished with diapers, you know?"

"You'll do fine," Hilary said. "You'll have a great time watching all those late-night movies. *The Revenge of the Ants*. That sort of thing."

After a moment, Pam said, "You had all the first things with Eric. You know how jealous I am of that."

Hilary looked at Pam.

"His first wedding. His first time making love with his wife. His first son."

"But look at you," Hilary reminded her. She placed a hand on Pam's belly where the baby was growing. "You're able to give him so much now. You both have a chance to make this really work. You have years left ahead with your children. For me, that time is gone. But now I'll have time to myself. Time to figure out what the next step might be." She smiled. "Another season. Another calling. We'll see."

Pam met Hilary's eyes. So, the two of them came to honesty. Together, they were the Father's pieces of artwork. "Everything's starting for you, Pam. While I'm learning how to let go."

Eric, Pam, and the kids were scheduled to leave town in an hour. But before they went, Seth was intent on getting Ben in the front driveway again to shoot hoops. "Can't go yet," Seth told his dad.

"This kid's got to practice his chest-high passes before he takes off."

Eric was in the kitchen filling the cooler with ice. Pam was checking the cabinets to make sure she wasn't leaving Tupperware containers behind. Hilary was keeping an eye on Lily as she toted her doll Ivy around the front yard. Lily had grown fond of Hilary. She had even begged her parents to let her spend the night at Seth's house last night and Pam had agreed. Now Pam had also given permission for Ivy to go wading in the cement birdbath in the garden.

Lily was holding Ivy's hands. Just as she dipped the doll's bare feet into the water, an unfamiliar car drove up and parked at the curb.

Seth dribbled the ball and bounced it toward Ben. The car door opened. Ben passed the ball to Seth, but the ball ricocheted off Seth's T-shirt. Seth wasn't paying attention to the game anymore. Abigail Moore was standing in the street. Hilary swept Lily and Ivy into her arms and headed toward their guest. But then Hilary stopped. Seth handed Ben the ball and told him to practice his shots. Abigail took three steps toward Hilary's son.

Seth's face had gone pale. He just stood there.

"Hello, Seth." Abigail closed the gap between them. She held a grocery sack toward him.

Seth eyed her with suspicion. It took him a good thirty seconds before he asked, "What's that?"

She jiggled the sack at him. "I want you to have it."

Gingerly, Seth took the bag from her. The item inside was enfolded in newsprint. It was rather large. Seth didn't take his eyes from Abigail's face as he peeled away the layers of paper.

Abigail said, "It's from her yard-art portfolio. It's one of the pieces that helped her get the scholarship. Laura told me just before graduation that you really liked this one."

Seth's hands paused. He stared at Laura's mother. "I can't take this." His nose had gone red. "You don't want to do this," he told her.

"Who says I don't?"

"I do."

"Well, you're wrong."

The last of the wrapping fell away. Seth lifted Laura's sculpture in the flat of his two hands as if the metal might sear him. "Yeah, I told her how much I liked this one. Her stuff is . . . was really great."

Seth held the piece toward Laura's mother, trying to get her to take it back.

"She made the choice to climb that rock, Seth. You didn't make it for her."

"She was scared," he said. "I told her I wasn't going to let her leave unless she called you. Nobody was in a position to drive. And there wasn't any cell service."

Abigail said, "Emily told me the story, Seth. I understand how it happened."

"She was afraid to go up. I told her I wouldn't let anything happen to her. I pushed her to do it."

"You pushed her in good ways, too, Seth. You encouraged her about this piece of art. You were a good friend to her over the years. You were trying to protect her. I want you to remember the good things you did for my daughter, too. I don't want you to forget that."

Seth stood with his feet planted wide in the middle of the yard, grasping Laura's statue.

Ben bounced the basketball a couple of times and then gripped it with both hands. "Can I see it?"

But Seth ignored Ben. He was watching Abigail traipse back to her car. She had her hand on the door handle when he said, "I don't get why you wanted to do this."

"Take care of yourself, Seth." Abigail shot him a sad smile. "Someday you'll understand."

If Hilary tried to pick one short sentence to describe Chicago, she'd say, *This is a city where people read.* Everywhere she went, she saw people with their noses buried in books. When you rode the L, everyone was either thumbing through magazines or peering intently into the pages of a novel. Along the Noble Square balconies with their arrangements of plastic furniture and roses in pots, people were creasing and pleating their newspapers, perusing the headlines. Here in Wicker Park, where there was the field house and a spray park for the kids and even the chance to dash through the fanciful cut-granite fountain, everyone had a bedsheet spread out on the grass and they were reading. Everybody had a book open.

Hilary was sitting at the cement table alone, waiting for John Mulligan. She was terrified John was going to come around the corner and give her more daunting trial-lawyer news that was too dire to be relayed over the telephone, something so critical that it had to be shared in person.

But when John stepped around the corner this time, his sleeves were rolled up, his arms were bare except for his watchband, and he was whistling. He was carrying two of those bullet-shaped red, white, and blue Popsicles.

"Here." He handed Hilary one. "You like these things?"

"What's wrong, John?" she asked. "What's so important that you needed to see me again?"

Two little girls went Rollerblading past them on the sidewalk. One was a pro and the other tried to keep up without having a wipeout. Hilary honestly wanted to follow the little girl with her arms out just in case.

"What's so important?" To John's credit, he seemed bewildered. "Oh. Did you think I needed to see you because of something about the case?"

Hilary nodded.

"Did I give you that impression? That this is because of the case?"

The Popsicle Hilary was holding was called a Firecracker. It reminded her of the third grade when they'd buy them in the school lunchroom and then laugh at one another when their tongues turned blue.

"You did."

"Nothing's important. Except that you're here. That's important. At least, it is to me."

Hilary's jitters started to disappear.

Oh.

Oh, I see.

Well, then.

His words evoked a twinge of surprising warmth in her. She leaned back and propped her chin on the heel of one palm.

"Did you know that some kid invented these things when he was eleven?" John's attention returned to the frozen treat he was wielding in one hand. "Kid stuck a stir stick inside a fruit soda and left it outside. He found it later, broke open the bottle, and voilà."

Hilary peeled the paper away from hers and bit into it. Then she leaned on her hand to watch John Mulligan. He straddled the seat beside her and waved at a cop who was cycling past. "A friend of my son's," John said, smiling. "You just watch. Give it twenty minutes; every cop in this precinct will meet at the fountain for lunch. You can always find them here if you need them."

"Thanks for the Popsicle," Hilary said, running the stick across her tongue, loving the smooth feel of it.

"They either meet here or they meet at that place around the corner with salads and chess tables. They go in there and play chess whenever it's raining. Do you like to play chess? I could take you there sometime."

Hilary asked, "Do they have black coffee?"

John laid his Popsicle stick on the cement table beside Hilary's. "I believe so. Or, if they don't, I'd find a way to get them to make some for you."

"So." Hilary smiled. At last. A chance to employ the master skills she'd developed from listening to the hordes of boys who'd frequented her living room. "If we visit this place, this chess place?"

"Yes?"

"Are we just hanging out together? Or are you asking me on a date?"

John threw his head back in a hearty laugh that Hilary liked. How long had it been since she'd been able to laugh like that?

"Did anyone ever tell you that you ought to be a lawyer? You *do* know the right questions to ask."

Hilary didn't let him distract her. She propped her elbows on the table. "Well?" she said, enjoying teasing him. "I don't go for false pretenses."

John picked up his Popsicle stick and pointed it at her. "If it's okay with you, I'd like to make it a date."

The ladies piled inside Spilling the Beans on a September morning and removed their sunglasses, shoved aside their windblown hair. Their eyes adjusted and (how could it be?) there were others chatting in their very private corner booth against the window. Didn't they know it was *Tuesday?* Didn't they know they were sitting in someone's seats?

They stood looking at one another, not knowing where to turn. They just sort of milled around for a few beats at the door, waiting for someone to take charge. Maybe they expected Gina to march across the room, place her hands on her hips, and let everyone know that this group of best friends had arrived. They were nurses or accountants or stay-at-home moms. Some had gone through their kids' graduations; some were newly divorced; one had a child in third grade. Some were Christians. A few weren't. There had been times the group had swelled in numbers, times those numbers had waned. They'd supported one another for two and a half decades, over coffee at Spilling the Beans.

"You're in our spot, you're not aware," Gina might have complained in one of her classic quips, *"said the table to the chair."* But that wasn't what Gina did at all. She headed toward the cash

register and ordered a chocolate mocha latte.

With the ebbing of spring into summer, Gina had been taking some time off from the hospital. She'd told all of them she wanted to give herself a seasonal makeover. She and her husband, Herb, had gone on a trip to a five-star resort in Branson. She'd been straightening her hair and carrying a metallic satchel bag that she'd found at Bess & Loie. She looked about ten years younger since she and Herb made that trip. And she picked a completely different table, one in the dead center of the shop. It seemed they had a new location today. Which Hilary guessed meant that they had a whole new view of things.

Hilary made her way through the line, and while everyone else waited for steamed milk, shots of espresso, streams of spicy flavoring, she gripped her cup of black coffee between two hands and stared at herself in the reflection. Even as they shuffled through the line, Hilary's empty-nest friends had their heads together, whispering. "That's a great idea," Fay was saying beneath her breath. "We can use my house. We'll make cookies and everyone can bring things to put inside care packages and it'll be a huge assembly line."

Julie added, "We'll do it next month after your kids all leave home. We'll all do it. No matter if we have college freshmen or not. All your kids will get care packages at the same time."

Hilary saw Julie clamp her mouth tight when Hilary approached. Hilary didn't blame her friends for changing the subject whenever she joined the group. She knew they were trying hard to keep from reigniting the pain for her.

So you've been grieving all this time because your son was leaving for college, how is it that you can also grieve because your son isn't *going to go yet?*

"I'll be there to help," Hilary said.

Fay jumped in. "Oh, Hilary. I'm so sorry. Maybe I shouldn't have brought it up."

"There's nothing to be sorry about, let me tell you!" Hilary couldn't keep her newfound confidence from shining through.

"Really?" Fay asked. "What are Seth's plans, Hil? What has he decided to do?"

Each time the door to Spilling the Beans swung open, new customers spilled in and joined the line. The proprietor had set wrought-iron seats and umbrellas outside where members of the crowd could return to sip their coffee blends. The colors on the umbrellas in the sunlight seemed to be throbbing.

"He'll stay home this first semester," Hilary said. "It was too late to apply anywhere else since he decided against Emhurst."

"Oh, honey," Gina said. "Are you okay with that?"

"I'm okay with whatever Seth is okay with," Hilary said. "He's applied for a paid position working with the kids at Clissold House this fall." The Clissold House was the center where Seth had completed his community service for the MUI, a center where he'd mentored at-risk middle schoolers. Seth had told his mom that he could get the kids to really talk to him when they were out on the court shooting hoops, their feet dancing across the pavement, their shirts soaked with sweat. He came home every night exhausted, and feeling he'd accomplished something.

Kim asked, "So he decided against Emhurst?"

"He did." Hilary's voice held steady. She felt certain of their future now, although it looked different than she'd once imagined. "Emhurst was too expensive without the scholarship. That's what started us talking about it. And it turned out that Seth had never really been sure of that school anyway. He'd agreed to it because he thought it would satisfy *me*."

"Oh, Hil," Donna said.

"He's been accepted to the University of Illinois for the spring semester. Pam and Eric are helping him with tuition. He's filled out the FAFSA to see if he's eligible for any grants or subsidized student loans."

Fay touched her hand. "Honey, that's so great."

"He'll have some catching up to do. He and Remy will be rooming together. And next year maybe they'll find an apartment."

"That sounds terrifying," Julie said.

"It *is* terrifying," Hilary agreed. "But I'm fine with it. We'll see how well they do. Whatever happens, they'll learn from it."

"*This* is the party we're going to talk about," Gina said. She was carrying a lemon bar with a lit candle stuck in the center of it. She set the plate in front of Julie while the crowd of coffee drinkers, including the ones in their corner booth, launched into a rousing rendition of "Happy Birthday." Of course the part of the song where everyone sings the name was left blank because nobody knew her name except for her friends.

"It's *Julie!*" Fay shouted to everyone. "Her name is *Julie.*"

Which made the people in the next booth sing it again. "Happy Birthday, dear *Jooo-lie.*"

Hilary would still have a difficult good-bye with her son when the time came. But it would be so different now than it would have been before. This schedule seemed right; it would give Seth time to heal. He'd have time for more sessions with his therapist. And whenever Seth needed to blow off steam or when he wanted to have one of his talking binges, Hilary would be there to listen. Who, except the Lord, knew where each day was going to take them? *Show me, Father, when I can love my son most by getting involved. Show me when I can love him most by standing back.*

In the morning, when Hilary worshipped, her heart touched on truth, that this pain of letting her son go could give her a hint, a finger touch, as if she were trying out the pain of a bruise, of what it must have been like for God to let Jesus come to earth. And yet . . . his love for us. His willingness to allow Jesus scorn, pain, separation.

Sometimes at night, when no one could see or hear her, Hilary still cried. Those were the times when the only prayer she could choke out was an exhausted, *Help. Oh, help. Please help us.* And every time, her Heavenly Father proved that he would.

Seth had found Hilary a few hours ago while she'd been wrapping Julie's birthday present. She had mitered the corners, taped the flaps on each end, and stretched the yarn lengthwise to make sure the bow would come out even. She was right in the middle of tying the first loop, pulling it taut, when Seth's finger landed on the yarn to keep it from slipping.

Hilary had pulled the knot tight and Seth had yanked his finger out just in time. He smiled and asked, "You okay, Mom?"

Hilary considered her answer. "Yes. I'm okay."

"You know," he said as he settled into the bed pillows to talk. "I've got to thank you for something."

Hilary had been rummaging in the drawer to

find a pen to sign Julie's card. She lifted her eyes to his.

"You're the coolest mom."

"Me?" Hilary asked, feigning surprise. "You're talking about me?"

"Mom. Quit joking around. I'm serious. You know you're cool. All my friends tell you that."

"Is that what you're thanking me for?"

"No."

"Well, what then?"

"I'm thanking you for the way you look at me."

Hilary narrowed her eyes at him, confused.

"It's been different lately."

"How so?"

"You look at me like I'm your son. But you also look like I'm a grown-up who has to take care of myself. Like you trust me enough that your emotions aren't riding on me all the time."

Hilary shot him a little salute. "For noticing how I'm making progress I give you *my* thanks."

"It's like I don't have to be the one to make life come out all right for you anymore."

And Hilary couldn't help thinking, *This is what comes in the end, isn't it?* Because, before, her prayers had only been the night prayers: *Help me get through this, God. Show me how to handle what comes tomorrow.* And now she had the morning prayers, too. *Oh, Father. I couldn't have done this alone. Oh, Father. Thank you for changing me.*

・ ・ ・

Not long after Seth and Hilary took their voyage on the four-masted topsail schooner, he started bugging Hilary for another trip. Only this time he wanted to go when his father had flown into town. He wanted to show Ben how to trim the sails. He wanted to hold Lily and help her take a turn at the wheel. Which meant he also wanted Pam to stand on the deck during the voyage, he wanted her to feel the sails being silently pushed by the wind. He wanted Eric's other wife to stand in this place where Hilary first began to find so much peace.

So, on a blustery fall day after they'd convinced the entire Wynn family to return to Chicago and visit them again, on a day after most of the senior class had departed and Seth's part-time job was under way, the entire family boarded the boat. Pam had signed the kids up for an educational program, which included their captain giving ten-minute talks on maritime history, sailing, maritime arts, physics, navigation, and seamanship.

"Mom," Seth teased Hilary. "How come I never got to do anything like this for school?"

Hilary swatted him on the behind with her sweater. "You got to do plenty of cool things in school. Don't rile me up."

Overhead, the sails were beginning to unfurl. Eric stood on the starboard side, watching

Chicago slip past. They all held their breath as they stared up at the masts, watching while wind inflated the sails. Once the sails were set, the engine was turned off. Silence, all was beautiful silence, as the prow sliced through the water and their course was chosen.

Seth lifted Lily and she gripped the wheel with tiny, knobby fists. "I'm driving!" she shrieked. "I'm making us go where I want us to go!"

Hilary's son kissed Lily on the top of the head. "That's what you think, munchkin."

Ben craned his neck and peered straight up through the riggings at the flags while the captain explained to him what each of them meant. Eric turned to Hilary and smiled. She knew what he was thinking. He was thinking how, here they were, the entire Wynn family, the first wife and the second, all these kids, crashing forward through the waves of Lake Michigan, with their faces turned into the wind.

When Hilary looked for Pam, she found her at the bow of the boat, looking straight out over the open water. The spray was splashing toward her. She was getting wet, but she wasn't flailing or backing away. She was letting it soak her. She was wearing maternity jeans with a placket of stretch knit at the front. And the knit was stretching. Her pregnancy was starting to show. Lake water glistened on her neck.

After Hilary joined her Pam said, "I wish this

could last forever." And Hilary was thinking, *Maybe it will, Pam. Maybe it will.*

Hilary reached across the gap between them and took her hand.

Author's Note

❧

*F*or a long time, I've been intrigued by the story of Hannah in the Bible. The account of Hannah's life, as she aches to have a baby, as her husband's other wife constantly reminds her that she isn't good enough, is often overshadowed by the stories of her son. God had bigger plans for Hannah than the woman who provoked her. When at last Hannah gave birth to a child, a boy named Samuel, she handed him over to God. Samuel became one of the greatest prophets ever to lead Israel.

My favorite part is how Hannah's circumstances don't change, but *she* changes. Hannah must learn to trust God *before* he changes the situation around her. She finds her peace *before* she sees any evidence that her family relationships might get any easier. Hilary needs to learn the same lesson that Hannah did. Having Hilary go through feelings of shame, of not being a good mom, of having to prove herself to another woman who is constantly judging her, seemed a good way to parallel the two women's lives. This is how *His Other Wife* was born.

Writing a contemporary novel based on a biblical character is no easy job! I felt God leading me to tell this story although there were times I wanted to give up! Many thanks to my two amazing editors, Anne Goldsmith Horch and Christina Boys, for their meticulous work over the past two years and for helping me make this novel the best it can be.

It can be so hard to feel peaceful when everything around you is in turmoil. In the middle of difficult times, if you invite God to take charge of the situation, you can trust this: What happens in the end will be for good.

At the end of this story in the Bible, Hannah says a prayer. She says, "My heart rejoices in the LORD; in the LORD my horn is lifted high. My mouth boasts over my enemies, for I delight in your deliverance."

Know this: If you seek peace from Jesus Christ and not from the world around you, you will be like Hilary and Hannah. You will always be able to boast over your enemies. You can rejoice and delight in the Lord.

I love to hear from my readers. You can e-mail me at deborah.bed@bresnan.net. Check out my Web page at www.deborahbedfordbooks.com or join us on www.facebook.com (Deborah Bedford and/or Deborah Bedford Fans).

Delighting and rejoicing right along with you,
Deborah

Group Discussion Questions

1. Read 1 Samuel 1:4–20. Name three ways that Hilary's story in *His Other Wife* differs from the story of Hannah. Name three ways that Hilary's story resembles Hannah's story. Why do you think these similarities jumped out at you? Why do you think the author chose these similarities?

2. At the beginning of the book, it is easy for Hilary to be grateful to God for her husband, her job, and her son. But when Hilary's life changes it becomes harder for her to be faithful. Do you think God allows difficult things to come into the lives of his people? Why?

3. Near the beginning, the author shows Hilary counseling her friend Julie as Julie goes through a divorce. Julie is hurting; Hilary speaks as though she's come through to the other side. Why do you suppose the author chose to show Hilary doing well before she showed Hilary floundering?

4. Who is most to blame for Hilary's pain? Is it Pam? Eric? Seth? Is it Hilary herself? Explain.

5. During the course of the story, Seth writes an essay about his mother and father taking

him on a rafting trip to the Grand Canyon. Why do you think Seth would make up something that wasn't true? What was Seth trying to say when he wrote the essay? Why do you think he would submit the essay in class but not talk about the idea to his parents?

6. On page 130, Alva asks her daughter, "How long has it been since you've listened?" When Hilary doesn't understand Alva's question, Alva continues. "Christians stay so busy trying to think what they should *say,* what they should *do*. But they don't always think how they should *listen*." What is Alva trying to tell Hilary? Discuss ways that you've found to listen to God.

7. After Laura's accident at the party, Hilary wants "the sort of faith that made her expect something beautiful to come from broken places." In chapter 14, what questions does Hilary ask God as she stands clutching the pew? Do any of these questions relate to what Alva said to her earlier? How? What is the answer that God whispers to Hilary at the hospital? Why do you think this message is difficult for Hilary to hear?

8. How do you think Pam's relationship with her own father and sisters affected her relationship with Eric? With Seth? Discuss Pam's point of view. She obviously has faith,

too. So why would she choose to have an affair with Eric? Why do you think she feels like she has to compete with Hilary?

9. Hilary and Seth are on a sailboat together when the captain tells Hilary, "Being a sailing captain makes you understand certain things. Makes you understand how even though you can't always see the wind, it's still there to propel you forward with power." Was the man talking about the wind or was he talking about something else? Explain. What is it about the man's words that makes Hilary begin to see herself differently? Why do you think Hilary's heart is open to this message now when she couldn't hear it before?

10. A major theme in both Hannah's story and Hilary's story is woundedness, how God can encourage someone who is being continuously hurt by another person. Hilary was wounded by Pam's actions. Toward the end of the book, Hilary's circumstances don't change, but *she* changes. Can you think of a specific moment in the book when Hilary began changing? Why is this significant? Is there an area in your life that resembles Hilary's struggles with Pam? Do you have an idea of how you might change? If you feel comfortable, share this with the group.

Center Point Publishing
600 Brooks Road ● PO Box 1
Thorndike ME 04986-0001 USA

(207) 568-3717

US & Canada:
1 800 929-9108
www.centerpointlargeprint.com